THE EXECUTIONER'S

RACE

ANDREW BYNOM

In this impressive debut novel, Andrew Bynom captures both the mystery of nineteenth-century Istanbul and the magical qualities of a Hans Christian Andersen fairy tale. Weaving together the stories of an exiled female calligrapher and Andersen himself as he tours Ottoman Turkey, Bynom provides an artful and captivating meditation on aesthetics, politics, and faith. It's hard to believe *The Executioner's Race* is a first novel.
—David Anthony, author of *Something for Nothing*

Andrew Bynom's *The Executioner's Race* is an inventive and beguiling mystery about the self transfigured by art. Every carefully wrought sentence speaks of our ongoing struggle to tell our own story while joining it with the stories of others. Bynom's novel transports us, as the best novels do, to places we've never been, allowing us to see our own in a new light: Constantinople and its shimmering strait of Bosphorus, through the mysteries of Sufism, and into the gloriously serpentine heart of Zeynep, its calligrapher hero. A fine and startling debut.
—Scott Blackwood, author of *See How Small*, a *New York Times* "Editor's Choice" pick and a 2015 Best New Book selection by both Amazon and *People Magazine*, et al

Andrew Bynom's debut novel expertly braids the epic love story of an exiled calligrapher with an audacious reimagining of Hans Christian Andersen's travels in Istanbul. The late Ottoman setting is haunting and fantastic, and the prose flows with the vibrancy and elegance of calligraphy, delivering a steady stream of tangible delights for the reader. *The Executioner's Race* celebrates the magic of writing and storytelling, but it is also a demonstration of that magic.
—Eric Lundgren, author of *The Facades*

THE eXECUTIONER'S RACE

ANDREW BYNOM

Aqueous Books

Birmingham

Published by Aqueous Books
P.O. Box 170607
Birmingham, AL 35217
www.aqueousbooks.com

Published in the United States of America
ISBN: 978-0-692-51040-7

First edition, Aqueous Books printing, Aug. 2015
Editing, book design, and layout: Cynthia Reeser
Text is in Adobe Caslon and Akhenaton
Cover illustration by Paul Sloboda. Used with permission.
Interior maps by Kay Carr. Used with permission.

Aqueous Books

For Holly

CONTENTS

Chapter 1... 9

Chapter 2... 19

Chapter 3... 47

Chapter 4... 69

Chapter 5... 86

Chapter 6... 109

Chapter 7... 135

Chapter 8... 147

Chapter 9... 181

Chapter 10....................................... 201

Chapter 11....................................... 226

Chapter 12....................................... 239

Chapter 13....................................... 258

Chapter 14....................................... 266

Chapter 15....................................... 295

Chapter 16....................................... 365

Chapter 17....................................... 380

Chapter 18....................................... 386

Arabic Alphabet..................................... 416

Glossary of Turkish & Arabic Words   418

    & Phrases...

The 99 Names of Allah......................... 421

Map: The Bosphorous........................... 426

Map: Ottoman Istanbul........................ 427

Acknowledgements................................ 428

Chapter 1

W omen in the sultan's capital, no matter their rank, tended to die uneventfully: strangled in the dead of night, sewed neatly into weighted flour sacks, tipped into the Bosphorus along with the rest of the week's refuse.

A calligrapher, imprisoned for reassembling the word of God, might have expected the same treatment. She had drawn human and animal forms from holy words and invocations, compact chronograms with diacritical marks for eyes and letters for limbs, but the holy men didn't care to see the *Bismillah* reflected in their own faces. Their God belonged on the page, as immobile and resolute as a citadel. They sentenced the calligrapher to death.

Her jailers talked of the Executioner's Race. She begged them to pass a message to the *Bostanci-Bashi*, the Chief Gardener, who doubled as the sultan's executioner.

"Let me race," she said. "Let me die an honorable death. After all, as a woman I have no chance of winning, and think of the spectacle you would have on your hands as I flounder through the bushes, thorns, and weeds."

Her jailers shook their heads and said the race was the privilege of condemned notables—a deposed vizier, perhaps, or a chief eunuch—not for someone as ordinary as her.

The calligrapher scratched a petition on the walls of her cell with the husk of her reed pen. She called in the jailers and they, unlettered and afraid, ran to the Bostanci-Bashi. The Chief

Gardener examined her markings by candlelight and clucked his tongue.

"Is this the way you honor your master's profession?" he asked. "By daubing God's script on prison walls?"

"I'm sure you are right, sir," the calligrapher said. "Women are always impatient. I simply couldn't wait for the right conditions."

"The right conditions?"

"As a gardener, you wouldn't plant and sow unless the soil was favorable?

"Of course not."

"And you wouldn't use an inferior spade and hoe?"

"No."

"And as an executioner, you wouldn't slice off my head with anything but the sharpest blade."

"Woman, what are you saying?"

"That you, sir, possess infinite patience and expertise. A lesson I would do well to learn."

An hour later, a sheet of paper and a tortoise shell full of ink arrived at her cell.

The calligrapher licked and spat on her right hand until her mouth drained dry. She removed the grime and dead skin of the dungeon the best she could with the hem of her *ferace*. She looked down at the materials sent by the Bostanci-Bashi and sighed. The ink was thinly mixed and flakes of soot floated to the surface like crumbs of bread in a bowl of soup. The paper was coarse and unburnished, lacking the shiny finish of the quince kernels and egg white she was accustomed to working with. The pen was unkempt; she longed for a penknife to trim its rough edges, to hone it in preparation for the words forming in her head. She sat cross-legged and balanced the paper on thigh and knee. She felt it tremble a little and waited for it to settle. She began to write.

When the Bostanci-Bashi looked at the bold strokes and curving letters climbing the page, he had to blink twice before he saw that the calligrapher had woven her petition into the shape of a flower, of a type that his predecessors had once grown in the palace gardens. In his dreams he had felt the texture of this flower on his fingers, breathed its slight scent. He arranged for the petition to be framed. Eventually he sent word that the calligrapher would race against a *bostanci*, a junior gardener. They would begin on the top terrace of the palace's outer garden and run down to the fish-house gate in the sea wall. If the calligrapher reached the gate first, her life would be spared.

The calligrapher stood at the apex of the palace gardens and looked down at the sea. Half-starved, eyes burning in the sun's glare, she could barely stand. Her green *ferace* was torn, her shoes and veil had long since disappeared, and her hair, hacked off by the jailers, grew like black gorse across her skull. Only her hands remained defiant. Her fingernails were dark, henna-stained tips. On her left palm she had painted the letters of her name; on the right, the words *Insha'Allah*— God willing. The junior gardener stood at her side, broad-shouldered, his bare arms a document of cuts and scratches from the flora in his care.

At midday, a cannon boomed and the two figures began their descent to the shoreline. The young gardener was racing for pride; it had been many years since his brethren had lost the race against a condemned man, let alone a woman. The runners passed through and around thorny rose bushes, woods of guarded cypress, and, massed like vast armies reposed after battle, beds of hyacinths, narcissi, and tulips. *Bostancis* stood guard at each tier. Men dressed in similar sleeveless tunics and blue breeches were differentiated by the color of their belts: red for the Corps of Vine Grafters, yellow for the Corps of the Haystore, and blue and green for the rival Corps of Okra and Cabbage.

If the calligrapher veered from the path onto the sultan's flower beds, she would be struck down by the axe of the nearest *bostanci* before the race had run its course. She weaved around the aprons of attentive tulips, moving sideways and sometimes backwards to find a path, constantly thwarted as she tried to break into a steady run.

The junior gardener had already passed between the ranks of the Grand Turk's tulips—the Delicate Coquettes and Pomegranate Lances with their taut stems and silken petals. He knew the narrow paths well; he had worked this soil since he was a boy. His mind began to wander. Tomorrow he would be permitted to collect, cut, and place five of the finest specimens in filigree glasses in the sultan's private kiosk on the top tier of the gardens overlooking the Golden Horn. The sultan himself would choose one of these flowers to be placed in his private chamber. It would be a great honor for the young *bostanci*, a mark of the respect he could then expect from his colleagues.

But something was happening behind him. The calligrapher had arrived at a bed of the sultan's most prized tulips: the reddish/orange *Mahbub*, or Beloved, a single bulb of which a collector once offered one thousand gold coins to possess. The sultan himself had named this particular cultivar; its petals reminded him of the curve of the new moon that crested his beloved city on spring evenings. The calligrapher stopped dead in her tracks and stared. To the observing *bostancis*, it seemed she had given up on the race and decided to spend the remaining moments of her life enjoying the tulips' beauty. The calligrapher took a few steps back as if to gain a better perspective. The young gardeners nodded to each other. The woman was misguided and perhaps crazy, but she could appreciate beauty and was courageous; she would die a noble death. Then, without warning, she dashed toward the tulip bed, *ferace* billowing around her, hennaed fingers glinting in the sun.

The *bostancis* drew their axes; it seemed, after all, that the woman was a reprobate and would care no more about crushing the sacred flowers than stepping on a beetle. As they advanced toward her, the calligrapher began to dance, spin, and skip between each row of tulips. There was certainly no path cut through the meticulous flower bed—even a rabbit could not have forged its way between the tight ranks—but she pointed her bony toes downward and landed on the tiny strips of earth separating each line of flowers. The *bostancis* raised their axes and waited for the calligrapher to crush even a single petal. The Mahbub swayed and dipped their heads as if caught by a sudden breeze. In a few seconds, the calligrapher had traversed the flower bed without damaging a single bloom.

When the calligrapher passed in a flurry of silk and skin, the *bostanci* felt the earth exhale. Standing in her wake, he understood, for the first time, the true nature of the soil.

The *bostanci's* colleagues, not believing the evidence of their own eyes, surrounded the calligrapher. They prodded her with their rakes and hoes as if she were a snap-jawed plant. They might have returned her to the earth had not the Bostanci-Bashi arrived on the scene. He hadn't seen the calligrapher dance over his precious tulip beds; he had been waiting for her at the fish-house gate, garrote in hand, a woven sack crumpled at his feet like an exhausted dog. The reaction of his men told him that he would not have the pleasure of tightening the knot around the woman's neck and consigning her memory to the Golden Horn. But he restrained his young charges in case the calligrapher had some strange, magical attribute to use against him.

{

A week later, after the calligrapher's sentence was commuted to a seven-year exile, an envelope arrived at the Bostanci-Bashi's quarters. It contained one sheet of thick, creamy paper, emitting the faintest aroma of quince. He recognized the loops and curls of the script immediately, the elasticity of letters that could not be contained. Above a short note that read simply, 'from the beneficiary of your expertise,' the Bostanci-Bashi beheld a stork in full flight, its plumage a network of loops, lines, and dots, its fragile, fluted neck curving into a tipped beak.

CHAPTER 2

*T*he man told stories about flowers to help them bloom. Andersen had picked him out from the line of passengers sidling along the gangway toward the ship's mouth. Unlike his compatriots in their crimson fezzes, he wore a turban of deep blue, stacked in a whirl.

The voyage from Smyrna to Constantinople would take three days. In the harbor at Smyrna, the steamships rested at anchor like floating fortresses. Andersen stood on the deck of one of the biggest, *The Pegasus*, watching gondola-shaped boats skim back and forth between the ships, peddling newspapers, watermelons, and dates. When all the passengers were aboard, the captain asked them to surrender their weapons. This they did willingly, but not before firing a parting fusillade that rang through the old city with a *whip* and a *crack*. Andersen watched one of the Turks remove a feathered pen and an inkwell from the handle of his dagger before tossing the weapon onto the pile of pistols and cudgels in the middle of the deck. He set his writing materials in front of him with great care, as if not to upset their potential for transmitting his thoughts.

The man in the blue turban stood in the middle of the deck. His friends sat cross-legged before him, watching as he produced a flower from within the folds of his kaftan. The flower was still in its bud, hunched and quivering.

The man caressed the backs of the petals with the pads of his fingers as he spoke, holding the flower up to the light to reveal a glow of orange inside the curled bud. Andersen listened, uncomprehending, to the soft enunciation of his words, aware of the rise and fall of the man's pantaloons like a pair of silk lungs. He thought of his own, more physical, performances at dinner tables back home: pointing his nose into the air to form a swan's beak or dropping a shoulder for a humpbacked witch—the audience listening intently, dessert plates forgotten, children and adults peering briefly into each other's worlds. The blue-turbaned man reached the end of his story and bowed. Andersen joined the applause and felt the storyteller's green eyes rest upon him.

'I longed at that moment,' Andersen wrote in his journal some time later, 'to call out to this flower man, whose head was wrapped in blue silk, to tell him that I, too, told stories of flowers and birds and creatures he would surely recognize. We wouldn't need a common language. We could rule the world with the gifts God has bestowed upon us!'

Up on deck children played, and veiled women unwrapped sweetmeats of flaky pastry, honey, and walnuts. They tucked their pantaloons into long, leather boots over which they added red or blue slippers. Their eyes darted around the ship, taking in each of the passengers. Andersen bowed his head when their gaze lingered upon him.

Embarrassed by the women's scrutiny, he took out a letter from his friend, Edvard Colin, and pretended to read it. At the time Edvard had settled at his bureau in Copenhagen to write it, Andersen was making his first train journey from Magdeburg to Leipzig in a coach that 'glided along like a sledge on a smooth snowfield,' as he would later write. Edvard's letter had finally reached him in Rome. Andersen's play, *The Moorish Maid*, had played three nights at The Royal Theater, Edvard wrote. Catcalls and critics ensured it did not play a fourth. Edvard, in a limp attempt to console him, said most of Copenhagen had already forgotten *The Moorish Maid* and was celebrating the publication of Heiberg's *Digte*. Johan Ludvig Heiberg was Denmark's leading playwright and critic; he loathed Andersen. He had led the criticism of *The Moorish Maid*.

Andersen had been re-reading the letter for weeks. He had carried it along rutted roads from Rome to Naples and on the long sea voyage from Naples to Greece. He had read it in Athens and again in Smyrna when his ship finally reached the western coast of Turkey.

It wasn't the critical backlash that hurt; Andersen had begun his journey to the Golden Horn well before the opening night, partly in expectation of this criticism. No, it was Edvard's tone that bothered him—the remoteness, the formulaic insensitivity to his, Andersen's, feelings. Even Edvard's handwriting was rigid and unfeeling: the spines of his b's and k's ramrod straight, the c's curved like an arthritic uncle hunched over a book. Sentences jostled together so as not to waste space, one sheet of medium-quality writing paper describing a failure, his only link to home.

On the second morning, the steamer sailed into the Dardanelles Strait, carving a narrow passage between Asia and Europe. On the Asian side, a huge fortress loomed over them: towers, gun emplacements, and thick stone walls. The deck was cast in shadow. There was an impressive line of cannon but none were manned. Instead, soldiers in Western-style uniforms and fezzes lounged in the sun. They could barely summon the energy to respond to the waving children. Andersen had set up camp by the gunwale, asking for his coffee to be brought on a trestle table along with two chairs. He imagined the flower man's sapphire-blue silk filling the empty place beside him, but the Turk and his entourage sat with their backs to him, feet resting in the gaps of the railing.

At breakfast the talk had been of unrest in Bulgaria, the growing Ottoman deficit, and from Constantinople, rumors of innovation and abominable practices carried out by the city's Sufis. Andersen caught these morsels from the Europeans on board. He was curious, but not curious enough to engage these noisy groups in conversation. Their Turkish dress—cotton kaftans, satin slippers, and occasionally, a fez—bothered him. The fezzes perched awkwardly on these European heads as if they had yet to find their groove.

He felt the *tap tap* of something sharp on his knee. A Turkish girl, no more than five or six years old, was standing in front of him holding out a clay teapot in the shape of a horse. She was wearing the same cotton pantaloons that served the Turks so admirably for traveling—tapering at the ankles but baggy at the thigh and knee. Tiny gold coins acted as buttons for her tunic and threaded their way through her hair. Andersen took the toy and treated the girl to his most engaging smile. She took a step backward. Behind each ear of the horse was stationed a tiny bird—one yellow, one green.

He asked her in German who had made the teapot. She stared at him blankly. Andersen tried another smile. How foolish to address this child in functional and terrifying German! He began a story about the horse-shaped teapot and the two birds in Danish, and the girl laughed, pointing at his mouth as the funny phrases came tumbling out, a special sing-song language for the tea-drinking birds. Soon, her sisters were crowding round to listen, and the adults too, standing at a respectful distance. They could not understand his words, but sensed the presence of a story as surely as the hovering gulls sensed the onset of lunch.

"The teapot enjoyed pride of place on the kitchen sideboard of a wealthy merchant family," Andersen began. "Although he was only made of clay, the teapot's unusual shape made him popular with everyone in the house. When the merchant and his wife entertained, the teapot was brought into the parlor, where he stood proudly with cups and saucers made of the finest china.

"The merchant's children loved to make up stories about the horse-shaped teapot and its tiny bird friends. The teapot, who had never been outside the parlor or kitchen, listened to these tales and imagined himself as a real horse galloping across the desert or carrying kings and queens through streets thronged with cheering people. When the birds heard this talk of far-away lands, they too got excited and chattered about flying around the world to see it for themselves when their wings grew bigger. But the teapot was a realist, and pointed out that they would struggle to survive outside the kitchen, where it was always warm and comfortable. 'It's all very well to dream of rich cities and vast rivers and seas,' he said. 'But we belong here, in this kitchen, where we have an important job to do.'"

Andersen was pleased with this opening. He pictured a Copenhagen audience nodding approvingly at the teapot's lack of ambition. But the little girl's attention had wandered; she was already singing softly to the birds and creating her own adventure for the teapot. Andersen patted his pockets as if he had misplaced something vital. He pulled out a pair of black scissors and a piece of thick, white paper folded into sharply creased sections. He got out of his chair to flatten the paper on the surface of the deck. He placed his thumb and forefinger in the eyes of the scissors and made them perform a ragged dance over the paper. The girl stared. Andersen picked up the piece of paper and placed it on his lap. Then, without warning, the paper, scissors, and his fingers were as one, dexterous and fluid as the component parts of a steam engine. His arm dipped and his wrist flexed as he made incisions, restraining the hungry blades when it seemed the paper would disintegrate into nothing. He made three more snips, frowned, and lifted the paper structure onto the trestle table beside his chair.

When he said the word in Danish for what he'd made, the children no longer sniggered at his strange tongue. They saw a mosque shaped like a fantastic ship with minarets for funnels. Emerging from the threshold of this paper structure was a dervish wearing a conical hat barely resting on his head, as if the merest breeze would cause it to float into the sky. On top of the hat perched a tiny bird. The girl laughed and held out her hand. More applause ensued. Andersen looked up and saw the blue-turbaned flower man standing at the back of the audience, sucking on his pipe. He nodded when he caught Andersen's eye.

❧

On the second night, the Marmara Sea seethed, forcing Andersen, in his cabin, to cling to the sides of his fixed bed. He lay fully clothed with passport in pocket, ready to make a dash for the lifeboats. The ship lurched to port and Andersen spoke reluctantly to God.

It seemed unreasonable, Andersen explained to his maker, for him to perish at this juncture of his life. Why, he had even found one of his own works in a bookshop in Leipzig! (He left out the part where the bookseller had dismissed the author as a 'Swedish upstart,' and offered to sell the book at an insultingly low price). What great work he would do if he were spared! He would rise above the critical setbacks. One of the reasons he had embarked on this long journey through southern Europe and into Turkey was to *think* about his writing away from the ciphers with their measly metaphors and dull axioms. 'Real genius,' a critic had written in response to one of Andersen's recent works, 'is not a tiny candle extinguished by any wind, but a fire which the wind merely challenges.'

What dullness! Andersen would return to Copenhagen a wiser man after this trip, refreshed and ready to work.

He felt a little better at this prospect and decided to make a determined effort to survive. He matched his breathing to the rolling of the ship, *in* as it threw him toward the far wall, *out* as it tossed him toward the edge of the bed; in this way he would establish a calming rhythm. It worked for a minute or two, but he was forced to take in ever-larger lungfuls of air, and soon, his heart began to race and his head to pound.

Just as he thought he'd pass out, Andersen heard a scratching sound outside his door. The first departing rat perhaps, or an intruder—a desperate stowaway planning to rob and murder him. He reeled toward the door, forced to take a step back for every two forward. Even in his turmoil, Andersen sensed somebody biding their time on the other side, listening, ear pressed to the wood. He pictured a pair of long fingers stroking the grain, as if caught between two minds as to whether to knock. He opened the door to the sound of receding footsteps, but a fragrance lingered in the passage. Something elusive, bergamot perhaps, blended with a sweetness he could not identify. Bleary-eyed, Andersen stood in the corridor with his nose in the air like a rodent.

Eventually he slept and was soothed by a dream in which the deck of the ship became the stage of the Royal Theater, and all of Copenhagen stood to applaud his story of the horse-shaped teapot and its resident birds.

᪲

Arriving on deck the next morning, he found the passengers in a state of excitement. The steward who brought him his coffee rested his hand on

Andersen's shoulder and said, "Soon, Monsieur, you will see the first minarets of Stamboul." Andersen nodded and settled in his position by the gunwale.

The flower man, his back to Andersen, stood with his friends, gazing out at the emerging contours of the city. Andersen closed his eyes and listened to the lapping of the waves. If he could only speak with this storyteller, he might form a lasting memory, an image beyond the physical, beyond the lilt of the voice that had danced around those impossibly long words and shaped them into a tale.

The crumbling walls of the city were visible now. Fishermen stood anciently in their shadows. Constantinople! Andersen had dreamed of this moment ever since leaving Copenhagen two months earlier. He had told everybody he met on the way—in Hamburg, Leipzig, and Innsbruck; in Florence, Rome, and Naples; in Malta and Greece—that he was going to the Orient, to the sultan's capital, to the Asiatic East. He had enjoyed the look of shock, followed by puzzlement and even distaste. His Danish friends believed he would not get to Constantinople— thwarted by a lack of funds, political instability, or the simple desire to return home.

Soon the walls of the city faded, and the fishermen and minarets vanished, one by one. Fog, thick and clammy, clambered over the boat's sides and tickled the sails. Andersen stood by the railing. The engines died and the boatswain shinned up the stempost, foghorn in hand. The passengers fell silent as the horn sounded, plaintive and distant, as if a recumbent beast were announcing its own demise. Voices called to each other, "brig a-hoy!" and the equivalent in a hundred tongues. Andersen gripped the railing so hard his knuckles drained of blood.

The flower man was standing next to him. Had he been there all along—staring, like Andersen, into the fog? Andersen sniffed, hoping to catch on the flower-man the bergamot-infused scent from the corridor outside his cabin. But he smelled only the salty tang of the sea.

"Do not concern yourself. The mist is capricious; it will soon tire of its trickery and move away."

He spoke in a modulated High German, carefully pronouncing each syllable as if it adhered to the end of his tongue.

"The other ships seem awfully close," Andersen said.

Ignoring this remark, the flower man said, "I will tell you my name. It's Musa *Effendi*."

Andersen introduced himself and offered his hand, which Musa held lightly as if afraid of damaging it.

"You are a German," Musa said, withdrawing his hand. "But when you told that story to the children, you used a dialect I didn't recognize."

"No. It was Danish. It is my native language. I am Danish."

Musa tilted his head to the left as if to consider this new information. "The Captain told me a writer from the German lands was aboard," he said.

Despite the slow lilt of his diction, he flattened the end of his sentences, giving his statements the air of irrefutable fact.

"Well, I am a writer—a writer from Denmark."

"A *renowned* writer, according to the Captain."

Andersen watched films of mist spell the word 'renowned' on the tips of the waves. A passenger boat went by in the opposite direction, so close he instinctively sucked in his cheeks. In its wake, he thought he heard the strains of a waltz, the orchestra struggling to keep pace with the boat's progress, footsteps shuffling around the deck.

"Have you heard of my work?" he asked.

"You are a writer whom some Germans know. But you are not known here."

"And you are a storyteller; perhaps a writer, too," Andersen said, unconsciously imitating the flat insistence of the other man's diction.

Musa turned from the rail and looked at him as if surprised by the observation. He was taller than most of the Turks Andersen had seen, slightly shorter than Andersen himself, but much broader. Broad but lean. His blue kaftan stretched snugly over his shoulders. A turban of the same velveteen blue pulled at the skin of his forehead and smoothed the lines on his face.

"I do tell stories, Herr Andersen," Musa said, angling his head to the left. "But they are not my business. No doubt you would like to know what my business is."

Andersen felt like a small boy about to receive a delicious confection.

"Yes, I would," he said.

"And I will tell you, but all in good time. It will give us something to talk about, should our conversation run dry. And I believe we have not finished talking about storytelling."

Musa tilted his head again and Andersen realized he was expected to respond.

"No," he said.

"As I thought."

The fog lifted to starboard to reveal gravestones, unevenly spaced and of different heights, pitching down a hillside.

"I saw you," Andersen said, "telling your friends a story, involving that flower you carry in your pocket."

"That is true. I was relating a tale that is known in my family as 'The Tulip with the Unbreakable Stem.' It was a story my father learned from his father, and is much loved in our *tekke*, the lodge of our brotherhood. When I tell it, I try to engage the memory of my audience. It is a tale they already know. I merely add whatever color and mood I can under the circumstances. You, on the other hand, are an originator. That is what I am told, although I do not know your work."

Andersen felt somehow at fault for this.

"And for your work, this original work, you receive payment?" Musa's eyebrow climbed sloth-like toward his turban.

"Sometimes I do, yes."

"But you make a living from writing. It is your profession. You do nothing else."

"Yes, that's true."

Silence while Musa pondered this.

"No doubt you would like to hear the story of the tulip with the unbreakable stem," he said.

"Very much."

"But I think now is not the appropriate time, as we are about to disembark."

"I suppose not."

Both men turned back to the rail just as the steamer entered the Golden Horn, the cornucopia-shaped inlet of water that divided European Constantinople in two, and whose entrance marked the confluence of the Marmara Sea and the Bosphorus Strait. On their left, jutting out into the water like the underjaw of a great and thirsty fish, the sultan's palace commanded a perfect view of the Asian shore.

"The paper cutting," Musa was saying in a low voice. "You were trained in this art? You studied under an *usta*, a master?"

"No. It's something I've always done. Since childhood."

Musa kept his eyes on the mosques and the dense, red-roofed buildings that seemed to mutate from within one another. "The ship you cut for the child. Can you re...recreate that for me? The same ship, the same holy man. Can it be done?"

Andersen could not suppress a smile. "Why of course, Musa Effendi!" His first use of the Turk's name fizzled pleasantly on his tongue.

Musa nodded and turned back to the rail, contemplating the ranks of stoop-backed porters on the dockside. "Then," he said, "perhaps we could meet."

The steamer maneuvered itself into docking position and Andersen glimpsed, on the opposite shore, the old city of Stamboul, its silver-tipped minarets craning through the thinning mist like the necks of great storks. They would disembark at Galata, the business quarter for European merchants. At the landing place, a line of gondolas formed a precarious bridge to take them to shore. Andersen worried for his hat-box and other valuables.

To Musa Effendi he suggested tea at his hotel, adopting a casual tone. Musa said he would meet him after evening prayers, and although Andersen had no idea when evening prayers were, he felt as happy as a child.

❧

Andersen engaged the services of an ancient porter and shuffled along behind the man's bent back, watching his luggage—trunk, overnight bag, and hatbox—sink ever closer to the ground. They climbed a steep hill while swarms of people passed by and around them on foot, horseback, and sedan chairs. Crooked wooden buildings arched their frames out over the street, and through the barred windows of their basements, Andersen saw figures pounding metal and fashioning wood, each domain a tiny workshop. When they finally reached the hotel, in what Andersen's guidebook assured him was the fashionable district of Pera, the porter straightened slowly, like a mechanical soldier, to receive his tip.

At the Hotel de la France, water tinkled in marble fountains and a string trio prepared to play. Tapestries and *kilims*, woven rugs with complex geometric patterns, hung on the walls. Cushions lay on the floor, if one tired of tables and chairs. Europeans lounged on these, blowing smoke rings into the air and supping coffee: Parisians pretending to be pashas, Savoyards dreaming of the Seraglio.

Andersen produced his passport, which no one had bothered to look at, let alone stamp, since he had left Greece. What if a Turkish official should demand to see it and accuse him of willfully promenading with incomplete documentation? Without a stamp in his passport, Andersen felt he had not truly arrived. The receptionist at the hotel desk gave his passport the most cursory of glances before returning it to him.

The monsieur would be staying at the hotel for six nights, *non*? The receptionist said this with a certain amount of scorn, as if Andersen, in his gray Western suit, was the traveling equivalent of a summer fly—to be batted away as a temporary nuisance. The monsieur's room would be ready in fifteen minutes.

Andersen strolled around the lounge, admiring the collection of bird cages placed on window ledges and nestled in nooks and crannies around the walls. He peered into one of them, through a dark façade of finely scrolled branches and leaves, startling the inhabitant. The dense facades of the cages, while beautiful, did not allow one a good view of the birds inside, nor a clear sounding of the creatures' songs. In fact, the birds did not appear to be making any noise at all. Their silence gave one the sensation of being watched by feathered sentinels from deep within the shadows.

Andersen decided to order coffee from one of the waiters shuttling back and forth, who switched tongues at will like stewards from Babel. He perched himself on a chaise lounge and surveyed the scene. A waiter came to a halt by his side. For a second, Andersen thought of testing the fellow with a burst of Danish, but settled instead for ordering his coffee in German. He sat back just as the musicians eased into a Haydn *Divertimento*.

Sitting opposite him was a man reading a very large newspaper, the city's weekly *Moniteur Ottoman*. The only portion of the man Andersen could see from behind the newsprint was a pair of legs tented by a bright green kaftan, and a flossing of red hair on his calves. He greeted the man in French but the man either did not, or chose not, to hear. Andersen looked at the back of the *Moniteur Ottoman* and blinked.

It was divided into three columns, but halfway down, the print was interrupted by a neat rectangle covering the width of the page. This was filled with various squiggles, loops, and lines, which at first seemed to follow no particular form or order, as though someone had given the newspaper an almighty shake, causing the print to disintegrate and reform in mysterious ways. It took Andersen a few seconds to realize he was looking at the outline of a large cat whose mane, whiskers, and facial features had been fashioned out of these looped markings. At the bottom of the rectangle was the following caption:

RETRAITE SE TRANSPORTE PLUS DE PRÈS A DIEU

To God? Closer to God? Something that transports one to the maker? A sacred place where one can find God? A retreat, perhaps a holy retreat.

He looked again at the cat. It seemed exhausted—black shading under the eyes, a sunken, jowly quality to the cheeks. One foot was barely raised off the ground, as if the next step were an immense burden. Even its claws appeared bitten down to the nub.

Andersen leaned a little closer. There was something not quite right about the image. The ink was a little darker than the surrounding print, and the beast seemed to glisten, as if its heavy tread and unhappy disposition were causing it to perspire. A trick of the light no doubt, yet Andersen had the uncontrollable urge to put his fingertip on the lion's mane to see if it was fully dry. He extended his arm toward the beast, who regarded him with a singular lack of curiosity. The man lowered the newspaper and met his gaze. Andersen, leaning forward with his arm outstretched, froze. The man showed no surprise at Andersen's behavior; in fact, he seemed to be waiting for him to speak. He had the same red hair on his head, and an eyebrow that grew in a continuous line above his eyes. He was very thin and pale and the glow of the lamp behind him made it seem as if he were lit from within.

Andersen wanted to say something, to explain his embarrassing invasion of the reader's privacy. But while he wondered how best to frame his apology, the man deftly folded his newspaper and left without a word.

§

When his room was ready, Andersen asked if he might acquire a timetable of evening prayers. No such article exists, he was told, but if the monsieur would care to retire to his room around sunset, he would be able to hear the *ezan*, the call to prayer, without undue difficulty. Perhaps the monsieur would like to take tea while he listened?

Andersen took off his boots, and, noticing they needed a polish, put them outside his door. To ensure they would not be sent back to the wrong guest, he wrote his room number on a piece of paper and attached it to the tassel of one of the boots. He went back inside and watched the shadows lengthen over the red slate roofs of the houses. Then a man's voice called to the faithful. For a few seconds, this quivering tenor sang alone, but then a second and a third voice joined the chorus until a hundred human clocks, turning slowly in their candle-shaped towers, united to proclaim the glory of Allah. Andersen waited until the calls faded and then attended to his dress. He would allow half an hour to pass before going downstairs and keeping his rendezvous with Musa Effendi, the flower man.

CHAPTER 3

*T*he calligrapher greeted her old friend, the Bosphorus, from the top of one of Istanbul's seven hills. One hill for each year she had been away.

She had walked for hours with only the trees, preening their new spring leaves, for company. But now she could see whitewashed farmers' houses with wisteria scaling their walls. She thought of the lives that went on inside and around these simple dwellings, lives unchanged and unchecked by anything that might have happened to her. And when she walked a little further down the hill, she saw it—a streak of metallic blue through the trees, silent from this height but visibly in motion, pushing its troubles relentlessly toward the Black Sea. It, too, like any good stretch of water, had gone on without her.

The calligrapher worked her way down toward its shore, listening all the while for the murmur of its current. She passed fishermen's shacks with mounds of freshly caught turbot piled outside their doors: dark, grimy fish with scales like the imprint of human thumbs. In the cemetery on the hillside, a gravestone informed her she was in the village of Bebek. The inscription, which included some erratic punctuation, lauded the deceased gentleman's piety, despite the gaiety of his surroundings.

Amid the green and red fishing boats and couples strolling affably along the shore, she realized what a sight she must be. The dirt and smell of her walk clung to her *ferace* and darkened her skin. Her hair had come loose from its scarf and bits of twig and leaf stuck to her sides. The calligrapher brushed herself down and took out the cypress cone she carried in the pocket of her *ferace*. Every morning she would find a fresh one and place it in her pocket, enjoying the ritual of selection and the light touch of the cone against her leg. Now she turned it over and over in her hands, feeling its ridges press into her palms. When she had finished with the cone, she licked her hands and rubbed them over her face and neck, inhaling the earthy, spicy fragrance.

The calligrapher breathed a lungful of cool, moist air. She was sure no one here would know her—she was still a day's walk from her old life. Even so, she could see, to her right, the distant domes and minarets of the city; there, amid the tangle of wooden buildings and stone mosques, was the place her home had once stood.

In Bebek, everywhere she looked, men were climbing ladders to hang strings of lights. The Prophet's birthday would be celebrated soon, and all the vantage points in the city, all the domes and towers and roofs, would light up in his memory.

On the waterfront two Greek fishermen were grilling their catch on the deck of a boat. In her mind, the calligrapher consumed the fish supper: the succulent, slightly charred flesh; the crunchy texture of the accompanying bread; the oil sliding down her chin. But the fishermen glared when she approached.

"She looks like a crazy Arab," one of them shouted. The villagers and day-trippers who had rowed over from their summer *yalis* laughed, pointing with crusts of bread or cobs of roasted corn.

The calligrapher ignored the comments and stared at the tiny figures on the opposite Asian shore, each standing beside the other as evenly spaced as ink letters. A rowboat piled high with something she could not see pushed off from that further shore: a lone rower, tiny toothpick oars passing through the water.

She looked into the green-blue water and pictured the murdered and careless reclining on the seabed. Fifteen years had passed since a fleet of boats carrying the old sultan's troops had also set off from the Asian shore, bent on destroying the Sufi sect of her father. The soldiers carried blazing torches and wore new, European-style tunics of pristine blue, but their evil was as old as the seven hills.

There had been nothing left of her parents after the sultan's soldiers had set their fires. Not a shred of clothing or a cup or a piece of her mother's jade. There were no charred remains for her to examine, no set of grinning teeth. Nothing but the blackened earth. The calligrapher had been sixteen years old.

Her parents had sent her away to visit a relative on the morning of the fire. They knew the men were coming. Her father believed he could talk them out of any brutality.

He loved words, her father; he chose them carefully, dispatching sentences like emissaries from a jeweled palace. The only time she could remember him falling silent was when she practiced her script. He had taught her to write as a child; taught her, through his speech, the power of letters. His own script was as bland as unseasoned pilaf. But his syntax was soft and textured. If a single soldier, at least one New Guard, had taken the time to listen to him, had caught an inflection, heard her father's rhythmic cadence amid the mayhem of burning wood and flesh, then he had not died in vain.

The rowboat moved toward her, laden with mounds of fruit, melons perhaps, great domes of sweetness stacked pyramid-style. She thought of the rower and pictured the rhythmic heft of his shoulder blades, the clench of his back muscles. He would reach her side of the Bosphorus, the European side, quickly as the strait was quite narrow at that point.

The water began to lap harder at the shore, causing the fishing boat to dip and sway. The Greek fishermen looked toward the open water, in the direction of the city, but saw no traffic other than the lone boat with its cargo of fruit, much too small to have caused such a wake.

The waves swelled and the fishing boat rocked as the fishermen held on with both hands. Fish slid across the deck and dropped into the water; loaves of bread were crushed underfoot. A wave pinioned the boat to shore and when it receded, the whole thing was sucked under the surface for a second.

The calligrapher looked for the rowboat, which had veered slightly to the left, circumventing the turbulent waters. When the water went calm, settling like soup after stirring, only one fisherman stood on the deck, his mouth open but no sound coming out. The second fisherman had vanished. The villagers and day-trippers dispersed, nodding like indulgent parents; how petulant the Bosphorus could be!

Whole fish and loaves of bread lay strewn on the shore. The calligrapher brushed off the fish and dried the soggy loaf on the sleeve of her *ferace*, just as the first of the cats darted in.

The fruit seller was pulling onto shore, laughing and shouting, "It's a great day to be out on the water, sister!" She smiled through a mouthful of fish and was about to continue on her way when the man arched his knife into the green hide of a melon. He held out the half-fruit to her like a freshly sacrificed offering.

§

The calligrapher planned to spend the night under a mulberry tree or in the niche of a stone wall. Her body was weary but her mind, fortified by the fish, bread, and melon, remained alert. The sun had lowered its eye to the west and the moon winked at her between the clouds.

The Bosphorus was as gray in the twilight as the suits of the diplomats who stood at the windows of their *yalis*, bemoaning the state of the empire. The calligrapher was cold, despite the mildness of the evening. She wanted seclusion, a vantage point from where she could watch the Bosphorus but not be seen.

She walked on and came to the battlement walls and turrets of a fortress. It was said that Mehmet the Conqueror ordered this very circuit of walls to be built in the shape of his own name. The calligrapher could make out only the first letter, *mim*; a conveniently placed tower formed its upper curve.

And suddenly she was envisioning the lettered plan of the fortress as it *should* be drawn, the Conqueror's name firm and unwavering. This rush of confidence in her ability to plan and shape letters was a surprise. In her seven-year exile from the city, she hadn't even looked at a pen or sheet of paper.

A line of abandoned cannons raised on concrete plinths stood on the shore in front of the fortress. Some fishermen, reeling in their lines and securing their bait, stood close by. The calligrapher settled her back against the trunk of a Judas tree, shaded and shielded by the pink leaves, and kept her eye on the dark cylinders of the cannons above, waiting for night to fall.

When the fishermen departed, she moved quickly. There were three cannons, each one slightly bigger than the last. The calligrapher ran her hand along the surface of one of the muzzles, tracing her fingers around the pendant of the maker's name at the base. There was a date inscribed too, but it had eroded away to a series of tiny marks; she could make out the tail of a six, perhaps, or the flourish at the top of a four.

A rustling noise came from inside the cylinder of the largest cannon. At first, she thought a cat or rodent was foraging within, but then a human voice boomed through the iron: "What are you?"

The 'you' of the question reverberated loudly through the cannon and echoed off the hills behind her, as though half the city were calling her name. The calligrapher gathered herself and said, "I'm a woman seeking shelter."

The person inside the cannon reacted to this by squirming and writhing to such an extent that the cannon shook, plinth and all. There was a pinging sound followed by a yelp, suggesting the occupant had bumped his head.

"Can't you help me out of here?" said the subterranean voice. "It's much easier to get in one of these things than out, you know."

The calligrapher peered into the open end of the cannon and saw a turbaned head and an upturned, furry mass of beard.

"What do you want me to do?" she said.

"Can you get your hands inside the cylinder and grab me by the sides of my head? Being a woman, you probably have small hands. Unless you're a char woman. They have hands like shovels. You're not a char woman, are you?"

"No."

"God be praised."

This short speech appeared to have taken its toll on the cannon dweller, as it was followed by some troubled wheezing.

"Are you alright?" asked the calligrapher.

"Yes, yes, yes," echoed the voice.

"I'm putting my hands in. If you're ready, I'll pull you out."

There was a grunt, and the calligrapher, with a tenuous grip on the sides of the man's turban, tried to pull his head clear of the cannon. The man inched himself along the inside of the cylinder until his head and shoulders appeared, followed by his arms, which he used to wriggle the lowest part of his body free. He then arched himself backwards so that only his feet remained in the cannon and his hands rested on the ground behind him.

Eventually, he freed himself completely, stood up, brushed himself down, and turned to look at his rescuer. Upright, he was tall, and despite his accommodation, he looked reasonably clean. His kaftan was crumpled but unsoiled and his turban was immaculate. Both were green.

"How do you normally get yourself out of there?" she asked.

"Oh, I'm not usually alone. There are two more of us who sleep here, each one a little smaller than the last." He waved a hand at the three cannons. "It's a very satisfactory arrangement."

"And where are your friends now?"

"Wandering."

"Wandering where?"

"Wherever the need arises. My colleagues are night owls; they prefer to roam by the dint of the moon. I'm older and keep more regular daytime habits." As if to confirm this, the man cast an anxious look at the moonlit sky and the phosphoric glow of the Bosphorus' surface. The calligrapher closed her eyes and imagined his face as she would have written it: a series of letters slotted into place like a mystic puzzle: the *nuns* of the eyebrows neatly punctuated by a tiny mole, the sagging *ayns* of his tired eyes, the bloodless *mims* of his lips.

She thought of another wanderer she had known, the man who had helped her after her parents' death. That man had called himself a dervish, one who renounced the world and felt the presence of God in his bones. She opened her eyes and saw in the green-clad figure standing before her the same personality in the loops below his eyes, the weft of his cheekbones. She would call him a dervish too. A green dervish.

"Is there something I can assist you with?" the green dervish asked. "You said something about shelter?"

"Yes. I was thinking of crawling inside one of the cannons myself, just for the night. But now I know they are occupied…"

The dervish gestured expansively at the row of cannons. "As I told you, my friends are out on their nocturnal roam. I see no reason why you couldn't squeeze into the smallest of the cannons there, on the right. I should imagine it's your size."

"I am very grateful."

The dervish once more allowed his eyes to range over the calligrapher, starting from her dirty headscarf and *ferace*, and ending with her ragged sandals.

"You cut a curious figure, my girl," he said. "Your appearance is squalid, but I hear from your voice that you are an educated woman."

The calligrapher lowered her eyes.

"Ah, another exile, I fear. Don't concern yourself too much," the dervish continued. "You are not uncommon, believe me. We're mostly all exiles here, of one sort or another. I've seen more than a few women seeking shelter on these shores too. How long has it been for you?"

"Seven years."

"And I'll wager that seven years ago, they told you at the palace to walk for a week in any direction."

The calligrapher nodded.

"And never to return on pain of death?"

"Yes."

"Humph! They always say that! As if after a week of pointless plodding you are going to say, 'That's it! Here I am! I have reached the point of exile and I will begin my life anew!'"

The calligrapher smiled. It was true the word *exile* had first conjured an image of adventure—fortress cities built on desert sands, camel trains, and convict ships—but in reality, her punishment had been to slip silently through the hole of people's memories, to become invisible, even to herself.

"You'd think they might vary their expulsion terms occasionally," the dervish continued. "Walk for two and a half weeks, for example, or head only in a southerly direction." He shook his head while the calligrapher looked longingly toward her allotted sleeping place. Someone nearby was coaxing sound from an instrument, a few delicate notes: woody, husky, and deeply familiar.

The dervish said, "I believe you have a gift that caused you to leave."

"I'm a calligrapher."

"Then I will ask you one question. Do you write from the heart? Because if you do, you threaten the sultan's holy men with their bird's nest brains of partially digested beliefs. You menace their fragile minds like a cat or a gust of wind with something as simple as love."

"I know no other way."

"Good!" the dervish said, brightening. He laid his hand tenderly on the cylinder of the largest cannon. "These are fine cannons, my girl. You might find it unusual that a holy man should seek sanctuary within weapons of such violent capacity. But there is something about these iron beasts that is quite noble. Why don't you sit a little, on this one if you like, and I'll tell you something of their story?"

The sound from the instrument grew stronger, and she heard a melody, a delicate daisy-chain of notes. It shook her so much that she had to turn away from the dervish to look across the moon-streaked water.

It was a reed-flute, a *ney*, like the one her mother had played at home when the calligrapher was very young. It was a private affair. She would play alone in a room when her family were busy elsewhere in the house or absent. Sometimes she would pick the instrument up but not play it, content to feel its lightness in her hands, pressing her fingers into the finely carved holes, fidgeting with it like a set of prayer beads.

The dervish, too, listened to the sound, his face solemn, hand still resting on the cannon.

The music stopped. The dervish, as if he had been waiting for this moment, started talking again. The calligrapher maneuvered herself onto the snout of the smallest cylinder and looked out over the Bosphorus. Exhausted, she would have given anything to climb inside and sleep, but she understood that, as a wayfarer in search of shelter, she had to pay appropriate homage to these cannons by allowing their custodian to be her guide.

"These weapons played an important role in the siege and liberation of our city," the dervish said, and began to tell her the story of the cannons, how they had once fired their huge cannonballs at the heads of the Christians. The men worked day and night to light the fuses while the Christians, like terrified sheep, ran back and forth as great stone projectiles rained down on them like the wrath of God. After two days of intense bombardment, the walls surrounding the city were breached and the sultan and his men poured in. The flag was raised and the muezzins climbed onto the roofs of the biggest churches and sang the first call to prayer.

"The cannon corpsmen were delighted with their weapons but a little too pleased with themselves," the dervish said, shaking his head. He told her that, although the order had been given to stop firing, the men saw some Christians trying to escape by boat—tiny figures heading up the Bosphorus as the city burned around them. They thought it would be good sport to try some target practice on these desperate and defeated men, so set about reloading their missiles and lighting the fuses. As the first boat of this forlorn flotilla passed into range, the corpsmen pointed the muzzles and released the triggers, chuckling to each other in a distasteful way.

The dervish paused for dramatic effect. The calligrapher saw three *caiques*, each containing a rower and one seated figure, converging from equidistant points toward the center of the water.

The dervish coughed, bringing her attention back to him and his story.

"The cannons shuddered mightily as they fired," he said. "And the men waited, expecting the Christians' boat to be blown sky high."

But nothing happened: the boat rowed on and there was no sign of impact in the surrounding water. Baffled, the men reloaded the cannons and waited for another boat to come along. Once again they fired, this time taking even more careful aim. Then a plopping sound echoed through the battlements; the cannonball had dropped harmlessly into the sea a mere ten meters away! Furious, the men reloaded and, in demented fashion, fired repeatedly, even though the Christian boats had long since passed. At each attempt, they were driven half-mad by the cannonballs dropping into the Bosphorus.

The *caiques* had reached the middle of the Bosphorus and were touching prows like hounds exchanging scents. From each boat, a seated figure rose. Each was holding a *ney*. Turning a full circle, all three figures made a series of elaborate bows to one another.

"Plop!" said the dervish. "Lovely! You see, God or these cannons, or perhaps both, knew that the battle was over and their job was done."

The calligrapher nodded and smiled, and patted the snout of her own cannon in appreciation. Now, in response to the neys, voices that she assumed belonged to the rowers rose from the water and attached themselves to the melody, drawing it outward and upward, lingering for a moment on its peak.

The green dervish also seemed transfixed by the performance. The calligrapher wondered briefly if this was a regular occurrence for him, but was distracted by another memory working its way through the deep sediment of her past.

She had been out on the Bosphorus on one of these boats with her parents many years ago. She could not remember the occasion, but the three of them had hired a *caique* and drifted out to the center in a similar way. Theirs had been a solitary boat, her father rowing strenuously against the current, her mother's *ney* resting on her lap. Her mother, who had never in her memory performed for an audience, was eager to play in this most public of private places where one could project sound so effectively but not be scrutinized.

Had her father sung a melody to her mother's accompaniment? He would occasionally sing in public, his thin, scratchy voice capable of surprising pathos. Only her mother's playing remained in her memory, though: those haunting strains, intimate to the boat and its passengers at first, but then audible to those silhouetted against the shoreline who had stopped to listen.

Now the musicians had finished and were rowing their *caiques* back to the points on the shore from which they had come.

"Why do they do that?' she asked.

The green dervish shrugged. "Why wouldn't they?" he said, and turned his attention back to the cannons, shaking his head in admiration and saying "Plop!" and "Lovely!" to no one in particular.

The calligrapher bade him goodnight and climbed into her cannon. As she wriggled around to make herself comfortable, she could still hear the mournful music of the evening in her head, as if from within the gray soul of the sea itself.

CHAPTER 4

*A*ndersen stood in front of a tall, oval mirror in the hotel lounge, stroking fingertips of cologne onto his cheeks and eyebrows. His best dark suit, freshly brushed, with its high collar and knotted cravat, was already causing his brow to spot with sweat on the warm spring evening. His soft face, devoid of whiskers, showed the beginnings of a flush. Staring into the mirror, he wondered if Musa had been struck, as most were, by his extraordinary nose, the beak-like protuberance that plunged his mouth and chin into shadow. Had Musa even noticed his pale blue eyes beside such a remorseless feature? Andersen sighed and turned away from his reflection.

In an attempt to change his frame of mind, he went over to the reception desk. Perhaps he would catch another glimpse of the cat-shaped image he had seen on the back of the local newspaper before Musa arrived. But when he approached the reception desk to request a copy, he was told of a "Turkish gentleman" already awaiting him in the small courtyard garden. A few seconds later the two men were shaking hands. Musa wore a claret-colored robe and turban, freshly wrapped, Andersen supposed, that evening. It was Musa who suggested they have their tea brought to Andersen's room where they would not be disturbed.

At the door, Andersen struggled with the brass key. His pulse quickened. He feared he would not be able to summon the energy or wit for the small-talk required on occasions such as this. To calm himself, he imagined his possessions neatly stored in their designated places: passport inside a sock, money-pouch pressed into the cover of his journal, soaps and lotions lined up by order of size on the sink. Nothing pleased him more than the proper arrangement of his things, especially when he'd been traveling and in disarray for so many weeks.

The lock finally slid, the door gliding open. Andersen beckoned Musa to sit, and was enchanted by the rustle and flow of the Turk's kaftan as it draped about the contours of the chair.

"Ah, *Dwarf's Purple*," Musa said, gesturing at the flower next to Andersen's bed. "Named because the stem is considerably shorter than other examples of the species." Andersen hadn't really looked at the flower, left by hotel staff, in its delicate filigree vase. The petals were a milky mauve color, stretching into stunted points like the antennae of a fading insect.

"I don't recognize it," he said.

"You are not familiar with the tulip?"

"This is a tulip? In Denmark we import thousands of tulips from Holland, but I have never seen one like this."

"Once, all tulips in Istanbul were shaped in such a way," Musa said sadly. "Only with much longer stems and petals. Colors, too, of every conceivable hue and combination. Now only this runt remains to remind us of what we have lost."

"And is that what you do for a living? Grow these tulips?"

"No, I merely trade in the bulbs of the more common varieties, specimens that would be familiar to you in Europe."

Andersen held the flower to his nose, but smelled instead Musa's fragrance, which was occupying the room slowly, exploring the surface areas and caressing the furniture. He thought of the smell of bergamot in the corridor outside his cabin, wanting it to be the same, but Musa's fragrance reminded him of Copenhagen and the elderberry tree that nuzzled against his study window back home, the one where swallows returned every spring to nest.

A waiter arrived with the tea in a silver samovar, polished and glinting, raised above a tray of sizzling charcoal. There were two tulip-shaped glasses. To Andersen's relief, Musa took charge, procuring a pair of tongs from a little door in the side of the contraption and rearranging the charcoal before venting a little steam from a mysterious switch. The samovar hissed and gurgled as if Musa had tickled it under the chin.

"What happened to the old tulips?" Andersen asked. "The ones that were lost?"

"They grew weary from neglect and stopped growing," Musa said simply. "You see, the tulips in Istanbul were descendants of wild species that grew on the steppe, at the foot of the mountains where the first Turks lived. Species much older than our people even, and with the most glorious names: *Light of Paradise, Diamond's Envy, The Blue Pearl, Rose of the Dawn.* So many colors too: apricot, purple, vermillion, and sulphur, and combinations of these you cannot imagine. They knew that, to men who craved variation, shapely evidence of the Creator, they would be irresistible."

It was the longest speech Andersen had heard his new friend give, and in response, the samovar whistled its appreciation. Musa placed the first tea glass under the spout, engaged another switch, and a deep russet-brown liquid emerged.

"Our ancestors brought the tulips to Istanbul," Musa continued. "They planted their seeds in palaces and parks. Soon, tulips lined the sides of our roads and filled the window-boxes of the city's poor. But over time, we Turks were seduced—not by the flowers' beauty, but by their value. We lost sight of their welfare. We forgot that the tulip, like any other plant—perhaps more so—requires care and attention: the right soil and nutrients, water and sunlight, the freedom to grow unhindered as they did on the steppe. Instead, we shut them away, forced them to breed into a decreasing number of strains. When this happened, the tulips began to wither and die until they disappeared from the city altogether. Today, those oldest species can only be found in the mountains of the steppe, where they can bloom in private, unsullied by avarice.

"When did all this happen?" Andersen asked as Musa handed him a tea glass on a saucer then filled his own.

"For a hundred years, we have not seen the old tulips in Istanbul," Musa said. "Only the commonplace varieties of yellow and red flourish now. There are those who have tried to cultivate the wild seeds here, but they refuse to take to the soil. Perhaps it is the damp climate, or the long journey from the mountains; no one knows. The pashas and the rich merchants still crave the exotic varieties for their dinner table vases. But to meet this need, I must import my tulips from Europe."

Musa added two cubes of sugar to his glass and stirred vigorously. Andersen did the same, although he never took sugar in his tea at home. He remembered his guest had come for a specific reason, to learn about Andersen's paper-cutting skills. He wanted to distract Musa, who had become maudlin recalling these old flowers.

Andersen's scissors were in his jacket pocket, as always, and the thick white paper he favored was on his bureau. He retrieved his tools and worked quickly, allowing the paper's creases to guide his scissors forward and back, sensing the contours of his creation evolving with each snip: the firm lines of the ship, the dome shape of the mosque-sail straining against the mast, the fainter folds of the dervish, who, in Andersen's mind, was now Musa, standing straight-backed against the breeze, kaftan billowing with the sails.

Musa propped himself forward and carefully followed the skipping scissors, switching his gaze from Andersen's face to his fingers as if to discern the sleight of hand or invisible thread that must hold this paper world together. When Andersen spread open the paper, he realized he had forgotten to include the bird who perched on the dervish's head.

"It is remarkable, Herr Andersen," Musa said, running his finger over the sharp edges of man and boat.

"I forgot the bird."

"It is hard for a bird to remain in one place for too long," Musa said with a trace of a smile.

Andersen went to his desk to sip his tea, feeling restless and uncoordinated now the performance was over. When he looked at Musa, intending to ask him more about his work as a florist, he saw the face of someone whose thoughts had set sail. His visage reminded Andersen of a church façade he had seen in Italy, grooved and ribbed but still in its original bare stone because no one could afford to fill it with marble.

Andersen thought over his meager vocabulary of consoling German phrases, but none seemed suitable. Instead, he crossed the room and placed his hand on Musa's shoulder, brushing his fingers over the kaftan's silk, an enquiry rather than a touch. Musa looked up, still engrossed by the paper cut, before a half-smile and a shake of his turban brought him back.

"Watching you work, Herr Andersen," he said, "has reminded me of another I once knew, who could also summon life from a sheet of paper; one who could transform the words of a simple prayer, sentiments as dry as sand when intoned by others, into something striking and fluid. Even the way you looked with the scissors in your hand brought the memory of this person back to me. The slight tremor around the lips. The hint of the smile to come. It was, and forgive me for putting it this way, what my mother used to term a *sorcerer's look*."

Andersen laughed. "I like the phrase. Who was this person?"

"A writer like yourself. A calligrapher."

"I would like to see your friend's work, and meet him too," Andersen said.

Musa moved his head in a slow circle. "I can show you my friend's work, parts of it at least. But it is beyond my power to manage an introduction." He picked up the tiny silver spoon and stirred the remainder of his tea, rhythmically tinkling the metal against the glass.

"Your friend," Andersen ventured, "is he—"

"My friend was a woman, Herr Andersen," Musa said, looking up from his stirring. "A woman I knew for a long time. Her name was Zeynep."

The samovar murmured and spat and Musa released some steam.

Andersen, who had imagined a whiskered scribe with mischievous eyes and brisk hands, asked Musa to repeat the name.

"Zeynep."

Again the smile played upon the Turk's face, as fleetingly as a bird passing a window frame. "I would like to repay your generous gift, Herr Andersen," he said, "with a small offering of my own."

From the pocket of his kaftan, Musa produced a sheet of drawing paper he had folded into neat quarters. He opened it onto the desk. Andersen saw the ink outline of a flower: tall-stemmed with three feathery leaves and almond-shaped petals that pinched slightly at the waist and stretched into six points. The colors were remarkable: from the deep green of the stem and leaves to the golden, harvest orange that framed the petals. Yet, the more Andersen stared at the flower, the greater his awareness of its components became; the petals had not been shaded in, so that one could see the inner workings of the creation, the intricate network of lines and tiny loops hinting at pollen receptacles and reproductive systems.

"The flower is composed of calligraphy, Herr Andersen," Musa said, tracing the outline of the image with his finger. "Of letters and words that proclaim its allegiance to God. The stem is always formed from the *alif*, the first letter of the Arabic alphabet, which, like the stem itself, refuses to buckle to any gust or passion. You can see the inverted shape of the two *lam-alifs* here in the shape of the leaves. And the final letter of God's name, *ha*, is represented at the base of the petals."

"And the inside of the flower," Andersen asked. "These markings. What do they say?"

"The inner workings of the flower reveal God's true identity," Musa said. "In this case the word 'generous,' which, in our script, is seven letters long."

"'God is generous?'"

"*Al-Karim*, 'God *the* Generous.' It is one of the ninety-nine sacred names we use for the Creator. The forty-second one, in fact."

Andersen marveled at the delicacy of the ink strokes, as thin as the legs of an insect where they merged and mingled with the flower's anatomy. What kind of nib had Musa's calligrapher friend used to achieve such a lightness of touch?

"Tell me, Herr Andersen, are you pleased with my gift?"

"Yes I am, Musa. Thank you. And I would like it if you could call me Hans."

Musa nodded and the samovar, starved of attention, hissed and shuddered.

"I think it wants us to have another glass of tea," Musa said, and poked at the coals.

Andersen asked about Zeynep's work and Musa told him about the great task she and he had set out to accomplish when they were students at a type of religious monastery—a *tekke*, he called it. The two of them had worked on a book depicting all the old tulip strains in calligraphic form. The Book of Tulips. From

Musa's loving descriptions, Zeynep had chosen just the right word, and drawn each specimen with her intricate script. Musa had offered to show his friend miniature replicas of the ancient, dagger-shaped tulips; he recommended reading the work of poets who paid tribute to their beauty, but she refused, claiming his words were all she needed to recreate the flowers.

Musa talked of their student days, how they made fun of their teachers and elders, Zeynep drawing wobbly letter-shapes of relatives' heads and the bow legs of the *imam* from the mosque across the street. After their education was complete, Musa took over his father's garden and Zeynep became a calligraphy apprentice to the *usta* who had taught them both the craft, a man whose very face was a document of grooves and creases. The *usta* had sensed Zeynep's innate skills, and under his tutelage, she mastered her gift.

But the friends drifted apart. Musa continued to cultivate the stories of the old tulips and the gardeners who tended them, while Zeynep stayed in her room to write.

Andersen listened to Musa's careful phrasing, which increased in confidence as his German began to flow more naturally. Musa hadn't said it in as many words, but it was clear Zeynep was dead, and had met her end at a young age, too. Why would he tell Andersen this? He didn't know Musa well, after all. Perhaps his visit to the hotel was motivated by more than a simple desire to acquire one of Andersen's paper cuts. Yet the Turk seemed to sense that Andersen would be taken by his friend's calligraphy, and he was right—Andersen was curious. When Musa asked if he wanted to see more of her work, Andersen readily agreed. Besides, he wasn't quite ready to let this man, with his flowing silk and mysterious scent, drift across and out of his life like a warm breeze.

Musa nodded and said, "I will send a boy to collect you here at the hotel the day after tomorrow."

As Musa prepared to leave, Andersen looked again at the golden tulip and its tightly scrolled lettering. In the bottom right corner was something he hadn't initially noticed: a face about the size of a large coin, formed from tiny lines, curves, and ligatures.

"Her signature," Musa said. "It is formed from the invocation, 'Oh Muhammad-Ali.' She inscribed it whenever she completed a work."

Andersen looked at the eyebrows lifting in surprise, the fluid strokes of the cheekbones. The eyes, which Musa said spelled the name Ali, twinkled in joyous swoops.

"Zeynep's signature," Musa repeated as he opened the door to leave. "It is as unmistakably her mark as a royal *tughra* belongs to a sultan."

Musa stepped outside the room, but a pair of boots arrested his progress, cavalry boots adorned with a series of silver buckles and studs, polished to a fine sheen. Musa handed them to Andersen. "Fetching," he said. "People will certainly know you have arrived." Andersen smiled thinly.

Despite his precautions, the hotel had indeed sent back the wrong boots.

CHAPTER 5

ncased in her bed of iron, the calligrapher awoke to a Bosphorus morning. The sea lapped against the shore; seagulls danced a *ping, scrape, ping* rhythm above her. As from a distant cloud, the first *ezan* of the day called to the pious. From inside her cannon the calligrapher could hear hawkers and hailers, the metallic bark of Bosphorus dogs. She edged her way along the cylinder of the cannon and into the light.

Her neighbors in the other two cannons were still asleep, their breathing strangely amplified, as if a cemetery stirred in purgatorial slumber. Who would rise first, and, as she had occupied the remaining cannon, where had the third dervish slept?

Slowly, a pair of feet emerged from the muzzle of the middle-sized cannon, then the lower half of a blue kaftan. A man of medium height wriggled free without difficulty. He was younger and slightly shorter than the green-turbaned dervish she had met last night and dressed all in blue. He looked at her, stretched, and embarked on a bout of scratching. Then a voice called for assistance from the longest cannon. There was a thud of bone on iron and a familiar yelp, and the blue dervish pulled his green friend clear of the cannon with practiced expertise.

"Not a bad spot for a night's rest, is it, my girl?" the green dervish said, brushing himself down. He made no attempt to introduce the calligrapher to his colleague in blue.

"I hope I didn't steal anyone's shelter," the calligrapher said, but the green dervish seemed not to hear. He returned to his cannon and pulled out half a loaf of bread and a slab of cheese. "Don't you have the cucumber and olives?" he said to his friend, who rummaged around inside his own cannon before producing the items. Then the dervishes ordered tea from a man patrolling the shoreline with a silver urn slung over his shoulder and tulip-shaped glasses clipped to his belt.

"You don't prefer to pray first, do you?" asked the green dervish.

The calligrapher shook her head.

"Good. You see, I already have. Prayed, that is. You may have heard me mumbling. And my friend here," he said, nodding at Blue, "never prays before a meal. After all, so he argues, God can hardly be expected to hear him over a stomach growling like a camel's."

The blue dervish began to lay out the breakfast food on the base of the largest cannon. He presented the calligrapher with an olive, large and fleshy, which cleaved cleanly from its pit on first bite. A signal of some sort passed between the two dervishes, and the one in green turned to the calligrapher.

"There is a third member of our little tribe here, as I think I mentioned last night. He hasn't joined us for breakfast and may well not make it for lunch."

The calligrapher nodded. "I will, of course, move on today."

The green dervish smiled. "My dear, that is not what my friend is suggesting at all! No, he merely points out that, should you see a man dressed in a red turban approach the cannon you slept in last night and climb wearily into it, do not be alarmed. Another space will become available, as my friend here often wanders at night, especially if the moon is favorable."

She smiled her thanks. They ate in silence and breathed the freshness of the sea.

"What do you do when you go wandering?" the calligrapher asked.

The green dervish laughed and a cheese crumb settled on his beard. "That's a good question. Sometimes I ask the very same thing after a long day. We don't roam with any definite plan as other dervishes do; some set out to visit all the local tombs of the order, say, or to make a pilgrimage to a distant *tekke*. No, my friends and I prefer to let God decide how we should serve on our walks around the city. Sometimes we come across the hungry and we help them find food, or a quarreling couple might seek our counsel, or we may restrain a man intent on revenge in a blood feud. People often ask us for directions or a short-term loan. Occasionally someone will approach us with a line of poetry or a few notes of a song and ask us if we have heard it on our travels. Once, a man insisted that he had lost his memory, and we walked around his neighborhood until he saw the house where he had grown up. We spent the night gradually revisiting all his old haunts, piecing together his youth and bachelorhood, the early years of his marriage, until he recognized the midwife who had delivered his first child buying a loaf of bread." The green dervish smiled at the memory and sipped his glass of tea.

Blue again communicated something to his older colleague, who nodded thoughtfully as if the former had completed an interesting disquisition. "I have mentioned your profession to my friend," Green said, "and he wonders if, after breakfast, of course, you could write something in a little book he keeps with him. Something that shows the skill of the trained calligrapher."

"It's been a long time," the calligrapher said.

"My friend senses that," the green dervish said. "We both do. But you will write again. You have no choice. Writing is the purest form of expression and the trained calligrapher is especially blessed, because his pen reflects the word of God. He molds it into delectable forms; he imbues it with energy so that even the illiterate are struck by its power. If a calligrapher doesn't write, if he needs to take a rest, then God will be patient. He too will rest. He will find a cushion in the calligrapher's soul until those fingers start to twitch again."

The calligrapher wondered what she should write, what would be a comfort to these two holy men, as she partook of the meal. One of the shorter *hadiths*, perhaps, a prayer from the Koran? She ate the bread, cheese, cucumber, and olives and drank the tea; it flowed into her fingertips and warmed them as writing *nastaliq* script used to warm the nib of her pen. *Nastaliq* was always her favorite writing style because it had big loops and curves. It was a style that hated borders and scoffed at margins; it stole, unchecked, across the page like wild ivy spreading over a house.

The blue dervish reached inside his cannon and, to the calligrapher's amazement, brought out an old leather notebook, a *kalem* to write with, and a writing case from which he extracted a large tortoiseshell inkwell, stippled with tiny pots containing a myriad of colors. The nib of the *kalem* was honed to a sharp point and the inks were of a good consistency. The blue dervish had filled the reverse side of each page in the notebook with close lines of minuscule script: words nuzzled their neighbors, sections jostled for space, diacritical marks coaxed their way into gaps. The calligrapher felt as if she had lifted a piece of wood and exposed a colony of ants underneath. Yet the front sides of the pages remained unmarked, ideal for her purposes, and she smoothed the first page with the flat of her hand, trying not to think of the chaotic scrawl on the other side.

But she still didn't know what to write. In her exile, she had not wanted to pick up a pen; she had consigned her writing to the corner of her memory as an amputee tries to forget a missing limb. She flexed her fingers. The dervishes put down their tea glasses to watch her, and she felt the power of their gazes, heard the swell of the sea against a passing boat, saw the silvery glint of fishing line sprats arcing through the air. The calligrapher picked up the *kalem* and her hand shook. It had been seven years since she had made these gestures, the flick of the wrist, the blot of the ink—at least as a free woman. The last time she'd tried to write, two uniformed men had stood behind her at the *tekke*. They had not said a word as she worked. They must have spoken, she supposed, to have confirmed who she was, but she had never been able to recall the sound their tight mouths made, the tone and inflection of their command. The two men had moved around her desk to examine the paper she worked on. They had stood close to her as she twisted and twirled her letters into the image of a face. When they saw what she had done, one of the men smiled a half-smile, a twist of the lips that creased his left cheek like a tiny fish parting a stream.

She had always disliked an audience. Once, her *usta* had made her enter a calligraphy contest. The judges stood in a line and pontificated on each candidate's work. One particular judge gave her a fragment of scorn she would never forget. "Your letters take up too much space," he had said. "They are languid; they stretch over the page like a harem girl." She had imagined herself standing up and hitting him across the face. Hard.

When the two guards led her away, there had been no judgment on her work, or at least no spoken appraisal. Just that little quiver of the lips, the cleft in the cheek that marked the end of her freedom.

After that came prison and exile. She had vowed never to write again and had kept to her word, until that time in prison when there was no choice.

Her audience today—two dervishes—had been kind. Yet she could not keep the *kalem* still in her hand, and she had to concentrate to remember the shape of her grip, the way the *kalem* used to fit between her forefinger and thumb. She had to ask God to help her do what had once come naturally.

She wrote an *alif*, a bold line on the first page of the blue dervish's notebook, to the exact dimensions she had been taught: five rhombic dots long and two wide, curving slightly at the bottom like a seahorse's tail. The calligrapher held her pen above the page and watched the ink of the *alif* harden and dry. She listened to her breathing; her pulse began to slow. She turned the page of Blue's notebook and tried to ignore his dense and unruly script. The second *alif* would be the same as the first; it always was, yet the calligrapher felt like she was back in her cramped room with the *usta* standing over her—a demon keeping watch. A hundred times he would insist she write the first letter of God, and a hundred times it had to be identical or she could not eat or sleep. She drew the second *alif* on the dervish's page perfectly, and relaxed a little. The green dervish bent down and gently took the notebook from her. He passed it to his blue friend, who nodded.

"My friend says you are a true calligrapher," the green dervish said, and signaled for more tea.

{

When the two dervishes left for their morning roam, the calligrapher sat with her back against the Judas tree, drinking tea. The Bosphorus was a glittering blue. The calligrapher held out her hand and saw that the simple act of inscribing the *alifs* had steadied it. After all these years, perhaps she was ready to write again. She sat with this simple, life-affirming thought in her head and watched the people stroll by, snippets of conversation catching in the pink blossoms above her head.

Vendors hawked their wares: strawberries and cherries, yogurt carts with their tinkling bells, and heavier vehicles laden with onions or potatoes pulled by old horses whose tails hung limply behind them.

Only the distant shapes of the city to the east spoiled her contentment. The minarets of the great mosques and the headland of the palace, from which she was exiled seven years before, fussed at the corner of her vision like an inflamed eyelid. Had these wandering dervishes guessed something of her history and befriended her for a reason?

As the calligrapher was mulling this over and wondering if she might borrow the blue dervish's notebook once again, she spotted the two men walking slowly along the shore toward her. The green dervish had his head cocked toward his blue friend as though listening intently, but the calligrapher had yet to hear the blue dervish utter a word. The two approached the Judas tree and interspersed their low conversation with frequent looks in her direction, as if weighing the various options her arrival had presented them with.

"My friend suggests that you join us on our wanderings," the green dervish said without preamble. "He feels that your skills as a calligrapher would complement the work we do."

Before the calligrapher could respond, the blue dervish moved swiftly to his cannon. He returned with his notebook, complete with inkwell and a supply of *kalems,* and presented it to her as if he had read her mind. He indicated she should bring the writing materials on their walk.

To the calligrapher, this gift of paper and pen was as satisfying as the tender slice of lamb her mother had served on the holiest night of Ramadan, or the soft pulse of her father's voice reading the Koran. For the second time that morning, excitement prodded her heart. She would write again, something beyond the simple *alif*, although she had no idea where her pen would lead her.

The dervishes set off the way they had come and the calligrapher fell in behind, breathing the lilac and cherry blossoms and resting her eyes on the green-gold of the budding plane trees and the darker, more protective green of the soaring cypresses. It was a Bosphorus spring, fleeting and sweet. She remembered how, as an apprentice, she had sailed up from the old city on one of her rare afternoons of freedom and walked along this shore, noticed only by the gulls basking on the rooftops.

After fifteen minutes the trio reached a small bay, where a group of fishermen were pointing at a structure further out to sea, which the calligrapher recognized as a fish trap. The contraption consisted of four poles that rose high into the air with nets slung across the top. Between two of the poles someone had nailed a wide wooden plank, on top of which a man sat on a comfortable-looking chair. This man's job was to wait for a shoal of fish. When he spotted one he pulled a cord, which released the nets and trapped the fish between the poles. The nearby fishing boats thus alerted, they moved in to collect the catch.

Unfortunately, as the dervishes soon learned from the fishermen pointing and scowling from the shore, the man they had assigned to sit on the plank too often dozed off in the sun, and thus failed to sight the richest shoals of fish. He had also established something of a nest up there: as well as the chair, the man had hauled a tea pot and water pipe to the platform, and, even though he couldn't read, had been known to turn the pages of the *Moniteur Ottoman* newspaper to pass the time.

The green dervish enquired why one of the other, more reliable fishermen did not take his place.

"Look at us, *Hocam*," said one man. "Can you imagine men of our age skinning up that pole? Our younger friend here, for all his flaws, climbs like a gibbon."

The green dervish moved aside to consult with Blue. There was much head-scratching and gesticulating between the two men. After a minute or so of this, the calligrapher noticed the blue dervish trying to catch her eye. She had a vague image in her mind, but was unsure of the words that would form it, and thus give the image its meaning. She took a *kalem* from the case and inscribed the letter *wah* unevenly, so it appeared to be tottering; underneath, she drew one of the fisherman's poles as if it were supporting the letter. When she showed this to the dervishes, they nodded approvingly, and to her surprise, Blue tore out the page (which had his dense letterings on the other side) and gave it to one of the fishermen.

"Your monkey-like friend will have to dispense with the wooden plank, the chair, and the teapot, gentlemen," the green dervish announced. "He should balance himself at the top of one of the poles, rather than in between them. For imminent catastrophe is a good guarantor of wakefulness."

The fisherman thanked the dervishes profusely, and one or two even nodded in the calligrapher's direction.

"You would be surprised how many people forget the advice we give them," the green dervish said, explaining why Blue had torn the page from his notebook. "We've lost count of the number of times folks have said to us, 'You were such a help with my dilemma the other day, *Hocam*, but do tell me again what you said, just in case I make the same mistake.' Now, at least for the time that you are with us, they will have your letters to remind them."

The calligrapher and the dervishes walked on, occasionally leaving the shore to visit fishing villages further inland, or nestled higher up the hillside. The dervishes were well-known, and many people stopped to chat or ask them a question, looking at the calligrapher curiously as they did so. The calligrapher knew her association with these holy men would grant her temporary acceptance among the villagers of the Bosphorus, one she could not have gained on her own as a returned exile. It would also guarantee her food and, perhaps, further use of the smallest cannon, should the red-turbaned dervish not return.

She kept the blue dervish's notebook ready at a clean page during the walk and made sure at least one of his pens was moistened. After each consultation she wrote something in the notebook in support of the dervishes' advice—a stork or a lantern constructed of simple sayings or prayers that were meant to lodge in the supplicants' minds—and the page was duly detached and given away.

Once, she drew a mosque with a human face, minarets for ears, and the eyes of a man who had told the dervishes that he always cried when he prayed in his local mosque because he couldn't believe God was listening. While the green dervish praised him for his fervor, the calligrapher drew his irises with a darker green hue and added two tears on his cheeks. The man took the sheet of paper eagerly, weeping at the truth of what the calligrapher had written.

They stopped for lunch further along the Bosphorus in Arnavutkoy. The people here originally hailed from Albania and wore the white breeches of their former countrymen, with orange sashes to carry their pistols, while the women's snowy *yashmaks* rested lightly on their faces and necks and offset the spring cheer of their *feraces*: pale pink, violet, straw-yellow, and sea-green. The Albanians had set up their tiny charcoal grills by the seafront and roasted cubes of liver with onions and red pepper. Every grill was of the same dimension, and each man cooked identical fare, yet the green dervish walked slowly along the line of vendors as if conducting a military inspection, wrinkling his nose and making eye contact with each cook. The blue dervish looked at the calligrapher and rolled his eyes. Once his friend finally made his selection, they ate their liver atop a piece of flatbread and washed it down with hibiscus juice.

When the calligrapher looked once too often at the gauzy outlines of the women's faces, at the smooth contours of their cotton and silk, the dervishes led her to a tiny shop in which a merchant was busy measuring strips of cloth. The calligrapher chose a purple *ferace* and two pieces of white cotton to cover her hair.

"You might as well blend in," the green dervish said. "Just in case you…if you ever feel safe enough to cross the Golden Horn and go back to the city."

The calligrapher thanked him, noticing that, although the dervishes never paid for anything, the merchants seemed flattered to surrender their wares.

The dervishes tactfully invited the cloth merchant for a glass of tea so the calligrapher could use his shop to change into her new clothes. In the mirror, the bones of her shoulders poked through the silk. Her hair had never grown back properly in all the years since her imprisonment. It sprouted in uneven patches, dark brown wired with gray, making her palms tingle as she ran her hands over her scalp. But she pressed the clean *yashmak* as carefully over her head as any woman.

There was color in her face now, weathered into her skin by the sun and the wind, but her eyes were as cool as she remembered them. When had she last looked in a mirror? It must have been just before the soldiers arrived at the *tekke* to arrest her; she had known they were coming, and had just written the final mark on one of her faces, the *ayns* of the eyes shining with ferocious green, before they burst in. She had taken comfort from those eyes, the way they had looked at her from the paper: assured. Unafraid.

Once dressed, she washed her hands and face in a bowl of water the cloth merchant had kindly left for her. She stood in front of the mirror and was aware of something missing, something that would complete her ablutions. Then she remembered the cypress cone in the pocket of her old *ferace*. She worked it into the lines and crevices of her hands before massaging her face and neck. The woody, slightly sweet fragrance reassured her.

The calligrapher emerged from the shop to find the green dervish alone in the midst of a daydream, a half-smile flitting across his face, an empty tea glass balancing on the palm of his hand. Blue was nowhere to be seen. She coughed. The green dervish turned to look at her and broke into a grin.

"You are a respectable *hanim* now! A new woman. And too good to sleep in a cannon!"

"Perhaps I should look for another accommodation. What if your friend in the red turban returns tonight?" the calligrapher said, lowering her gaze.

"Oh, who knows what's going on in Red's mind! He's probably lost again. That man has no sense of the compass points; the sun and the moon are irrelevancies to him, the stars mere baubles. He is apt to wander around in circles until someone points him in the right direction."

The green dervish waved his colleague's difficulties aside with a flick of his wrist. "Why don't you join me for an afternoon walk? There's a place where one can stand and watch over the Bosphorus from a great height. You can return

the notebook and writing case to Blue's cannon—
it's on the way. Come, the climb will do us good."

CHAPTER 6

On his first morning in Constantinople, Andersen slept through the dawn call to prayer. He imagined the *imams* announcing the day, blowing sleep from the eyes of the pious while he slept irreverently on, oblivious to God or anything created in His name. At eight o'clock, he stood on his hotel balcony watching the commotion in the street below. People walked, shoved, jostled, and leaned into one another. Priests and *imams* used the elbow of God to carve out their passage. Trays of fruit, bread, and mussel shells wobbled on human backs. And everywhere there were hats—maroon fezzes with tassels oozing from their crowns, stovepipe hats, European top hats, turbans, and military kepis—a rolling parade of headwear that made him feel quite dizzy.

Andersen had fallen asleep thinking of the calligrapher, Zeynep, painstakingly fitting her letters into the head of a tulip while Musa stood over her, extolling the virtues of the city's exotic floral history. What a pair they must have made: Musa, tall and angular in a kaftan of sapphire blue or crimson, his turban bobbing rhythmically as another tulip took shape in his mind; Zeynep, bent over a page of The Book of Tulips, visualizing the letters, the holy phrase that would best reflect the flower's configuration and character. Musa had not described his friend's appearance, but Andersen imagined her with deft features, nut-brown eyes, and hair loosely bunched under a headscarf of pale blue. Had Musa loved her? He surely felt something; his harrowed face, when he used the past tense to describe her, told Andersen that. Perhaps they had been husband and wife, or engaged to be married, before some tragic illness, some terrible accident, had befallen her.

But Andersen wasn't sure. Musa had spoken of Zeynep as one might speak of a dear friend. He sensed Musa had admired her, perhaps from a distance, and that these feelings had not been reciprocated. Andersen himself had endured many such relationships with women, praising them and fawning over their beauty while they remained oblivious of his existence.

Andersen felt the Turk was encouraging his interest in the calligrapher, although he could not be sure. Last night, when Andersen had asked if people in the city knew her story, Musa had smiled, little furrows forming in the cheeks of his beard.

"It's too good a story for the peasants and idlers at the coffeehouse, Herr Andersen," he said, tipping his head to one side and fixing Andersen in his sights. "Adventure, persecution, incarceration, not to mention sacrifice and pain.

Shapes turning into letters and letters becoming faces, people, and animals. Her life's work to create the perfect image: the supreme manifestation of God in an earthly form. An audience would be spellbound, Herr Andersen, *spellbound*. Tea would go cold and meat congeal on the plate, wives would neglect husbands, the muezzin would call in vain to the faithful! But when the storyteller reaches the part about Zeynep's detention, the very moment when he has the audience at his mercy, someone would be sure to call out: 'But that is unbelievable! You are describing a *tekke* not two kilometers from here, and a woman, to boot!'

"This voice would soon be joined by another and another until the audience were clamoring for something more familiar—a saint or a dervish, or a warrior with a fleet-footed horse."

Musa scratched his beard, tilted his head again. "Audiences like to listen to dramatic stories while they are smoking their *nargiles*, Herr Andersen, just as long as those stories are not too close to home."

Andersen thought over this exchange as he went to his dressing table mirror to adjust his tie. The drawing of Zeynep's flower was propped against two bottles of cologne. He tried to recall how the Arabic letters of Allah had formed the stem, leaves, and base. Within the slim yellow-orange tinged petals one could make out further markings—what had Musa said they meant? Generous? God, the generous?—finely-nibbed curves and loops in black ink. Framed in their slim capsules, the letters looked like the bone structure of a small aquatic creature, a seahorse perhaps, lit from within.

Again he marveled at the delicacy of the penmanship. He took the paper flower to the window. Had its golden color of yesterday faded a little? He rested the paper on the window sill; perhaps the brightness of a new day would have a restorative effect. Smiling at his own thoughts, he turned back to the mirror and imagined his teeth as lettered keys on a stencil; if only dentists knew how to read teeth, they could predict the toothaches that so bedeviled him.

1

Andersen was to be welcomed by the Danish consul, Jensen, who had arranged to show him the old city. They would meet in the hotel lounge, but first, Andersen needed to see about his boots. He had informed the hotel of its error last night and was assured that the correct boots would be delivered to his room in the morning. But they had not appeared. So he was wearing his light shoes, made of very soft leather with thin soles, unsuitable for the long walks planned for the day. The receptionist, with a gray lick of hair curling away from his forehead, listened—rather casually, Andersen thought—to his complaint, and then surprised him by producing a sheet of paper and a pen.

"Why don't you write about these boots, Monsieur?" he said brightly, the lick of hair bobbing as he spoke.

"I beg your pardon?"

"Well, Monsieur, you are a professional writer, if I am not mistaken, from the German lands…"

"Denmark."

"…who would be more than capable of an engaging paragraph on the aforementioned footwear. The shape and size, for example; the accoutrements that allow one to secure the boot; perhaps even a line or two about the tread…"

"I really…"

"Consider the position of the hotel, Monsieur. We have 310 rooms, and let's say that eight out of ten gentleman leave their boots out for cleaning. That makes, hmm, let me see…"

"Two hundred forty-eight pairs," Andersen said, badly wanting to cut off this man's needless swirl of hair with a snip of his scissors.

"Exactly, Monsieur. You make a strong case with such an impressive number. We are presented with boots of every description to be cleaned and polished. Riding boots, boots with straps, buckles, or laces up the sides. Hussars and Hessians, boots with steel-toe caps, and those fancy ones that cut away at the calf for mobility. Marching boots that step majestically…"

"Yes, thank you. I will write a brief description," Andersen said. He stood at the desk and composed a short account of the boots, including something of his own history with them. By the time he returned to the now-deserted breakfast room, he had but a few minutes until Jensen's arrival. He paced the room, noting that bird cages adorned this part of the hotel, too; near his table, a bird sang mournfully behind a ribbed façade of dark mahogany. When did the hotel feed these creatures? he wondered. He spent a few minutes chopping the remnants of a stale breakfast roll into miniscule portions and, keeping an eye open for waiters, unfastened the cage door and deposited the crumbs. The bird inside was small and grey, and nibbled at his offering.

Encouraged, Andersen filled a discarded plate with more crumbs and fed a few more birds, opening and closing one cage door after another. He put down his plate and drifted into the lounge, wondering whether he should tend to the birds there, too. In a corner near the piano, Andersen saw a cage he hadn't noticed on his arrival: tall and handsome, and built like a miniature palace in dark, polished wood. Andersen admired the floral patterns woven into the façade, which contained windows and a door. He was about to slide a finger under the tiny catch when someone tapped him on the shoulder.

"Allow me."

A small man with a wax-tipped moustache worked his fingernail under the catch and opened the door. He had spoken in French.

"You will find much to admire in here, but, alas, no bird to enjoy it," the man said.

Andersen looked inside. It was indeed empty, but he was surprised to see that the attention to detail inside the cage was even greater than that of its exterior, as if the architect possessed an intimate knowledge of a confined bird's needs. There were perches on display at various levels, viewing galleries and feeding areas, a swing, and even a water chute in which the bird could slide and bathe at the same time.

"It is beautifully constructed," Andersen said, also in French.

"I am happy to hear you say that. I made it. Giacomo Taranto at your service." He held out a hand almost as delicate as one of his cages. "My family are descended from the Genoese that traded here in Byzantine times. I myself was born in Constantinople."

Andersen introduced himself, hoping as ever that his name might be recognized. It wasn't.

"I speculate you are a German speaker," Taranto said in that language.

"Actually I am a Dane, but my German is better than my French."

"Denmark!" Taranto said, as if Andersen had discovered a new land.

Andersen smiled politely. "What happened to the bird you designed this cage for?"

"That's just it!" Taranto said with a sad smile. "The hotel wanted me to design a structure for a toucan they had purchased at discount from the sultan's aviary. Unfortunately, the toucan, after initially welcoming its new home, was overcome by an intense bout of melancholy. For days, it refused even to squawk, but when it did deign to speak, it was only to use language unfit for a hotel of this rank. We could not understand how this bird, formerly so taciturn, could have acquired a lexicon commensurate with that of a seaman. Then we discovered the toucan had briefly fallen under the tutelage of the palace gardeners—a foul-mouthed lot, to say the least. Something or someone in the hotel must have triggered its memory. Toucans, as you may be aware, are impressionable creatures."

"So they keep the cage empty?" Andersen asked.

"Yes. I encouraged them to give it to a smaller bird—a canary, say—but they claim the cage is too big, and that guests would struggle to locate the bird inside. Still, I make a point of taking my morning coffee here every Wednesday in the hope of hearing a birdsong, but I am constantly disappointed. The cage has wonderful acoustics, you know."

Taranto offered Andersen his card and invited him to call on his workshop near the Galata Tower. He left with a bow as another man, surely Jensen, advanced toward Andersen. There was something unmistakably Danish in his confident stride and look of icy efficiency; even the charcoal frock coat looked like the work of a Copenhagen tailor. Andersen bent toward the cage, pretending he hadn't seen Jensen, and out of the corner of his eye, watched the man's features rearrange themselves into a frown; he noted, too, the paunch straining the buttons of the diplomat's waistcoat.

Jensen introduced himself with a click of the heels. There was much to see, he said, and they could not afford to dawdle. He made no mention of Andersen's work as a writer, even though his embassy must have briefed him on it. Perhaps this was because none of Andersen's books had the words 'Very Important' emblazoned on the front cover in big, red letters.

When Andersen asked if he should bring his passport, Jensen said it did not matter either way—an answer Andersen found unsatisfying. He debated on whether or not to keep Jensen waiting while he retrieved the document from his room, but thought better of it.

§

The two men walked through Pera's streets, so narrow in places that opposing neighbors could lean across and offer each other snuff. Here, one moved in a perpetual state of temptation and distraction—amid shops and donkeys hauling timber, roving musicians blowing bagpipes or plucking at lutes—while the great human wave parted around them. The crowd would not get out of Jensen's way quickly enough, but Andersen, following a Turk in silk robes whose servant carried his tobacco pipe like a holy relic, felt comfortable with its rhythm.

It was a five-minute sail across the Golden Horn to Stamboul through a mass of gondolas and the larger craft basking at anchor. Jensen had commandeered their gondola, or *caique*, in which they lay on cushions and rolled from side to side like a pair of restless corpses. From this position, Andersen watched their rower pitch his oar into the waves, arms flexing at each stroke. He wore, like all his colleagues, a tunic with short, knitted sleeves that cut off just above the bicep. The current flowed relentlessly across the bows of the boats, yet each rower negotiated his passage with ease.

Jensen pointed out the kiosks and pavilions of the sultan's palace overlooking the shores of the Golden Horn. On the steamship, Andersen had glimpsed the other side of the palace grounds, the thickly wooded hills spilling down to the Marmara Sea, and wondered about the secrets within.

"One can find cedar, turpentine, fig, olive, and various fruit trees growing there," Jensen had said when Andersen asked about the palace gardens.

"What about the tulip gardens? Can one see them from anywhere on the water?"

But Jensen, a lackluster guide, had already started barking docking instructions at the boatman, who grimaced at the imperious tone. Andersen thought again of those precipitous slopes on the other side of the palace; he imagined a series of terraces woven through with tightly ranked flower beds and streams—descending tapestries of color that ran all the way down to the sea, secluded from prying eyes by the cypresses and plane trees standing like sentinels on the slopes.

A steep hill welcomed them to the old city. Every mosque and public building was bedecked with rows of unlit lanterns strung between minarets or placed on hooks over windows and doors. Jensen told him the city was preparing for the Prophet Muhammad's birthday, five days hence. The celebrations would begin the night before with the lighting of the city. Anyone out walking on that night was required by law to carry a candle or lantern. Andersen only half-listened.

He was enjoying a vision of Musa and he strolling through the illuminated streets, carrying candles, laughing at a story one of them had told. And what a city this was for storytelling! The tang of spice in the air, the sun reflecting off the marble and gold of the minarets, which in turn replicated themselves as shimmering columns in the water: it was not such a leap to imagine the two of them spinning yarns of glass palaces and hanging gardens, or as protagonists in their own stories, passing through the thousand and one nights of Andersen's youth.

In the square of Atmeidan, the old Hippodrome, Andersen saw the red-headed man from the hotel leading a group of Europeans toward the Egyptian Obelisk. The party, about ten strong, shuffled along in his wake in their fezzes and colorful kaftans, occasionally picking up their hems to stop them dragging on the ground. But the red-headed gentleman wore his kaftan with confidence; it fitted perfectly, as if he had trained it to move with the rhythm of his body. Andersen watched the procession reach the end of Atmeidan and disappear over the lip of a hill like a line of diminishing fireworks. Odd, he thought, that he should see this man again. But the thought disappeared into the swirling crowd.

Jensen had arranged for them to enter the Hagia Sophia, the former basilica of Holy Wisdom, converted by the Turks into a mosque. They shuffled to the end of a long line of worshippers and visitors, all of whom were quickly swallowed by the cavernous interior. The light, filtered through arched windows in the base of the cupola, was milky gold. Giant black discs covered in Arabic script hung in midair as if by supernatural threads.

Andersen had expected to see the white-backed ranks of Islamic worshippers praying in unison, as high up under the shadows of the dome as the Christian saints who frowned in ghostly mosaic. But the faithful lay scattered across the vast carpets, and the walls, as far as he could see, had been whitewashed of their biblical images.

When the worshippers finished their prayers, they did not head directly to the exit but shuffled behind one of the huge columns, where a whole army could lie in wait, or padded the floor in slow circles, relishing their insignificance. Andersen watched a man move slowly around the perimeter of the building. He seemed to be in charge of the lanterns, checking the flames and adjusting the wicks. How long would it take him to complete his rounds?

Inside, Jensen left Andersen alone with his thoughts. But outside, blinking in the brightness, his host was anxious to return to his fixed schedule, in his European progression from one site to the next, as if the act of standing still and looking at a part would upset the balance of the whole. Jensen was a little way ahead of Andersen in the square in front of the basilica, gesturing at Sultan Ahmed's mosque just in front of them, sumptuous on its domed haunches, six minarets pointing into the sky.

"If we move quickly enough," Jensen shouted over the turbaned heads of the departing faithful, "we can see Sultan Ahmed before lunch."

Andersen called for him to slow down. It was too much, leaping from the porphyry columns and burnished gold of Hagia Sofia to that sun-drenched construction of stone and marble. He needed to rest and collect himself.

Andersen again called Jensen's name, but the thickening crowd exiting the Hagia Sofia pushed him further away, and Jensen soon vanished from sight.

Andersen forged his way into the Hippodrome, as far as the rusty iron rings that once bore the splendor of Constantine's column, but there was no sign of his host. He waited, expecting at any moment to see Jensen's long stride aimed toward him. When Jensen did not appear, Andersen imagined he was playing a game, some petty revenge for Andersen's lack of gratitude, his failure to honor the man's courtly status. In that case, let him have his fun. Andersen would not be so easily found.

Andersen cut a path through the crowd and away from the Hippodrome. At the northeast corner of Atmeidan, he took a cobbled street leading down to the sea. There were plane trees here—poplars too—growing from patches of earth on the sides of the street, casting spidery shadows from their low-slung branches. A mosque, slightly raised above street level, lay hidden among the foliage of these trees, a single minaret poking through the leaves.

Andersen paused, intrigued by the seclusion of this small mosque. After the overwhelming grandeur of the Hagia Sophia, he imagined a peaceful place, a gentle suggestion of piety. He stepped between two trees and saw the outer wall of the mosque and a set of stone steps leading to a portal or gate shaped like a key. He was halfway up the steps before his courage failed him and he turned back. What would the worshippers think if he were to stand at their door, dressed in his infidel suit?

He had reached the bottom step when a small, barefoot boy burst through the trees and ran straight into Andersen's legs. The boy, who showed no surprise at his presence, spoke in rapid Turkish interspersed with a few words of French.

He beckoned Andersen back up the steps, brushing aside his objections. The boy, Andersen understood, would serve as his guide and show him around.

Through the key-shaped gate, the boy and Andersen stepped into a compact courtyard of smooth stone slabs built around a black marble ablution fountain. Although he wore rags, the boy took his time washing his hands and feet at the fountain. Andersen wondered if he should do the same, but the boy merely indicated for him to remove his shoes, looking disparagingly at their flimsy construction and thin soles. There was no door to the mosque, but a thick, leather curtain, which the boy pushed aside with difficulty for Andersen. Later, Andersen would admire the cool, white stone of the walls, the symmetry of the stained glass windows. But upon entering, his eyes feasted on a thing of beauty: a multi-colored shrine, a prayer niche encased by the finest set of glazed tiles he had ever seen. The tiles depicted a garden of spring flowers on a background of snow-white enamel: roses, carnations, and tulips;

sprays of fruit blossom and branches of pomegranate in emerald green and cobalt blue, turquoise, mauve, and a glorious bolus red that dominated the scene.

"*Iznik*," said the boy, beaming from ear to ear. "*Iznik fayans*." Next to the prayer niche was a slender, pulpit-like structure with a conical hood made from the same bold tiles of deepest red and blue on spotless white.

As Andersen approached, the boy leapt prodigiously to touch a tiny black stone embedded in the base of the hood.

"*Kaba*," he said, gesturing again at the stone. Andersen had heard the word before. Was his guide showing him a stone from the holy site in Mecca? The boy held up four fingers, then ran around the mosque like a gazelle, pointing at three other tiny pieces of black stone: two buried in the walls, and another over the doorway.

Andersen ran his hand over the clear glaze of the tile, marveling at the intricate brush strokes, the vivacity of the colors. He tried to ask the boy the name of the mosque, but his guide had stepped into the shell at the heart of the prayer niche, in which he seemed to fit exactly. From this alcove, he gazed at the ornamental columns placed on either side. Then he applied his palm to the column, making it turn on its vertical axis. With the column still spinning, the boy mimed the collapse of the building, a surge of energy whipping through his thin frame, his arms flailing. Earthquakes, Andersen understood the motion to mean. The revolving pillar was an indication that the foundations of the mosque were still perfectly aligned.

Andersen tried to tell the boy that he wanted to go outside and search for a plaque, something that could tell him more of the mosque's history, but the boy held up his hand and pressed his ear to the column.

"*Fayans*," the boy said and pointed at the wall. He began a ragged, uncoordinated dance, his thin arms describing wild shapes in the air.

"Oh," said Andersen, not sure if his guide were demented or overcome by religious fervor.

The boy stopped moving and gave the pillar an almighty swivel.

"Look!" he said in French, but Andersen thought he was going to start dancing again. Unnerved, he wanted to keep the boy in his sights.

"No!" said the boy, pointing at his own eyes and then the tiles to indicate what Andersen ought to be doing. "Look!" He rotated the column again.

Andersen focused on the area to the left of the niche where the tulips and cherry blossom looked almost moist under their glaze. The column's rotation began to gain in speed, although the boy did not reapply his hand. Andersen heard the keening sound of stone against stone. Then, the tiled flowers on the column began to move, bending at the stems and flattening their narrow petals against the heavy leaves, pushing them aside as through craning for more light, more air. For a few seconds—or was it longer?—the whole wall, both sides of the prayer niche, were in glorious motion, a field of enamel tulips swaying in the house of God.

A breeze blew against the back of his neck and instinctively, Andersen turned to the leather curtain to see if someone had entered. The mosque remained empty, and when he turned back, the movement had ended; the tiled flowers stood pristine against the wall, still as stone.

The boy did a little jig of his own. "I told you," he seemed to be saying, gesturing at himself and the tiles while Andersen stood, unable to move or even think about what he had seen, what he had felt.

Andersen tipped the boy and went back to the Hippodrome. Jensen was pacing around the Egyptian Obelisk, pocket watch in hand. Andersen approached and smiled. He was about to describe the tulips on the tiles in the mosque and the incredible illusion he had witnessed when he saw the curl of the Danish Consul's lip, the slight crack in his veneer of indifference. Andersen nodded at his compatriot and decided not to explain or even apologize for his absence.

1

At dusk, the Hotel de la France suffused its lounging clientele with a soft and intriguing light. Having taken his leave of Jensen, who mentioned another visit as if administering a threat, Andersen walked through the lounge, nodding at a few familiar faces, although he had yet to introduce himself to any of these Europeans. Andersen's room had been cleaned thoroughly, his possessions left neat and tidy. The paper flower remained exactly as he had left it: on the window sill, basking in the remains of the evening sun. Andersen examined the drawing carefully. The tiny markings inside the petals seemed more pronounced than before, as if someone had applied an extra coat of ink. The orange hue of the petals' edges, too, appeared rejuvenated after a day in the sun. A trick of the light, no doubt, but Andersen would keep a vigilant eye on Zeynep's tulip just the same.

CHAPTER 7

*T*he green dervish wanted to climb the stone walls of the Rumeli Hisari, the ruined fortress overlooking their cannons. As they ascended the crumbling steps, the calligrapher saw men securing strings of colored candles around the rims of the various towers. She shivered despite the warmth of the evening. On the eve of the Prophet's birthday, everyone would be outside carrying a light. If she were going to be recognized, if her old humiliation were going to return, it would be on this night, when there were no shadows to protect her.

At the crest of the highest tower, the calligrapher and dervish stood pasha-tall amid the crumbling battlements, above a sweep of Bosphorus blue. To their right was the peninsula where the sultan's palace stood, and behind it, the imperial mosques of the city silhouetted against the reddening sun. Was there anywhere in the world as high as this? The calligrapher looked at the green dervish, whose turban seemed to be resting against the sky.

"I have always wondered what it would be like to see my city, my old home, from the vantage point of a bird," she said.

"And is your home still there," the green dervish said, waving his arm in the general direction of the city, "after all these years?"

"It was destroyed."

"What about the place where you learned your script?"

"I don't know. It survived the violence of the last sultan. I lived there, in the *tekke*, after my parents were gone. They gave me a room and were happy to keep me as long as I practiced every day, every hour."

"Would they take you in again?"

The calligrapher shook her head. "I would not expose them to more shame than I already have."

"They might welcome you back," he said. "Things have become easier since you left. For all of us."

In his last sentence, the green dervish had slipped seamlessly from the formal 'you' pronoun, *siz*, into the familiar, softer *sen*, startling the calligrapher like a slap from a gloved hand. She was afraid of this intimacy, but forced herself to look at him. His eyes were trained, not on her, but on a green and yellow butterfly hovering just above his sleeve.

"Do you know who I am?" she asked.

"Not at first. But when we watched you work, how could we not know? The letter *wah* on its pole, the forlorn stork, the mosque with a human face."

Again the informal *sen*, as permanent between them now a mole on the skin. "I will leave you," she said, and started to rise.

"That would be a shame. Blue, especially, would be most disappointed."

"He told you this?"

"He wants to tell you. We both do." The butterfly turned a half-circle above his head before coming to rest on a large stone. "You may not hear it directly from him, but you will know."

"But..."

"How can a man with no voice make himself understood?" The green dervish smiled. "He was not always like this. My blue-turbaned friend had the most beautiful singing voice I ever heard." And, as a line of storks flew heavy-winged over the fortress toward the Black Sea, he beckoned the calligrapher to sit to sit on the battlement wall beside him and listen.

"In all the years of our friendship, I only heard him sing once. That was in the prayer hall of a *tekke* in Merdivenköy where we were guests for the night. One of the worshippers knew of my friend's gift and asked him to sing the *zikr*, the ninety-nine names of God. The chanting of these blessed appellations is always inspiring, but that evening, my friend's tender voice filled us with awe. He began slowly, but then settled into a rhythm and a tone so sublime that the holy names soared over us like the individual beats of a swallow's wing.

"I can still hear some of the names from that evening—Allah, the first and purest, *Ar-Rahman* (The Compassionate), *Ash-Shahid* (The Witness), *As-Sabur* (The Patient)—names that brushed us with a divine grace. I can still see the faces of the worshippers rocking gently back and forth in the lamplight. But what I remember most were the pieces of colored cloth hung across the niche of the prayer hall to remind the *tekke*'s saint to bless the worshippers.

As my friend pronounced each name of God, I looked at these bright squares of blue, red, orange, and yellow and felt, with a blind man's instinct, the *essence* of these colors as I had not experienced before, nor have again since that evening.

"It was around this time my friend was overcome by restlessness, a spiritual stagnation that could only be assuaged by travel. He was gone for many years, and wherever he went, the reputation of his voice preceded him. People waited anxiously for his arrival; he could not enter a *tekke* in search of lodgings for the night without first reciting the *zikr*. When he sang the names of Allah, people were transfixed. In the bigger towns my friend found himself in even greater demand. He finished a *zikr* at one establishment, only to dash across town to sing at another. His voice began to crack and he croaked the last ten names of God like a holy frog. Still, the people thought this was beautiful and were disappointed when he could not sing for them every night.

"Then my friend returned here and found the city much changed. He saw huge ships sailing through the Bosphorus, belching steam. In the coffeehouses, smokers no longer sat with their *nargiles* and told stories, but crowded around newspapers and talked of other, far-away cities and the people who lived there. Frockcoats and fezzes sprouted like weeds. The colors bled from people's clothes, the bright reds and greens and blues replaced by shades of gray. My friend and I decided to visit the *tekke* where I had heard him sing. We arrived in the middle of the chant of the ninety-nine names and heard the familiar beat of the drum, the plaintive call of the *ney*. The people swayed to the rhythm of the chant, but the voice intoning the names of God did so with a peculiar lack of passion, as if each moniker were a diner to be seated at a royal banquet.

"But we could not see who the singer was. The voice was not coming from any of the worshippers in the room. When the ceremony was over, we asked the sheikh to introduce us to this new singer and enquired what innovation had occurred in our absence that necessitated his standing outside like a naughty child. The sheikh laughed and told us that since my friend had sung the *zikr*, they had invited many other worshippers to lead the chanting, but none had been able to recreate the same joy and abandonment as my friend. Some singers were too maudlin, others excitable, while still others, encumbered by their village dialect, struggled with their enunciation of the sacred syllables. Then one evening, a young man, a devotee who was studying at the engineering college, presented the sheikh with a glass box in which a number of coils, springs, and cylinders had been ingeniously arranged. The young man proceeded to wind this contraption as a child winds a clockwork toy, whereupon it produced a series of whirring sounds, convulsed slightly, and then intoned the ninety-nine names of God without so much as a pause.

"At first, the sheikh wanted to destroy the young student's glass box; not only did it sound ungodly, but the sheikh doubted whether the divine could hear something that did not come from within the human soul. But then he recalled the more unfortunate *zikr* evenings they had endured since my friend's departure. The sheikh decided to keep the glass box in reserve for days when no suitable singers could be found amidst the congregation, which happened just a week later.

"The sheikh told the student to place the box behind the curtain of the prayer hall; the young man was to wind it before entering the room. The sheikh himself would clear his throat to cover the initial splutter of the contraption. That first time, he held his breath for most of the ninety-nine names. It wasn't until the glass box moved smoothly into the eighty-ninth, *Al-Mughni* (The Enricher), that he began to relax. The faithful, who kept their eyes closed during this portion of prayer, each believed one of their neighbors had performed the rite, someone with a clear, even voice, if somewhat lacking in nuance. Soon the worshippers began to ask for the singer with the strong, steady tone. The Sheikh found it easier to wind the machine before *every* recital, place it behind the curtain, and, coughing lightly, let the rite of *zikr* begin.

"The sheikh told us this story, I believe, to compliment my friend's gift, to imply that no human could register the same level of emotion as he had managed that night. But my friend shook his head and offered the sheikh a sad smile. 'I congratulate you on your glass box,' he said. 'My voice is weary now and you have saved it from further strain.' The sheikh looked aghast at what he had done, but my friend had already commenced his vow of silence and it was too late."

༄

When the green dervish finished his story, he and the calligrapher sat in silence, the imprint of the conqueror's stone on their backs. The calligrapher thought of the holy names clicking and whirring in endless repetition, all because men no longer had the patience to talk to God. She remembered the look on her *usta*'s face when he first saw a printed copy of the Koran. It was like someone had stolen his identity, and sold it a thousand times over. *Who trained this paper machine?* he had asked her. *Who gave it the permission to write?* She had turned the pages herself and found the script of the printed book dry and without soul. There had been no smell either. No hint of quince or the fragrance of an ink lovingly mixed.

ﻝ

Blue was waiting on the shoreline when the pair returned from their walk. He smiled at the calligrapher and pointed to the muzzle of her cannon. Inside he had deposited his notebook, pens, and inkwell. The calligrapher understood that the dervish, as her *usta* had once done, was examining her work, checking on the shape of her *alifs* and the lines of her prayers. She had always liked to have the approval of another. It was lonely writing only for oneself, like having an idea and no one to share it with.

She went to the cannon and took up the writing materials. Testing the thickness of a turquoise ink with her finger, she wrote a practice *alif*. She thought of Blue and the joy he must have felt while singing the ninety-nine names of God. A joy similar to what she felt now, *kalem* poised above the paper, her mind wandering over the possibilities offered by the blank page. "If your brain were paper, my girl," her *usta* had once said upon catching her adrift like this, "you'd be the most prolific calligrapher in the world."

CHAPTER 8

The following morning, Andersen was up well before the hotel restaurant opened for breakfast.

In an hour Musa would send a boy to bring him to the ferry landing near the palace. From there, they would cross the Bosphorus to Uskudar, the location of the monastery where Zeynep had been a protégée to a master calligrapher, and where Musa himself had been a scholar.

As he shaved and dressed, Andersen wondered what he would find at this *tekke* on the Asian side of the city. Was Musa going to ask him for something at the monastery, a donation perhaps, because of the common misconception that European travelers had money to spare? Andersen did not like the idea. He hoped, though, that another of Zeynep's lettered flowers might be for sale. His friend Edvard would love the intricate design of the tulip's component parts. He brought his own paper tulip out to the balcony, placing it on the tabletop and weighing it down with a glass. The afternoon sun would do it good, he thought, and turned his gaze to the street.

The hotel across the way was very close. It was in a different class than the Hotel de la France, Andersen was pleased to note; paint was peeling off the walls of the building and the windows were too close together.

A man holding a sketch pad in his hand appeared on the balcony opposite. He stood in profile, looking back into his room as if admiring—no, assessing—something inside. With a start, Andersen recognized the man. His red hair and green kaftan were unmistakable. The edge of his impressive eyebrow twitched as his pen jerked across the surface of the notebook at a rapid pace. In his haste, the man jabbed a hole through the page with his pen, then promptly tore it out, crumpling it up and throwing it to the ground. He was about to begin again when he turned toward Andersen. Some seconds passed, the two men regarding one another in cautious silence. Andersen considered raising his hand in greeting, but before he could, the red-headed man ducked back into his room.

Somewhat rattled by the man's odd behavior, Andersen left the balcony and returned to the room.

"*Bottes, Monsieur!*" said a voice, followed by a knock and the sound of retreating footsteps. Andersen opened the door to a pair of boots so much like his own: sleek, calf-length black leather, tassels for tightening at the front, thick heels for support. The hotel had even tied the tops of the boots together with a bright ribbon. But the boots were the length of Andersen's hand, miniature boots that a well-heeled dwarf might wear around town.

§

In Uskudar, on the Asian shore of the city, the boy led Andersen along cobbled streets escorted by a troupe of dogs, who, until roused by the scent of a Frank, had been content to idle away the morning sprawled on dunghills or sniffing the husks of rotting vegetables. Musa, resplendent in a kaftan-turban combination of dark green, was waiting for him at the gates of a dervish *tekke* set deep in a cypress wood. He explained that, as his guest, the holy men would tolerate Andersen's presence within the *tekke*. They walked through the wood, tall cypresses shading them on either side like an honor guard. As they walked, Andersen told Musa about the tiles he had seen in the small mosque near the Hippodrome. "Dancing tiles," Andersen said, and then into the pause that followed, "It was as though they were moving, right there in front of me."

"The mosque of Sokullu Mehmet Pasha," Musa said quietly. "Grand Vizier to three sultans."

{

Beyond the cypress wood, a cemetery set in a luxuriant garden greeted Andersen. A series of white gravestones had been carved into turbans and fezzes, the names and ranks of the deceased etched into the base. A second slab lay over the graves themselves, with hollows scooped out of the centers. Rainwater could collect here, Musa explained, for stray dogs to drink.

There were other graves too, simple slabs with no identifying script—nothing but a small lotus blossom carved into the corners. "For women," Musa said.

The cemetery was vast. Men, women, and gray wolf-like dogs strolled along pathways shaded with trellised vines, the dogs walking alone or in pairs. Andersen felt unexpectedly calm in this place. He noticed that the people paid little attention to the graves themselves, which were immaculate, but would bend to examine the curve of a flower, or stop to listen to the coo of a morning dove.

Musa showed Andersen a series of flower beds that followed no discernible pattern or order. Hyacinths planted with violets, roses with saffron crocus and narcissi, and Persian lilacs grew beside carnations, all in wild, furtive clumps. Andersen was bewildered at first, so accustomed was he to the regimented rows and orderly formations of European gardens, but he could not deny the beauty and vitality of these beds, a floral democracy of species and color.

"What a beautiful red," he said, standing beside a cluster of tulips growing alone as if refusing to conform to the mixed-bed policy. To his surprise, Musa bent and plucked one of the tulips from the ground.

"You mentioned the tulip tiles of the Sokullu Mehmet Pasha mosque, Herr Andersen," he said, running his fingers over the petals. "And although the red tulips in this garden are striking, they cannot compare with the color you saw there."

"No, I suppose not," Andersen said, knowing he was expected to respond.

"As a writer, I'm sure you have already tried to compose a simile to capture the color of those tiles: 'as ripe as the tomato plucked off the vine,' perhaps, or 'as distinctive as the wax on the sultan's seal.'"

"Yes. I was thinking in those terms."

Musa rolled the stem of the tulip back and forth across his palm. "I will never forget my first visit to that mosque either, Herr Andersen. That leather curtain, set so deep into the doorway that one emerges right in the middle of the prayer hall as if propelled by a divine hand. Like you, I faced the tiles on either side of the *mihrab* and above the *minbar*. Green, blue, purple, and red, colors as clear under their glaze as the day they were applied." He transferred the flower to his other hand.

"Recall, if you will, the red of the giant tulips that bloom on either side of the *mihrab*. On that first visit I examined the tiles, trying to spot imperfections—an irregular curl of a leaf, perhaps—as I knew the artist had had but one chance to apply his fine brush to the surface. I must have been engrossed in this task because I hadn't noticed the *imam* standing at my shoulder. He told me this particular hue of red could be seen at very few mosques in the city. 'Think, *bey effendi*,' he said, 'of the tiles you have seen elsewhere, at the Sultan Ahmed Mosque, for example—think of the dullness of the red there. It is like blood diluted in a wash basin, or the bruised skin of an apple.'

"'How is it possible,' I asked this *imam*, 'that no one has managed to recreate this color in the three centuries since these tiles were painted?' He told me that if I cared to return to the mosque later that day, I could see for myself."

Musa tapped the tulip gently against the palm of his hand. "Shall I relate the story of the

Lost Red of Sokullu Mehmet Pasha Mosque, Herr Andersen?"

"I'd like that very much."

"Then I should add the caveat that this is a slightly unusual story."

"Oh?"

"It is a story in which I myself appear."

"I see," Andersen said.

"As a professional writer, you would no doubt scorn such an approach. If you were to compose the tale, I would appear as someone other than 'I.' A philosophizing baker, perhaps, or a traveling salesman."

It was a strategy Andersen had employed many times in his own work. Musa seemed to know quite a lot about writing. He wondered, not for the first time, if Musa had lied about never having read his work. If not Andersen, then who had Musa read in the German language?

He said, "That is what many writers do, yes."

Still holding the tulip, Musa began: "The secret of the Iznik red died along with the craftsmen who painted the tiles of our mosque.

Before that time, people were satisfied with fewer colors—turquoises and blues, the occasional yellows. When they saw that red, though, the men of wealth, the viziers and pashas, flocked to Iznik, which prospered like never before. But the craftsmen kept their secret, and as quickly as the red had appeared, it disappeared, as if the inventors of this new color and taken its recipe to their graves.

"Generations of subsequent Iznik tilers tried to recreate the glaze, but to no avail; their tulips, roses, and cherry blossoms were pale and sickly in comparison. When, in desperation, the head guildsmen began to solicit the advice of outsiders, many traveled to see for themselves the apotheosis of the Iznik red at the Sokullu Mehmet Pasha Mosque. Indeed, at the time of my first visit, dozens of so-called experts had already gathered at the mosque hoping they could succeed where many others had failed.

"A team of wool merchants huddled together by the screen of tiles around the *mihrab*. Like performers in a shadow puppet show, these dour guildsmen held red socks and waistcoats against the spirals of the tulips, searching for a likeness in tone. They returned with red dye, thickened with gum from the acacia tree, but they could not get the right hue. Then, a group of tea merchants from Rize claimed the long stem of the Black Sea tea plant, when mixed with red pigment and a sprinkling of the wet, fertile earth from their hometown, would do the trick. I watched them sitting by the *mihrab*, stirring their concoctions in glass jars like apothecaries. But they, too, failed to produce the desired red.

"Over the next few days, I returned again and again to the mosque to observe ever more desperate gentlemen mixing and stirring, sniffing and scratching their heads, coloring the air with profanities when they could not match the color. The *imam*, meanwhile, ignored their folly: as long as these men did not encroach on the *namaz* prayers, he let them alone.

"But watching these failed attempts made me wonder if I, an educated man with many contacts among the city's guilds, should not also try my hand. I visited a friend in the Grand Bazaar, a silk dyer who worked with pigments derived from beetles. He ushered me into a back room and showed me a glass pepper jar. Inside was a pair of purple-colored beetles, the female of which, according to my friend, was about to hatch her eggs. These beetles were from the Americas, he told me. He kept only a small supply to produce pigments for wealthy clients, which was strictly against the practices of the guild, who are bound by law to use registered sources for their pigments. My friend sold me the beetle, instructing that when it was ready to lay its eggs, a white secretion would appear on its underside; when this was wiped off and the beetle crushed, the resulting color would give off a favorable match.

"I smuggled the jar into the mosque, along with one of my shoes, which I intended to use as a means of dispensing with the beetle when the time came. But, as one day passed into two, the beetle showed no signs of cooperating, refusing to eat the food in its jar and exhibiting such torpor I thought it had already died. Still, I sat by the *mihrab* peering into my glass jar until, about to give up, I saw signs of the white secretion my friend had told me to look for on the beetle's underbelly.

"I unscrewed the lid of the jar, only for the beetle to leap from its glass prison. It scuttled across the floor toward the *mihrab* tiles, proceeded up the wall, and paused on the very red of the tulip I hoped its sacrifice would help replicate. I stood with my shoe at the ready, aware the *imam* had seen me and I was about to soil the tiles we both revered.

"The *imam* reached up and cupped his hand around the beetle, returning it gently to the jar. He told me the beetle's death would not prove a thing, but instead of berating me for my foolishness, he invited me to sit on the floor by a window where he kept a cut tulip in a filigree vase. And in that flower I saw the red I had been seeking, red in its original form without shading or blending, free of corrupting hues and polluting dyes.

"The *imam* told me to take the flower and examine it by sunlight. 'Perhaps you would be good enough to let me know what you see,' he said. Outside in the courtyard, feeling like a dismissed child, I held the tulip up to the light and blinked, wondering if my eyesight was deteriorating since, instead of the red I'd seen in the mosque, the flower had turned pale as if experiencing a terrible shock; that deep, immortal hue had faded into an unpleasant umber, an unholy alliance of pigments that pained the eye to see.

"I went back inside and found the *imam* sitting in front of the *mihrab* with the jar on his lap and the beetle gamboling along his outstretched arm. He nodded and suggested I place the tulip back in its vase. The secret of the Iznik red would remain intact, he said. Safe within the confines of the Sokullu Mehmet Pasha Mosque and others like it, in which the Iznik tilers, the men of that golden generation, had worked."

Musa gave no further explanation for the tale.

He continued to massage the stem of the tulip between his palms, as if trying to absorb the flower's essence. Then he smiled, broke the stem of the red tulip, and inserted the flower into the lapel of Andersen's jacket. For a few seconds, his fingers remained locked under the head of the tulip so that they rested against Andersen's chest.

Musa and Andersen walked through the rest of the garden, toward a rectangular stone building covered with wisteria and vine. They would enter the *tekke* shortly; everything had been arranged. Andersen watched turbaned holy men— dervishes?—standing in groups by the door, holding glasses of tea.

They entered the prayer hall of the *tekke* through an anteroom bisected by a thick, red carpet and plywood shelves full of shoes. In the prayer hall itself, the walls were lined with low benches covered with brightly colored *kilims*. Worshippers lolled on these, some chatting happily, others lying on their stomachs staring hard at the bare wooden floor. Those in more upright positions were removing hats or unwinding turbans.

Musa and Andersen waited at the back of the prayer hall. They stood very close together, effigy-like in the curve of an alcove. At the other end of the room hung a pair of enormous green discs displaying loping white calligraphic script. Musa pointed out a latticed gallery running along one side of the room where the women prayed. Andersen imagined he could see shapes moving behind this barrier, the glint of watchful eyes.

A hush descended on the room. The worshippers had replaced their hats with soft white skullcaps and were now perched on the edge of the benches, alert. A figure dressed in a blue tunic, green turban, white skirt, and red slippers strode to the middle of the floor and held up his hand. A low chant worked its way around the room, rippling and insistent: *Ja hu, Ja hu*.

"The sheik," said Musa. The worshippers advanced to the middle of the room and began to circle the holy man, who had sunk to his knees. *Ja hu, Ja huuuu*, they sang to their prostrate leader. Musa whispered, "They will pace the floor for a while yet. Now will be a good time to see Zeynep's work." They retrieved their shoes, opening the door to a stream of worshippers making their way in from the graveyard.

Outside, Andersen was surprised to see more buildings extending off a courtyard: kitchen, store room, library, school—even an infirmary. A small structure no bigger than a hut, with a slit for a window, stood at the very back of the courtyard. Musa led Andersen into this structure, which from the inside, was a rectangular room with two walls supporting shelves of tightly packed books. A divan and desk and chair stood in front of another wall. Musa, with difficulty, lit a lamp in the corner, casting a huge, turban-shaped shadow behind him. He motioned Andersen toward the desk while he squinted at the books. A writer's room, no matter how ascetic, stirred Andersen's heart, and now here he was at the desk of a Turkish calligrapher! Musa pulled out a green volume. There was a single line of letters braided in gold on the front cover. "'He Practiced It,'" Musa translated. "Or I should say, 'She Practiced It.' This was Zeynep's notebook as an apprentice calligrapher."

Musa moved behind Andersen's right shoulder and opened the book. A faint *Ja hu* could be heard from the main prayer hall. The paper was dry with a smooth, creamy surface. The pages fell with a crackle, each one revealing a single vertical line, black and bold, drawn parallel to five rhombic dots.

"The *alif*," said Musa. "The first letter of God. It must be practiced until the calligrapher has fully internalized the letter's dimensions, until the pen *becomes* the letter. Here," he said, pointing to the line on the page. "The height is equivalent to five dots, the width two. When the calligrapher has perfected the *alif*, then other letters may be formed, all to be drawn within the *alif*'s invisible circle, in perfect proportion." He began to recite in a low voice, his breath gently probing the tip of Andersen's ear:

There is on the tablet of my heart nothing but the alif of my beloved's stature—

What shall I do? My teacher gave me no other letter to memorize!

The *alifs* and the guiding dots looked like a series of tiny kites floating, one on top of another, beside a cypress tree. Andersen began turning the pages. When the apprentice became more confident in her depiction of the essential letter, the kites floated away, until finally, the cypress-like *alif* stood alone, page after page, in identical upright beauty. And then, slowly, the *alif* began to change. From one page to the next, a new version appeared. It grew bold and nimble, slanting into the wind, curling and looping, floating on its side, coiling its neck like a cobra, arching into eyebrows, angling into gallows, sprouting into branches, reclining like a sated lover, spooning and sawing, gaining heads and sloughing tails, as sharp as a scimitar, as soft as a sliver of moon. Each of these shapes, Musa said, was a new letter.

"Say it again, Musa. That couplet you just recited"

Musa recited it more slowly this time, letting each word resonate:

There is on the tablet of my heart nothing but the alif of my beloved's stature—

What shall I do? My teacher gave me no other letter to memorize!

Andersen had never considered the individual character of a letter before, its fluidity and power, its independence from the word it helped to build. He thought of the letters that Zeynep had used to create the flower in his room; each one was integral to the whole in the same way a real flower would wilt and die if one of its components were missing. And now Musa, a man he had considered solemn until this moment, even distant, was reciting poetry to him in this simple room where one could study a single letter and achieve happiness.

Musa closed the book and carried it to the shelves. He was efficient, business-like again, and the moment passed.

The chanting from the prayer hall started up again. *La illah illallah*: a low, continuous mantra.

"How long did she practice?" Andersen asked.

"Until she got it right."

Musa placed another volume in front of Andersen. On the cover page, amid scrolling branches and small polychrome flowers, was a single line of script. "'*Katabahu*. She Wrote It,'" said Musa. "It is the final permission, the highest rank a calligrapher can attain. From the moment she received this, everything she wrote could be signed with those words." He pointed to a smaller, spidery line at the bottom of the page, nestled between a red tulip and a cluster of feathery leaves. "The signature of the *usta*, his seal of satisfaction. Now we must find the caveat."

"The caveat?"

"There's always a caveat."

Musa turned one of the heavy pages. Andersen caught flashes of black cursive script.

"Here it is," Musa said. "It is not so restrictive, as caveats go." Peering into the book, he translated the following:

The calligrapher should not divide a single word onto two lines because this is unseemly, even if the price of paper is now an affront to us all. She should begin each new piece with the words 'God bless this pen and give it peace' and never mention the Prophet without asking first for his blessing. I recommend the calligrapher sprinkle some sand on the completion of each page for protection.

Under no circumstances should she adopt a haughty attitude to her craft or to fellow calligraphers. Many young calligraphers believe the kataba gives them the right to criticize older colleagues, who have spent half a lifetime laboring for little reward, since calligraphers, alas, remain terribly underpaid. They would be better off remaining at home to practice than lounging in coffee houses expounding on affairs of the realm. Why, only recently I witnessed a young apprentice holding forth

*on the voraciousness of Armenian bankers with his
pen tucked behind his ear like a gypsy's trinket!
Fortunately I knew his master, who, on hearing my
report, did not spare the rod on the impudent wastrel.*

Musa's face underwent an alarming metamorphosis. His cheeks and chin undulated, lips twitched, nostrils flared, and his eyes became liquid and bright. He was laughing, Andersen realized with relief. Three staccato sounds wheezed through the Turk's pursed lips like a locomotive's horn. Andersen felt he too should laugh, but could not bring himself to do so.

"It is amusing, if a little sad, to recall the *usta* in such fine voice," Musa said.

"What else is inside the book?"

"Verses from the Holy Koran, special prayers. Perhaps even a little poetry."

"No flowers?" Andersen asked hopefully.

"Not for *Katabahu*," said Musa. Everything would have to be rendered exactly as the *usta* taught her."

The successful completion of this book would have meant Zeynep's release from her apprenticeship, Andersen thought; it was the strictest examination of her craft. What a difference from the West, where almost anyone with half an idea or legible handwriting could claim to be a writer or a scribe!

"When did Zeynep gain her permission to practice?" he asked.

Musa started to remove books from one of the higher shelves, placing them in a neat pile on the floor. "It must be ten years now," he said.

"You must have been very proud of her."

Musa grunted, reaching into the shelf space above his head.

"Did you know she was special, more gifted than other apprentices, at that time?" Andersen asked.

Musa pulled out a cylindrical metal case. "She was fourteen when she arrived at the *tekke*," he said, placing the cylinder on the desk. "A thin girl. We never knew about her parents or the home she grew up in or how she learned to write. A wandering dervish brought her in. He said the two of them had been roaming around for weeks, learning from each other. We doubted this at first; what could a young girl like that teach an old sage?"

"But later?"

"Everyone who saw her work learned a little, I think. We looked and we saw something of *ourselves* on the page. That is the true skill of the calligrapher—to reflect and illuminate not just the word of God, but those who seek it."

Try as he might, Andersen could not grasp the meaning of Musa's words. He felt like a student again, in the mathematics class back in Copenhagen, trying desperately to make sense of the symbols and formulae, hoping the esoteric affinities between x and y would suddenly declare their intentions to him.

Musa unscrewed the lid of the cylinder. He extricated a scroll of manuscript paper and flattened about three quarters of it onto the desk. "Perhaps this will better illustrate what I mean," he said, resting a finger on the roll. "Do you have your scissors? To hold the paper in place, not to cut it," Musa said with a smile. Andersen removed the scissors from his breast pocket and wedged them against the roll of paper.

He was struck first by the colors in what lay before him: a lush mélange of jungle green, orange and yellow, purple and gold. Scrolling branches bent over a waterway of intense blue. There was life in and around the water: prowling, perching, and poised. A lugubrious stork stood at the forefront of the scroll, one wing outstretched toward the river, as if introducing the delights within. The stork's black and gold plumage, Musa told him, was composed of the *Bismillah*, a phrase meaning, 'In the name of God, the Merciful, the Compassionate.'

On the river, a swan enjoyed a morning swim, seven cygnets following in her wake. The cygnets, tiny blobs of script, were composed of the most miniscule configurations of lines and dots, almost imperceptible to the naked eye. Each of the birds, Musa assured him, proclaimed the *Bismillah* in full. Andersen wondered about the delicacy of the nib that had drawn these birds. How was it possible to cut it so fine? Had Zeynep required a magnifying glass to see what she was doing?

Still other, more fantastic, creatures lurked in the depths of this waterway or patrolled its banks. Fire-red *Bismillah* parrots basked; shoals of green and yellow fish broke the water's surface with their scaly script; grey spider monkeys dangled from low, overhanging branches. If Andersen stared hard enough, he could see tiny birds stirring within the trees—compact chronograms with diacritical marks for eyes and letters for feathers. He realized he was looking for something else, too, amid this profusion of life. And soon enough, his gaze found what he'd been seeking. Small yet powerful, Zeynep's signature face looked down from the top of the scroll, peeking over the riverbank like a rising sun.

Andersen put his finger on the welcoming stork. He had always been fascinated by the creatures. Their ungainly appearance belied their great determination and patience. As a boy in Odense, he had watched the storks rebuild their nest year after year on the roof of the town hall.

They were at once great migrators and impeccable homemakers. His grandmother had told him that storks liked to nest in chimneys because this was the aperture through which they delivered babies to lucky households. The sight of a stork gliding over rooftops always made his heart skip a beat. What good news would they bring?

And yet, the stork was mute. It lacked the distinctive call of the heron or ibis, but when it clattered its bill together, the noise travelled up and down one's spine and rattled one's teeth. Everyone knew when storks were coming.

"And I always thought the stork could only say *lak lak lak*!" he said to Musa.

"It is reassuring to know the stork can be understood in many tongues," Musa said dryly.

"Musa, why are you showing me all this?" The question came quickly, unplanned by Andersen.

Musa frowned. "You said you were interested."

"I am."

Musa put his hands on the edges of the scroll, which had tipped over the side of the table; he was shaking his head slightly. Andersen knew that if he didn't mention it now, if he sat and watched Musa roll Zeynep's scroll back into its cylinder, the moment would be gone and with it, the opportunity of ever drifting along this riverbank with all her creatures again.

"Your friend. Zeynep. How did she die, Musa?"

Musa smiled his partial smile. "She died the death of most women who aggravate the men of this city, Herr Andersen," he said. "Drowned like an unwanted kitten. But I have never had the opportunity to confirm this fact."

"What do you think happened, Musa? Did she disappear?"

"She was abducted by soldiers from the New Guard—the sultan's police—and kept in a prison somewhere in the outer gardens of the palace. I have never been able to determine where exactly, or for how long. But I do know she was there. When they were done with her, she would have been taken from the prison down to the shoreline, put in a woven sack, and loaded into a boat by two *bostancis*, the palace gardeners who also served as the sultan's executioners. It is possible they strangled her first—they sometimes do—or she might have been alive and suffocating inside the sack. They would have rowed out a little, and then they would have thrown her overboard." Musa's tone was flat and lifeless; he might have been describing the various means of planting a successful tulip.

"But what had she done?" Andersen's voice was shrill in comparison.

"The New Guard took some papers from her room when they came for her. I assume the papers contained writing someone deemed impure."

"Impure? She was persecuted for her work? By whom?" Andersen could hardly control himself.

"The religious authorities—the *ulema*—consider it profane to turn the holy script into human or figural form. But their reasons for this are selfish and motivated by power. The holy men who advise the sultan are frightened that the word of God will slip from their grasp. When the prayers are written in their prescribed fashion, the holy men can determine their meaning for the faithful. You see, these men don't want the public to be able to understand the word of God for themselves. A calligrapher with enough skill, one who could form shapes and images even an illiterate public could interpret, could make these men of God irrelevant. Then, what would they do?"

"Because Zeynep's writing was unorthodox, because she wrote for people to understand, she was killed?

"That is my theory, yes."

"What about this scroll, what about all this bird-life?" Andersen asked, pointing at the lettered stork. "This cannot be impure!"

"What we think or believe doesn't really matter, Herr Andersen."

"How did these guards know about Zeynep's work?"

Musa shrugged, a gesture Andersen found both odd and disconcerting.

"To have her killed," Andersen persisted, "there must have been something else, don't you think?"

"If you have another theory, Herr Andersen, I would be delighted to hear it."

"I'm sorry. I didn't mean…"

"Because I can assure you I have turned over every stone searching for a reason. It's the insignificance of her death that I come back to, as if they killed her between jobs, murdered her to fill the time. I don't know why they took her, but I'd like to think that, once imprisoned, she troubled them somehow. It reassures me to think she might have given them nightmares. The sultan, the religious men, the politicians in their Western suits—all of them." He picked up the scroll case and pointed it at Andersen. "I hope she did something to make them mad."

Andersen shook his head. What could be so maddening about a riverbank like the one on the table before him?

"Have you seen enough?" Musa asked.

"Is there any more to see?"

Musa raised his eyebrows and unfurled the last part of the scroll, pushing the paper halfway to the floor. A boat of billowing sails and fluted funnels appeared further up the river. The hull was a labyrinth of geometric lines and tiny, open-ended squares, its sails swarming with cursive script, supple spirals, and ligatures.

Musa stood beside him and read the mainsail. "'Whoever is kind to the creatures of God is kind to himself,'" he translated softly.

"It is the most beautiful thing I've ever seen," Andersen said. "The boat, the animals on the riverbank—why wasn't it taken by the guards when they came for Zeynep?"

"Because it was hidden away."

"And who knows about it?" Andersen asked.

"The sheikh, who knows all the business of the *tekke*, and I, and now you."

He was party to a secret, a potentially dangerous one, but Andersen felt the warm glow of one specially chosen; he must be the only writer in Europe to have sat in a Turkish calligrapher's chair, the very one where Zeynep had threaded her script into the sail of this boat. He sensed her struggle in rendering the curves and flourishes into a recognizable shape, the many false starts and discarded sheets of paper, the nibs scratched to a nub.

Andersen swallowed, and as with his first meeting with Musa on the steamship, he felt like the Turk was taunting him with a delicious sweetmeat, some delicacy beyond compare.

"Musa, are you asking me to write Zeynep's story?" Andersen's heart began to race. He had never attempted a story like this, one that made him feel so close to another writer—a calligrapher, the purest form of writer.

"As a professional writer, you will not be able to resist."

Musa began to roll up the scroll, the ship sailing backwards on its paper river, the birds and animals disappearing one by one.

CHAPTER 9

The calligrapher's second morning on the Bosphorus was very much like the first. She assisted the blue dervish in extracting Green from his cannon and waited patiently through the rituals of preparing and consuming breakfast. No one mentioned Red, or seemed particularly bothered by his continued absence. Blue then left on his own, which did not seem to surprise the green dervish.

The calligrapher and the green dervish spent the morning walking along the same stretch of shoreline as the day before. The calligrapher carried the notebook and writing materials, imagining her pen scuttling over the quandaries of a new day. It was the perfect weather for advice-giving. The clouds moved briskly across the sky; the Bosphorus was slick and businesslike.

But when a woman stopped the green dervish to ask him about ancient remedies for a sore throat, the latter seemed at a loss. The calligrapher moved to open the notebook, but the green dervish shook his head. A similar thing happened with the next three supplicants they encountered along the shoreline. The green dervish, without Blue to support him, seemed to be the one most in need of counsel.

At eleven, the green dervish said, "I'm getting tired of hearing people grumble. How do you feel about taking the rest of this morning off?"

The calligrapher was disappointed. "Is my presence a distraction?" she asked.

"Not at all. It's just that the act of giving, whether advice or time, can be draining. People expect you to know everything. They think because you refer to God's will, you must have the maker's ear." The green dervish was looking at Blue's notebook, tucked under the calligrapher's arm, as he said this.

"Is there something I can write for you?" she asked, thinking she might shape the *Bismillah* into the shape of a turban.

He nodded, keeping his eyes on the notebook. "But first, I want to show you a place where I used to spend a lot of my time. It is important that you see it."

The calligrapher imagined he would lead her to the tomb of a venerable saint, like the men in her *tekke* used to do: a pilgrimage to a gravestone or small sarcophagus where they would have a picnic and a glass of tea before offering a quick prayer to the deceased.

They set off along a steep lane of wooden houses, past workshops and mosques. The green dervish greeted flower sellers and shepherds, all of whom eyed the calligrapher discreetly. They made an interesting pair. The calligrapher felt as if she were serving another apprenticeship, that the people were assessing her potential for wisdom; perhaps they saw her as the replacement for the missing red dervish.

On the far side of the small village, they came to a wooden house with a small blue door, the top of it barely reaching the calligrapher's shoulders. The green dervish worked an ancient-looking key around the lock. He bent almost double to fit through the doorway. They stood in a passageway lit by tiny glass skylights.

"It's something of a labyrinth, I'm afraid," said the green dervish, who still could not stand to his full height. They turned into another corridor with a ceiling slightly higher than the last, but just as dim. The calligrapher's spine turned to ice. Beyond the walls, in rooms she could not see, a hundred muted arguments were taking place, stone-dulled voices insistent, moaning, accusatory. She and the green dervish zigzagged through more passageways. The voices slowly gained definition until the calligrapher could hear a man denouncing the ineptitude of contemporary philosophers, while in a separate dispute she was able to make out a woman railing against the shortcomings of her husband. What kind of holy tomb was this where the occupants were so querulous?

They arrived at a doorway that opened to a square room with unadorned walls. On the floor, five people sat with their legs crossed, facing something that looked like an artist's easel. To the side of this, a man fiddled with an olive-oil lamp. Then the man with the lamp picked up a reed pipe and played a tune, high-pitched and fearless. He trained the lamp onto the easel, which turned out to be a white screen of transparent material raised slightly off the ground. The room filled with a bitter, grassy smell. As the light illuminated the white easel, the audience applauded politely, and the man disappeared behind the screen.

Two loose-limbed, silhouetted figures appeared. The figures advanced toward each other. The first, resplendent in gilded kaftan and satin turban, recited a love poem featuring dancing flowers and burbling springs. The second, a character with threadbare clothes and a rugged beard, launched into a strong critique of this poem, rejecting its flowery language, florid metaphor, and unrealistic portrayal of relations between the sexes. Emboldened by the diffused light of the screen, the puppets looked to the calligrapher like miniatures cut from stained glass. She admired the fantastic detail, from the folds and weighted texture of the poet's dress to the dilated pupil of the critic's eye, which lent him an artful, cynical expression. A furious argument ensued between the puppets, ending with Black Beard administering a sound beating to the poet, who nevertheless struggled to his feet to deliver a final couplet. At this, the green dervish edged along the wall, and the calligrapher followed. She was shaken by the eruption of violence on the shadow screen.

From the corner of the room, they could see behind the screen. They watched as the puppeteer manipulated figures with horizontal rods connected by string to holes in the joints. The puppets appeared to have been rendered from flat pieces of animal hide.

"Camel is the best," whispered the green dervish. "It is more transparent when baked in the sun." He nodded at the puppeteer, who bowed in return. By now, the majority of the audience had risen to their feet and were exiting through a side door. This led to another room, similar to the first, with a white screen mounted at the back and a second puppeteer, this time aided by an assistant. In this production were four silhouettes: the same poet and critic as before, plus a dandyish figure in a Western-style waistcoat carrying a cane. The fourth, a smartly dressed woman with fine hair falling from her *yashmak*, stood slightly away from the action and delivered pithy indictments on the men's attempts to sound cultured and worldly. This discussion, too, ended in violence, the three male characters falling on one another in a squalid heap while the long-suffering woman shook her head.

Still more rooms branched off from this one. Peering through one of the many doorways, the calligrapher saw that the building was a honeycomb of tiny theaters. The audience drifted from one room to another, sometimes settling on cushions, sometimes leaning for only a few minutes against a piece of wall before moving to the next theater.

"This is where the puppeteers spend their winters," the green dervish explained. "They practice here, honing their skills for the summer and trying out new material. Now they are busy with their final preparations."

"Where will they perform?" the calligrapher asked.

"Some will go to theaters, others to coffeehouses. But most of the people you see here will perform wherever they can. On a quiet bank by the Bosphorus, in a soup shop, on top of a hill, next to a tripe stand, under the statue of a frowning sea captain, at guild meetings and garden parties. They will shout in bazaars and whisper in libraries. I know one who plans to perform on a moving sedan chair so that he might reach a larger audience." The green dervish gave the calligrapher a crooked smile. "I was among their number once," he said.

"A puppeteer?"

The dervish nodded.

"And you…practiced in one of these rooms?"

"Yes. *Inshallah*, it is still here. I keep telling them to let someone else use it, but puppeteers are a sentimental lot."

The green dervish returned to the corridors, leading the calligrapher deeper into the structure until they found another room, dimly lit like a shrine. The green dervish adjusted the wick of the oil lamp as the calligrapher approached the screen at the back of the room. She ran her finger along its surface. It was made from a very fine cotton— as transparent as the veils she had seen on the women in the Albanian village the day before— stretched onto a black frame. Behind the screen was a small wooden platform—the stage. Resting against this was a reed pipe.

"It will be a little dirty now," the green dervish said, gesturing at the screen. "I haven't used it for a long time. But there should be a cushion somewhere if you'd like to sit down."

The calligrapher sat in the middle of the room, still clutching Blue's notebook and pen case. The green dervish ducked behind the screen and blew some notes through the pipe. Then, modulating the timbre of his voice to sound at once low and quiet, yet deep and strong, he manipulated his own miniature shadow across the screen, the folds of the tiny kaftan sharp and new, thumb-sized turban bristling with purpose. The puppet's beard was blacker than the green dervish's, but its features were equally as restive. The eyes, tacks of filmy light, seemed to hold the calligrapher in their steady gaze. A figure in a kaftan of cheaper material appeared from the opposite side of the screen, and the two puppets exchanged glances as if to steel themselves for the telling of a familiar, but painful, tale.

"Once, in the golden age of shadow theatre," the green dervish began, "I roamed the city with my painted puppets and an apprentice who set up my stage for me and studied my methods. The figures were made in a workshop run by the puppet-maker's guild in the old city. In those days the guild workshop would produce any figure to order. No dress style, body shape or mannerism, no disfigurement or facial tic was beyond them. They were limited only by the puppeteer's imagination. What a pleasure it was to watch these craftsmen at work, crouched over tiny pieces of hide with paintbrushes as thin as a beetle's legs.

"You should have seen the wonderful characters that spread their shadows across our screens! And I don't mean the stock gentlemen you saw earlier, the type who solve their differences through blows or recourse to public humiliation. My apprentice and I"—here the green dervish puppet rested his elbow on his puppet-assistant's shoulder—"wanted all walks of life on our stage; no class or profession would go unrepresented, no corner of the empire would be left untouched. We walked around the city and collected people's stories, constantly creating new characters. Sometimes the audience themselves described characters they knew, and we had these made too. The puppet-makers could barely keep pace with our demand for new faces and forms. After a while, we carried a veritable army of puppets. We were prepared for every possible story.

"Our fellow puppeteers claimed we used too many characters; that the legion of dancers, djinns, witches, and monsters that crowded our stage would be better left to the imagination. The audience was overwhelmed by detail, they argued. Those who attended our shows saw in a nervous squint or a furrowed brow resemblances to people they knew. Children could not sleep after a performance for fear of fantastic nighttime visitors.

"Our rivals decided that, as an antidote to our brand of theater, they would kill off the minor characters in their own shadow-plays. They reduced their plot lines to a minimum so that the audience arrived at a performance already knowing what would happen. And as long as the characters acted their parts—the black-eyed hooligan losing his turban during a fight to expose his bald head, everyone misunderstanding one another's dialect with the predictable comic consequences—people would go home happy.

"As this prescriptive form of storytelling made its way through the city, our own audiences grew restless. They no longer had the patience to admire the realistic chopping technique we had perfected for our Anatolian woodcutter, say, or to analyze the ethics of our Greek doctor. Halfway through a play about morality or the difficulties of love, some wag would invariably shout from the back of the room for the black-eyed hooligan to come to the stage and incite a brawl."

The apprentice puppet moved to the edge of the screen and beckoned the imaginary audience toward him.

"In response," the green dervish continued, "I devised a show unprecedented in the history of shadow theatre. My apprentice traveled around the city announcing the performance, inviting everybody he met, from dignitaries and politicians to beggars and thieves. When our rival puppeteers asked the apprentice if yet more characters would appear on my stage, he told them I was locked away with my puppets, and that even he, my closest confidant, had not been permitted to see the rehearsals.

"I decided to stage my show in the courtyard of the Suleymaniye Mosque. Large numbers of people gathered there after prayers, and news of the performance would spread quickly. On the appointed day, my apprentice set up my screen under the shade of a pine tree, stretching a length of the finest Egyptian cotton over the frame. As the sun illuminated its gossamer threads, I remember feeling a sense of profound contentment.

"The faithful came out of the mosque. Word reached me that the Grand Vizier himself was among them, and soon a large crowd had gathered in front of the pine tree, including two puppet-makers from the guild. My apprentice beat out a slow rhythm on the tambourine, and I asked the audience to close their eyes. This they did without protest, although some of the other puppeteers in the crowd thought it their professional duty to close one eye at a time. I trained the lamp on the screen and intoned, one by one, the name of each character that had once flickered there. I recounted, one by one, each of their stories."

The green dervish puppet and his assistant moved off the stage, and the calligrapher shut her eyes as instructed. She concentrated hard, listening intently to the string of stories that poured forth from the dervish, scrutinizing each of the characters that made their way across her mind.

"The woodcutter who toiled without complaint," the green dervish began. "The sharp-tongued Circassian servant girl; the dervish with the self-winding turban; the sword-fighting *imam* and priest; the Georgian balladeer with the sore throat; the Armenian footman who recounted stories overheard through salon walls; the blind woman who wove carpets from memory; the vizier with two heads, one for good moods and one for bad; the philosophizing street dog fascinated by foreign visitors; the gardener growing invisible tulips; the polygamous wife; the sultan in his cage, drawing maps of the world; the Laz tinsmith who collected infidel coins; the exiled Arab princess practicing her calligraphy by writing love letters to herself..."

The calligrapher saw them all, one by one.

"As I reached the end of each tale, I told the audience to picture the figures on the screen, asking quietly, 'Can you still see them?' After a while, their breathing grew more relaxed; they nodded their heads to my repeated question and murmured *yes*, there was something forming in their minds: the soft folds of an aging woman's face, a boatman's smile, the tilt of a turban. 'When you open your eyes,' I said, 'the characters will be there, just as you imagined them.' I signaled for the tambourine to stop. The audience looked up."

The calligrapher opened her eyes. The screen was blank.

"Hushed, the audience leaned forward, searching for evidence of subterfuge, the ghostly outline of a puppet, the whiff of displaced drama. But there was nothing. Only the white cotton screen, illuminated to a golden hue. Then one of the puppet-makers stood to address the audience. 'Can you not see the figures in all their splendor?' he said. 'Think of how they looked with your eyes closed and tell me you can't see them. Tell me your imagination has failed.' There was a good deal of head-scratching, many people stared at the ground, but no one dared speak, not even the puppeteers. The second puppet-maker stepped forward. 'Once, my colleague and I made many of the characters you see before you. They were our life's work. Open your eyes and see them now, before it is too late.'

"Then a man raised his hand. 'I see them,' he said. 'I see them, and I have missed them like old friends.' A second hand rose, a third. Voices called out. 'We see the old characters,' they said. 'We see them as plain as the nose on the puppeteer's face.'

"In the middle of the crowd, there was a growing commotion. The Grand Vizier, aided by his secretaries in their pristine frock coats, was forging a passage through the throng. He had not seen anything with his eyes open or closed; he thought everyone was mad, but seeing how happy they were, he intended to crest the wave of contentment like a well-fed seagull. 'A brilliant display of the puppeteers' art!' he exclaimed, pointing to the empty screen. 'Let us salute the man behind it!' The crowd shouted their approval, but I had already fled, leaving my puppet-box and screen behind. Later, my apprentice brought them here. I like to look at the screen occasionally—it helps me to remember— but all the puppets, all the old characters, will remain in their box until someone has the imagination to put them to use again."

The green dervish raised his head above the screen, and as the light played over his features, the calligrapher saw him as he must have looked then: a young djinn breathing life into his puppets, making a thousand tiny wishes come true.

They exited the house of puppeteers without speaking. The muted squabbles of other shadow plays seeped into their thoughts as they went. Once outside, the green dervish was cheerful again, as if the performance had rekindled his energy. The calligrapher supposed that his old life as a puppeteer was not so different from the life he lived now—both involved a life of wandering, of dispensing wisdom to those lucky enough to understand.

The green dervish looked again at Blue's notebook, which she had gripped tightly during the performance in the puppet theater, too excited to write anything down. What could she create as a fitting tribute to his old life?

Before the green dervish climbed into his cannon for an afternoon rest, he stood on the shoreline and gazed from north to south. He had done the same thing the previous evening.

The calligrapher supposed this was another of his habits, scanning the horizon for his friend in red before the gloom of the cannon consumed him. The calligrapher took Blue's notebook and pen over to her Judas tree and sat with her back against its trunk. Behind her, the sunset tinged the continent of Asia a warm orange. Nearby, a kitten picked over the bones of a fish. She felt herself slipping into the comfort of a daydream. She opened the notebook and the cat stopped its licking, regarding her reproachfully. She nodded at the little creature and began to write.

CHAPTER 10

ndersen would have to wait two days before seeing Musa again. The Turk had invited Andersen for Saturday lunch, just a day and a half before he was due to leave Constantinople. Musa had issued his invitation carefully, first checking Andersen's departure time, then closing his eyes as if solving an arithmetic puzzle. "Saturday afternoon," he had finally said. "After lunch when the sun is full and strong. I will send the same boy to collect you. Please be ready."

But ready for what? Andersen thought as he sailed back across the Bosphorus and returned to the Hotel de la France. He took a seat in the lounge and ordered tea in a tulip-shaped glass, requesting it be strong and black, like Musa had served. He secretly hoped Musa had invited him over to show him The Book of Tulips. But if that were so, what did the time of day and the strength of the sun have to do with anything?

Andersen thought about the lettered creatures on Zeynep's scroll and the mission Musa had entrusted him with: to write the story of Zeynep's life. But what did he know of that life? He knew about her early years in the *tekke*, her long and exacting apprenticeship, the many hours spent alone in her room threading the letters into that intricate scroll. He could write for hours about the magic of her calligraphy, fill sheet after sheet of the sleek, faintly perfumed paper embossed with the watermark of the hotel.

But when he thought about Zeynep's arrest and the subsequent time until her death, he was on less firm ground. Her alleged crime of—what had Musa called it?—impure writing, work deemed unorthodox and threatening by the authorities; this seemed vague and unconvincing. Surely there was something else?

Perhaps the answer was in her calligraphy, Andersen thought. The paper tulip in his room, the beautiful riverbank scroll: these he had found transformative, life-affirming. But Andersen was not a religious man. Musa had suggested others would see Zeynep's work as a conduit for interpreting God's word. *A calligrapher with enough skill, one who could form shapes and images even an illiterate public could interpret, could make these men of God irrelevant.* Somehow, her calligraphy had engendered suspicion and condemnation that had led to her death.

And it was Zeynep's death, or more precisely the *way* she had been murdered that bothered him the most: summarily executed in the palace prison and tossed into the Bosphorus like refuse. This seemed extreme to Andersen, although certainly possible, he supposed. *I hope she did something to make them mad*, Musa had said. He *must* know more. Perhaps he was teasing Andersen, waiting for him to discover the truth like a detective.

Andersen took a sip of tea. He would have to wait until he saw Musa again; he would insist the Turk tell him everything about Zeynep's last hours before he agreed to write her story.

In an attempt to distract himself, he asked the waiter to bring him a copy of the *Moniteur Ottoman*. He wondered if those loops and lines, those markings he'd seen on the back of the red-headed traveler's copy, which he'd taken for a lion, might have been a form of representative calligraphy similar to that of Zeynep's scroll. He imagined the beast sauntering down to Zeynep's river, scattering all before it: pink tongue thick and sinuous, whiskers moist with spray, green eyes narrowing in pleasure as it lapped at the cool water. The image of this larger, fiercer beast would turn the scroll into something more primal, Andersen thought, the law of the jungle expressed in zoomorphic form.

The waiter delivered the newspaper and Andersen smoothed it flat on his knees. He looked around the lounge. The English guests at the hotel had commandeered the afternoon tea hour, sprawling themselves on divans with their china cups and a look of vacancy peculiar to their countrymen at rest. Someone began a smooth, meandering piece on the piano; it was familiar, but not quite right, the timing somehow elongated.

Andersen looked at the front page. The Egyptian renegade governor, Muhammad Ali, was withdrawing from Syria, leaving behind a collection of ceremonial camels and horses with jeweled saddles. He turned the page and glanced at an article outlining the building expenses of the new Russian and French embassies in Pera: the correspondent, as far as Andersen could make out, had issues with the flaunting of foreign wealth in the Ottoman capital—the colonnaded ballroom, Aubusson carpets, Sèvres vases, and gilded *tabourets*.

What *was* that piano piece? The *andante* was being stretched into a dirge.

His heart beating a little faster, Andersen turned the page for the third and final time. He thought his eyes were playing tricks, because where the lion had once been, a white rectangle now covered the page, as though someone had erased the animal with a rubber-tipped pencil. Only the caption remained: *RETRAITE SE TRANSPORTE PLUS DE PRÈS A DIEU*

That advice about retreating, or a retreat, bringing one closer to God. But where was the image? Had a new edition come out? *Moniteur Ottoman* was a weekly publication but this was dated the previous week. Perhaps this was a later edition of last week's newspaper and there hadn't been enough ink to include the illustration. Or did the city authorities have the newspaper censored? Either way, the illustration's absence came as a blow. Andersen had planned to ask Musa if the image were similar to Zeynep's work, but he could hardly show him an empty page.

He tried to read the text above and below the white rectangle, but his French was too limited to glean much of what was written. From what he could make out, the article was an account of a debate in the Ottoman parliament. Dry, dull stuff about stamp duties and budget predictions. One name was featured numerous times throughout: Selim Ali Pasha. Andersen wrote the name down in his journal, as well as the caption from the missing image, reminding himself to find a fluent French speaker to confirm his translation.

The pianist continued his painstaking playing of what should have been a compact, palate-cleansing piece. Was he trying to play a Chopin prelude? Andersen could contain himself no longer. He would offer the piano player some advice, maybe sit down and play a few bars himself at the right tempo.

He rose with the newspaper in hand and turned toward the piano. To Andersen's surprise, the player was the red-headed traveler from the evening of his arrival, the one who had crossed his path both in and away from the hotel. Andersen studied the man's carrot-colored hair and single, continuous eyebrow, which extended across his forehead like a furry ledge. A Celt of some description, Andersen decided, an Irishman perhaps. A man who could not afford to stay at the Hotel de la France but passed his leisure hours here nonetheless. Spartan lodgings by night and the pretense of grandeur by day.

The Irishman, still bent over the keys, had not seen him approach. Andersen paused not five meters from the piano, hurriedly deciding what he would say in English: *I wonder if you wouldn't mind terribly...* The Irishman stopped playing abruptly and turned, raising the left edge of his great orange eyebrow and smiling at the newspaper in Andersen's hand. Andersen should have seized the moment; the man seemed friendlier now than when Andersen had seen him that morning, sketching on his balcony across the way, but he rose before Andersen could open his mouth. Taking a small leather bag from the top of the piano, he walked toward the door of the hotel. He moved like the notes of the Chopin prelude, languid and forcefully slow. Did he expect Andersen to follow? Andersen bit his lip, but made his way toward the door. Perhaps this fellow didn't care to talk in public spaces. He would follow at a discreet distance, just to see.

Andersen left the hotel and soon found himself on the road to the Galata dock. The Irishman was twenty meters ahead of him, his orange hair bobbing above the swell of fezzes. Close to the shore, Andersen was obliged to step aside for a troop of men dragging a block of marble on a wooden stave. The Irishman disappeared briefly from sight, and when Andersen next saw him, he was boarding a *caique* bound for the Stamboul side of the Golden Horn. Andersen quickly climbed into the next available boat, sitting heavily when the craft pitched backwards. Ahead of him, a flotilla of the canoe-shaped boats skimmed along, a muscle-brown rower at each helm, passengers sprawled on the cushioned bottoms. When they docked ten minutes later, Andersen gave his boatman the smallest silver coin he had and received an even smaller one in return.

He could just see the Irishman's head bobbing through the crowd beyond the docks. The man was heading up the steep hill in front of them, a street tightly thronged with fruit vendors and carts.

"Strawberries!" one of them called to Andersen as he scurried by. "Cherries!" said another. "Watermelons!" cried a third. The strawberry seller presided over a pyramid of the reddest, fleshiest specimens he had ever seen. The man made a sale as Andersen passed, scooping the strawberries from the peak with a small box.

The Irishman turned left onto a road with a more even terrain. They were approaching the Grand Bazaar, a tourist hub Andersen's guidebook had suggested he visit. This was hardly a quiet place to talk: perhaps Andersen had made a mistake and the Irishman didn't know he was being followed after all.

The bazaar was cold and uninviting from the outside. Its high walls were topped by cupolas with small, round windows to let in the light. Andersen passed through an archway covered with intricate calligraphy and painted flowers and found himself in a honeycombed world of arcaded streets, crossways, and cafés. Each merchant sector was carefully delineated: here saddles of Moroccan leather and buffalo skin; there a thoroughfare of boots, shoes, and slippers, catering to every size, from goblins to giants. Each street was marked with a signpost, and although Andersen could not read the script, he gave them all a colorful name: Bootstrap Street, Hill of Samovars, the Blind Alley of the Hookah Makers.

Andersen walked on through the din, resisting a pair of rose-colored trousers that would shock Copenhagen to the core. In the half-light from the cupolas and flickering stall lanterns, he thought he saw the Irishman examining a Damascene blade in the street of weapons, but could not be sure.

Was that him among the herbs and roots, dabbing a finger into a saucer of paprika? Andersen moved to a nearby stall, feigning interest in a brackish pepper the color of blood. Not wanting to appear suspicious, he walked on, and at the next intersection turned left, ducking behind another archway engraved with strange, floating letters.

"*Monsieur! Excellenza!* My Liege! You, sir, you!" A black-eyed salesman in an Arab burnoose approached from nearby. "Come." The man laced his fingers under Andersen's cuffs and slowly pulled him toward his stall. "You have the face of a Caucasian," he said in French. "You will require these pills not to become as hairy as one." The merchant held out a transparent bag of tiny white tablets. "You are prone to hair, Monsieur, unwanted hair, such as the resident of the steppe finds sprouting from his nostrils or curling around his ears. Take one a day for a year and you will never need to pluck!"

Andersen gave the man a banknote from his wallet. "For this value, I can let you take something else." He pointed toward the powders and perfumes, looked again at Andersen's face, and switched to German. "You will not find anything similar in the German lands," he said.

"Actually, I'm a Dane."

"A Dane!" he said in English. "Then you have come to us from as far as the Americas!"

"Not quite," said Andersen.

"You are married? I have *kohl* to fortify the lashes of your beloved, citron water for freshening the skin."

"I'm not married."

The Arab rested his dark eyes on Andersen's face as if solving a conundrum. "Essence of jasmine and bergamot," he said quietly, "is what you would know." He brought out a fluted bottle the size of Andersen's thumb containing a honeysuckle-colored liquid. With the tiny stopper he anointed the skin behind Andersen's ears.

Andersen closed his eyes. As a boy in Odense, he had once spent an afternoon obsessed with a yellow-white jasmine shrub. His grandfather had been sketching the plant, explaining its properties, while Andersen touched the fragile stem and petals; the fragrance had taken a day to die on his hand. And the smell of bergamot, native to Asia, with its clean, spicy kick—it was a fragrance that reminded Andersen of Musa, the warm essence that followed in the Turk's wake.

Andersen opened his eyes. Having completed his sale, the Arab had moved on and was now attending to an elegant French couple.

Andersen moved away from the corridor of spices. With the Irishman nowhere to be found, he no longer cared where he went. What a fool's errand! Perfume and newspaper in hand, he felt like a businessman shopping for a present for his wife.

He followed the general flow of the crowd exiting the Grand Bazaar. Whispers now, rather than shouts, from the stalls around him, subtle suggestions from the sellers. Some stalls had closed down for the evening, a piece of twine or a hung *kilim* separating one day's business from the next. Then, on the main thoroughfare, adjacent to another brightly painted archway, he spotted a small bakery and—he couldn't believe his luck—the Irishman was coming through the doorway carrying something delicate and steaming. Andersen waited across from the bakery while the Irishman stood in front of the archway's façade slowly consuming his food—some kind of a flaky pastry with a delicious aroma.

When the Irishman walked through the archway, Andersen followed discreetly. They moved deeper into the bazaar where the streets were much narrower. Here, various artisans and craftsmen had established workshops—iron workers bullying beauty out of sheets of metal, woodworkers whittling blocks of wood. Despite the late hour, they remained busy, perhaps completing pieces for tomorrow's bazaar.

The Irishman turned down an alleyway bisecting two of these workshops. Andersen was surprised to see daylight radiating from the other end of the passage. He pursued slowly, and at the end of the narrow street, found himself in a large courtyard in a hubbub of activity.

Men were unloading cargo from horses and camels, or stretching as if to loosen their limbs after a long journey. Everything smelled of animals. A few of the beasts, now free of their loads, were strolling, untended, toward a trough of water. Others were being led to stables on the far corner of the courtyard. The area was surrounded by buildings of heavy stone with wide, colonnaded verandas on their upper floors. Turbaned figures looked down from these vantage points—some alone and others in pairs, gesticulating expansively.

Andersen was struck by the timelessness of the scene; he could have been standing here watching the caravans coming in off the Silk Road. He imagined the men settling for the night here, discussing business and the state of the roads over coffee and pipes, swapping stories of brigands and taxes levied by unscrupulous tribal leaders.

In his wonder Andersen had forgotten the Irishman, until he spotted him moving toward one of these buildings—a hotel or inn, the sign seemed to indicate. Andersen hurried after him, wondering if his Western suit would stand out here, but the tradesmen in the courtyard seemed oblivious to his presence; a few even knocked heavily against him, hardly bothering to adjust their strides.

By the time Andersen entered the building, the Irishman had disappeared again. Men were milling about in a large, open space, and there was no sense of the order he might have expected from a hotel with paying guests. No one was dispensing keys or checking registers; the lobby had no seating area where patrons could rest while waiting to be served.

Eventually, the crowd thinned and some of the tradesmen made their way to the perimeter of the room where, one by one, they were greeted by others Andersen hadn't noticed until now. These others sat on the floor with their legs crossed. None of these men made any attempt to rise when the tradesmen approached, but listened intently as if the new arrivals were imparting important news. One of the seated men, with a swift nod of the head, balanced a stiff sheet of paper on his lap and picked up a brass writing case. He opened the case with a flourish and made a great show of selecting the right pen.

"Calligraphers!" Andersen said out loud. His heart beat a little more rapidly.

He watched the man cut and hone his nib with a small silver knife. He tested its sharpness by jabbing the point into the palm of his hand. From an inkwell, which looked to Andersen like a child's painting box with its miniature pools of color, the man selected an ink, then twisted a tiny wad of fiber into the well so that only its tip peeked from the top. He touched the nib onto the fiber, wetting the tip with ink. Then he began to write. Andersen couldn't see the script from where he stood, but the tradesman who had engaged the man's services appeared happy enough with the result and handed over some coins.

Andersen walked around the room. Twenty-five calligraphers either scribbled away or waited for business, all seated with their backs against a wall. It was an ideal place for professional scribes to hawk their talents. The tradesmen returning from long periods of travel would be anxious to send news to loved ones, or would need help filling out the permits necessary to conduct business in the empire's capital. Some of the calligraphers had a modest selection of their finished work for sale: prayers, he supposed, and some decorative letters written in giant fonts. Andersen searched the offerings for a calligraphic flower, or anything that reminded him of Zeynep's work, but the writing here was humdrum in comparison.

After completing a circuit of the room, he saw the Irishman standing in front of one of the scribes. The Irishman presented the scribe with what looked like a sketchbook, and the latter turned the pages, examining the contents from various angles. He returned the book to the Irishman with a slight raise of his head and click of his tongue, denoting a negative response. Was this the sketchbook Andersen had seen him use on the balcony at the hotel? He watched the Irishman approach a few more scribes with the same result: the sheets of paper were examined, a word said or a head raised, and the sketchbook returned.

Andersen could bear it no longer. He had to see what was in the book, even if it meant revealing his presence. He waited for the Irishman to finish with another scribe, then approached.

"Excuse me, would you mind terribly…" he said, pausing to clear his throat. There was just time to steal a glance at the paper—a series of heavy shapes in black ink, formless, like storm clouds. The Irishman spun around to face him, clutching the book against his chest.

His orange brow gave him an intense, feral look. Clinging sloth-like to the lower reaches of his forehead, it seemed an intense weight. For the first time in his life, Andersen understood the meaning of the phrase, 'his face fell.' Beginning with that eyebrow, his nose, his mouth, his freckles, his whole being plummeted in despondence. Andersen, alarmed that the Irishman's face was beyond recovery, moved away before he could do further damage. He hurried out into the courtyard, almost colliding with a loose camel that had wandered free from its owner.

‡

Somehow, he made his way back toward the shore, confused and embarrassed. It was he who had been shadowing the Irishman's every step, not the other way around: staring at him while he read the newspaper, spying on him from a hotel balcony, harassing him at the piano. Andersen must have misread the signals, the look they had exchanged over the newspaper, the casual exit from the hotel. He would make amends. He would introduce himself properly at the next opportunity, explaining he needed help with a curiosity he had seen in the *Moniteur Ottoman*.

Deferring to the Irishman's greater knowledge of Constantinople, Andersen would do his utmost to win the man's favor.

He turned onto the street leading to the dock, his steps ringing out against the stone, clear and solitary. What had been a pleasantly busy street populated by fruit vendors and strolling couples was now deserted. Perhaps it was prayer time, or everyone had gathered inside for dinner. Nevertheless, Andersen had an uneasy feeling, as though the residents of the houses were following his progress. A curtain fell back into place as he looked up at a window. He felt eyes peering from doorways, niches, and windows. He thought of those cool, clear summer nights in Copenhagen when he had walked home down the narrow streets by the docks, having spent his evening with a genteel couple and their children, earning his supper by reading his stories at their table. He had felt exposed on those walks back to his lodgings, and tainted, as if the householders, with each twitch of their curtains or casual glance from their windows, were judging him for his solitariness, a man without a family to call his own.

Two cats leapt from behind a wall to walk with him. He hurried forward, and did not breathe easily until he reached the dock. He found a boatman resting in his *caique* who was only too glad to take him back to Galata.

The short crossing landed him back on solid ground. It was early dusk, and people on this side of the Golden Horn walked the street idly. Now just four days before the Prophet's birthday, the residents, in preparation for the festival of light on the birthday eve, had covered their balconies with candles and lanterns and strung colored lights along the washing lines between houses. Flowers grew from every roof, scenting the air with jasmine and rose. The café courtyards were full and patrons spilled onto the street. Soldiers dressed in blue uniforms, some with slits in the thighs of their tight trousers, lounged on the ground with their pipes. Cheered by the sense of anticipation, Andersen tried to put the encounter with the Irishman behind him. He imagined

Musa and he together at the celebration. Arm in arm, they would stroll down to the shore after a good meal. They would take a *caique* across the Golden Horn to admire the lights from the water. He must remember to invite the Turk for dinner. The best restaurant in the city, Andersen thought—his treat.

He was halfway up the hill to Pera, near the sturdy, gray tower the Genoese merchants had built to proclaim their dominion over the port. There was a flash of light from the top of the tower that Andersen took to be a lantern; the huge blocks of stone were mostly in shadow and the light shone like a beacon. A figure stood on the viewing platform, perhaps a night watchman making his rounds. Again that flash of light, a glint of metal too, causing him to blink. At that moment, the call to prayer began as a whisper from a tiny mosque tucked away between two houses. The *imam*'s breathy persuasions were like a shared secret until the rest of the city caught on and the air was filled with voices.

He looked up to the top of the Genoese tower

and wondered how long it would take the night watchman to get down for his evening prayers. With a nod of admiration at the man's piety, he continued his walk up the hill toward his hotel. Men slid from doorways and shadows, magnetized by the call of God.

Chapter 11

here *was* the red dervish? The question stretched over the calligrapher's second night in the cannon and into the following morning. Every time she saw a flash of red cloth she thought of him, grim-faced and grimy, anxious to claim his iron bed. But he did not return.

The calligrapher had stretched and shaped her letters into the stories of Blue and Green, but she made no mention of the absent Red. She sensed his friends were waiting for her guidance, to see what she would write in Blue's notebook about him. She thought of the green dervish glancing up and down the shoreline for his red-turbaned friend and it pulled at her heart.

And so, before anything else this morning, the calligrapher wanted to suggest they look for Red together. She put her plan to the men simply: three pairs of eyes were better than two, and they'd be able to lift each other's spirits if the search proved difficult. The green dervish rubbed his thumbs in slow circles around his eyes as he listened.

"Yes, my girl, you may be right. I sense Red is like a misdirected bird on the wing; he will fly further and further away if we do not guide him home." Blue nodded his agreement, but again departed alone, leaving the green dervish and the calligrapher to search on their own.

"We should go to Eyup," the green dervish said. "It's a long way from here—half a day's walk and then a boat to the end of the Golden Horn. It is a place that Red knew well, and where he spent much of his early life. It's possible that he returned there and has forgotten the way back."

By sunset, they had arrived in Eyup, footsore but happy to stroll along the avenues lined with plane trees. A procession of pilgrims and villagers moved toward the mosque. Others meandered up and down the streets, searching for gifts and last-minute bargains.

There was an air of expectancy because a storytelling contest was taking place that evening in a coffeehouse close to the main square; the green dervish said that Red had always enjoyed these occasions. He had often entertained Green and Blue with his own version of these coffeehouse tales before they crawled into their cannons for the night.

Green brought the calligrapher down a side street lined with toy shops, each with a cheerful window display. Groups of children looked on, imploring their parents to bring them inside. The children were all dressed in white—oblong hats embellished with glittering sequins, white satin tunics, and purple sashes—and all carried white canes, which they swung around their legs or held to their shoulders as if toting narrow-bodied muskets. They were on their way to the Eyup mosque to begin the *sunnet*, the circumcision ceremony.

"Eba Eyup was more than a bearer for the Prophet. He was also the saint of children," the green dervish said, watching the white-clad figures. With his usual deliberation, he walked up and down the row of shops before settling on one in the middle of the street and walking inside.

Upon entering, the calligrapher was confronted by rows and rows of tin soldiers, all painted in the smart red trim of the New Guard. Each had its foot poised in midair, as if frozen on a silent, eternal march. The toymaker greeted the green dervish like an old friend, laughing the deepest laugh the calligrapher had ever heard. "The Janissaries are out back," he said, noticing her interest in the soldiers, "banging on their cauldrons and pots, but these men will creep up on you like undertakers." She looked at the other toys on display: whistles and drums and all manner of musical instruments, beautiful wooden boats with cloth sails and brightly painted prows.

"*Sunnet* is always a noisy time," the toymaker said, tapping a toy tambourine with his finger. "You can understand it after all those prayers the youngsters have to sit through, to say nothing of the prospect of the knife!" He laughed again, a warm sound that rose up from his chest like the sound of a gurgling water pipe. He had a thin, smooth face and a wedge of hair that looked like it had been pressed under the weight of a fez or turban for too long.

The toymaker locked the door of his store and invited them into his workshop, a room behind the displays. "The children can wait," he said, again with a wonderful bass laugh.

In the small back room, by the light of a single lantern, the calligrapher saw unpainted wooden figures resting on shelves and tabletops. "Look around if you want, sister," the man said and led the green dervish off to a corner. The calligrapher examined the figures while the men conferred in hushed tones. Some were no more than stumps of wood, while others were barely recognizable, the beginning of human forms with stump-like limbs. A few, though, were perfectly formed miniatures, waiting only for a paintbrush to bring them to life.

On a higher shelf, glinting in the yellow light, she saw another soldier standing on his own. She picked him up. He was painted in the full red and blue uniform of his colleagues outside, and at first, the calligrapher supposed he had been left behind by mistake. But while the toy soldiers in the shop had one foot slightly raised as they advanced, this man, although ready as the others, had only one leg. She studied his expression: tiny green eyes, moustache firm, a slight blush on his cheeks. The lack of a second leg seemed not to worry him; in fact, he looked doubly determined to carry out his duty.

The calligrapher put the one-legged soldier back on the shelf. The green dervish and the toymaker finished their conversation, which she supposed had concerned the whereabouts of Red. "No luck, I'm afraid," the green dervish said. "My friend here has not seen him, and there has been no word in the village."

The calligrapher must have looked puzzled because the toymaker said, "He used to work here, you know, in this very space before he received the calling. And what a craftsman! Half of the items here—the wooden boats with their silk sails, for instance—were made by our friend in the red turban. If I didn't need to eat and smoke the occasional pipe, I would never let a single of his pieces leave the store."

The green dervish smiled and said, "It is possible we will see him today at the storytelling contest."

They made their way back to the front of the store, but as they were about to leave, the toymaker clapped his hands. "Of course! She hasn't seen it," he said, looking at the calligrapher.

He went back into the workshop and brought out a wooden figure, the size of a hand, clad in a red turban and billowing kaftan of the same color. "Our friend may be absent, but an important part of him is still here." He placed the figure on the floor and gave it an almighty push. The doll swayed and tottered on its weighted axis, red turban almost touching the floor, before regaining its balance and composure. "Have a go, sister!" said the toymaker, as excited as one of his young customers. The calligrapher flicked the doll forward and watched it dip and sway like a drunkard.

"It never falls," the green dervish said, suddenly sad.

"*Haciyatmaz*," said the toymaker. "The pilgrim who won't lie down. Red made it many years ago. It has always been a good seller."

The green dervish picked up the figure and put it in the palm of the calligrapher's hand. "Take a good look. It might be the closest you get to him." The wooden version of Red wobbled in her hand and then stood perfectly still.

Outside, the calligrapher and the green dervish joined the crowds moving toward the coffeehouse where the storytelling contest was to take place. Opposite the coffeehouse was a *tekke* with a domed roof and projecting wings, which rose like a great bird above the outer wall. The green dervish wanted to go inside and pay his respects, but they could not find a way in. Then, as they walked along the outer wall, a stream of people filed out of a tiny opening, a small gate that had suddenly materialized in the stone.

The green dervish told her he would rejoin her later and hurried through the narrow door.

The calligrapher stood on the threshold and peered in. The people beyond were going about their business, enjoying the warm day. In another life, she would have been one of those carrying firewood or delivering vegetables; it was like looking through a window into her old life.

She remained in the doorway until an elderly dervish said, "Come in, sister. You are welcome!" The man ushered her inside as though she belonged. She walked quickly, avoiding eye contact, wondering if she should wait by the domed prayer hall for the green dervish to come out. Then she saw that the *tekke* had a garden and it was deserted.

The scents were familiar: the hyacinths bold and grasping, the carnations and roses gently reminding her of their sweetness. There was a pathway lined with pine trees, which she walked, enjoying the deep shade. Beyond the wooded trail a hill sloped downward, heavy with red, yellow, and white tulips. Riding a breeze, the tulips swayed and bent as one: forward and to the left, straightening in their resistance before yielding again. The calligrapher reached out for the nearby trunk of a tree, needing the support to hold herself upright, as though the wind pushing the flowers were pushing her too. The breeze relented, and the tulips and the calligrapher stood still and solemn.

She stepped from the trees and peered down the colorful hillside. She couldn't help herself. She took off her sandals and stepped into the first rows of flowers, bending the stems with the sides of her feet, pushing at their heads with her calves. Dirt worked its way between her toes. Another breeze, rustle-soft, and the tulips inclined their heads, but the calligrapher was waiting for something stronger. The wind blew again; the flowers leaned to the side. This time she leaned too, keeping her legs straight, her arms aloft for balance. Her hipbone popped, and the muscles in her thighs tightened. She straightened with the flowers and waited for the next gust. When it came, she bent at the waist, twisting further so that her spine stretched. She knew they were strong but their suppleness surprised her; they were as fluid and nimble as dancers. She wanted desperately to match their movements but couldn't keep up.

She stopped dead. There was a man on the hill. He stood twenty meters away with his back toward her, rooting among the flowers as if he had dropped something. A gardener, she supposed. She was suddenly ashamed of her bare feet and the way she had trampled through his carefully tended bed.

She backed away and found a spot behind the screen of pine trees where she could hide and slip her shoes back on. There was something about the man that caught her attention. He didn't move like a gardener; he carried no tools, and his clothes, burgundy turban and kaftan, were unsoiled. The man stood and turned to the side. He looked down at the tulips, then bent again, tending to a particular flower. He ran his fingers over the backs of the petals and pinched the base of the bud as if he were sizing it up. His mouth opened and formed inaudible words.

That was when she knew him. A man reduced by time to a fading collection of letters and lines, he was here now in front of her, as warm and distinct as the ink of a freshly-drawn face.

The green dervish, from somewhere behind, called out for her. The man stood quickly, disturbed by the sound, and looked up. She felt his eyes scanning the trees, stripping away the bark that concealed her. Even from this distance she could have captured the crease of his brow, the kindness that had once marked his eyes. He tilted his head to the left as if the weight of his thoughts pushed his head to one side, a gesture so deeply familiar to the calligrapher it moved her heart. He took a step forward. She pressed her body against the tree, its craggy surface digging into her cheek. She had recaptured his face in her mind now. She would not forget it again, whether she wanted to or not.

He had been looking for something among those tulips, something he still hadn't found, even after all these years.

When the green dervish touched her shoulder and led her away from the garden, the man was still standing there, his kaftan nuzzled by soft heads of red, yellow, and white.

CHAPTER 12

On Friday, Andersen had the whole day to explore Constantinople. His guide book told him there were mosques and palaces to visit, purifying sessions in baths, and bracing walks by the sea. But first, he needed to find the Irishman, to clear up the misunderstanding from yesterday. The Irishman seemed to be an artist of some description, even a calligrapher, since he had attempted to interest the resident scribes at the Grand Bazaar in his work. And if that were the case, then he might be able to tell Andersen something about that newspaper image of the lion and whether it had been constructed from script.

After Musa had shown him Zeynep's riverbank scroll, Andersen became convinced that what he had seen on the back of the *Moniteur Ottoman* was another example of this zoomorphic art—an image constructed from letters and words, perhaps even those of the caption about retreat and God.

But he also could not forget the lion itself; its gaunt, weary look and the way it could barely lift its paws off the ground. The beast had unnerved Andersen as much as Zeynep's creatures had delighted him, but both had captured an extraordinary essence of life. Andersen sensed he might understand more about Zeynep's art if he could study the image of the lion and compare it to the creations on her scroll. And he wanted to gauge his own reaction; had he only imagined the creature's haggard state because he, too, had been exhausted and disoriented from his long journey?

Before beginning his search for the Irishman, Andersen enquired at the reception desk about his still-missing boots. Since receiving the miniature pair yesterday, the hotel had been noncommittal about his boots' whereabouts. He was beginning to believe they were lost for good.

The receptionist with the unruly curl of gray hair who had first asked for the written description had not reappeared, and when Andersen mentioned having given this formal description, the other receptionist stared at him, uncomprehending.

"Try again tomorrow, Monsieur," was all he could offer. "*Inshallah*, your boots will find their way home." With that, the desk clerk handed him a letter from Edvard.

Two days ago, Andersen would have been wildly excited to receive a letter from his friend, but now it hardly seemed to matter. He read it standing at the reception desk, disappointed that this offering was just as supine as Edvard's first correspondence, received three weeks ago. Life in Copenhagen continued to move at the pace of a winter thaw. Heiberg's *Digite* was still attracting favorable notices; they had received Andersen's two letters (he'd sent three) and all was well among mutual friends.

What did people *do* in Copenhagen from one day to the next, Andersen wondered. Reading this letter from home, he was aware of the traveler's sense of superiority to those left behind, the sensory stimulation that had enriched his soul under the Eastern sky. At home, the Colin family, those closest to him in the world, would be sunk around the fire, waiting for sleep to snuffle the night away. Andersen could not imagine what they did to entertain themselves without him.

He took a seat in the lounge and read Edvard's letter again. There was very little reaction to Andersen's previous correspondence: no response to the bloodletting he'd endured in Naples when struck with fever, no reaction to the salvo of cannon fire that had welcomed his ship into the Valetta harbor. Even the description of the boy driving two ostriches along a busy street in Smyrna was batted away with: 'We can't quite believe you are in Turkey and look forward to the moment when you regale us with your experiences in person.'

Should he write back and tell Edvard about the woman calligrapher who had gripped his imagination? That he had stumbled on a writing project no one in Europe could dream up, let alone write? How he wished Edvard could see him now, resplendent among the travelers of the world. Perhaps he should extend his stay here, adapt his dress like his fellow guests, wear a fez, and smoke *nargiles* while sprawled on the floor.

How to describe Musa to Edvard? He decided to set down his feelings about his new Turkish friend now, because they might be harder to articulate later, once he'd left Turkey and there was distance between them.

My Dear Edvard, Andersen wrote in the hotel's black ink. But he didn't know how to continue. When Edvard addressed him, it was always in that damnable polite form: the *de* rather than the familiar *du*. Because Andersen was obliged to respond in the same formal manner, the *de* placed a genteel straitjacket around their feelings for one another. He yearned for the casual pronoun, something more intimate with which to explain his first sighting of the Turk on the steamer: the intricacy of Musa's turban, the smooth gestures of his story. "You would love to watch him tend to a tulip, Edvard," he could imagine writing to his friend, who wasn't a friend at all when addressed like this, but more like an uncle with a pockmarked face, or one of the benefactors Andersen had often had recourse to write to when short of funds.

Andersen gave up on the letter. It was almost lunch time and he had still not decided what to do with the day. He had hoped the Irishman might stroll into the hotel lounge for morning coffee, but Andersen's behavior in the Grand Bazaar seemed to have scared him off. Perhaps he had already packed his things in the cheap hotel across the street.

Andersen caught sight of the fluted wooden bird cage near the piano and remembered his conversation with Taranto, the Italian who had made the cage. He found Taranto's business card in the pocket of his coat. His workshop was located in Galata, close to the tower. Perhaps he would be able to give Andersen an exact translation of the caption in the *Moniteur Ottoman*, and he might remember the image of the lion, too.

{

When Andersen walked into Taranto's workshop, a short way from the hotel down a meandering series of streets, a cacophony of birdsong filled the small, rectangular space. He thought of the birds and the blue strip of river on Zeynep's scroll. The Italian was delighted to see him. They spent a few minutes gazing at the collection of cages, one crafted for every conceivable size of bird, while Andersen breathed in the heady fragrance of freshly planed wood, varnish, and glue.

"Imagine, if you will," Taranto said, pointing to the smallest cages, "the chirp of the blue finch, or the more harmonious tone of the common canary." The cages were empty, yet birdsong clearly filled the air in staccato bursts of sound, one for each bird Taranto had described. "Or how about the more emphatic squawk of the parrot family: the African Gray, for example, or the macaw?" There was a brief pause. Then, a new, tropical selection of bird calls sounded in the small shop.

"I'm impressed," said Andersen. "But I see no actual birds."

Taranto led him to a glass contraption in the back of the shop, full of whirring cylinders and busy cogs.

"I designed it myself," he said proudly. "It recreates the song of seven species of woodland and tropical bird and, when truly warmed up, will emit a series of sonorous squawks not unlike those made by the toucan that once resided at your hotel."

Andersen marveled at the breathtaking ingenuity of the machine, but could a mechanical bird replace the real thing, the flawless chime of nature that was, for example, the song of the nightingale? Perhaps this mechanization was the way of the future; people would be so satisfied with contraptions that sang on demand, they would stop listening to the live birds around them.

Andersen admired a small cage with fluted columns.

"Cypress wood," Taranto said. "Here, you must take it. A gift from me."

Taranto pressed the cage upon him, and Andersen didn't know how to refuse it. It was beautifully made, and would likely fit into his hat box on the journey home. The fact that Andersen did not own a bird seemed immaterial in the perfumed air of the Italian's shop.

Taranto was closing for lunch, he said, but knew a place they could go and sit together, an outdoor café secluded by acacia trees, but from which one had a good view of the Galata Tower.

Andersen agreed, and the two men made their way to the café, where they were quickly seated. At the top of the tower looming above them, tiny figures appeared and disappeared, like mechanical toy soldiers attending their posts.

The waiter brought *borek*, a flaky pastry with spinach and cheese, similar to what Andersen had seen the Irishman consume in the Grand Bazaar. "Your companion must bring you here when the sun goes down," Taranto said, after Andersen had explained his plans for the eve of the Prophet's birthday. "The tower and the city will light up more than heaven itself."

Andersen promised to do his best. Then, inexplicably nervous, he showed Taranto the *Moniteur Ottoman*, which he had stuffed into his jacket pocket. He pointed to the caption on the back page and explained how the white space above had once contained a lion, which he believed was formed from calligraphic script.

"A lion, you say?"

"Yes. And now it's gone. Sometimes I wonder if I saw it at all."

"Let me tell you something about the *Moniteur Ottoman*, Herr Andersen," Taranto said, sipping at his glass of tea. "It isn't much of a journal compared to European standards, hardly more than a pamphlet. But the editors and their backers are clever men. We Ottomans never had such a thing before. No one had thought to supply it, because illiteracy is rife here. However, the written word carries a certain amount of power and mystique in this culture, partly because it is disseminated by communal performance. The public reading of a newspaper is like a sermon given by an *imam*; few people would question the *imam*'s words—discuss and debate them, yes—but never doubt them. Going to these readings and being told what to believe becomes a habit, a ritual people quickly get addicted to. In fact, there is a regular reading of the weekly edition of *Moniteur Ottoman* right across the city, and not just for Turkish speakers. There is a Greek edition that gets read aloud, and I believe an Armenian one, too.

"I am telling you this because many people—Muslim, Christian, and Jew; literate and illiterate—have been influenced by a campaign that the newspaper has been running for the past year. Quite simply, the editors of the *Moniteur Ottoman* do not believe the Grand Vizier of the Ottoman Divan is fit to govern the empire."

"Selim Ali Pasha?"

"Exactly. What did the caption say again? *Retraite se transporte plus de près a Dieu?*

'Retirement brings one a step closer to God,' and that is precisely what many people want the Grand Vizier to do: step down and let a younger man take his place."

"And what about the missing image?" Andersen asked, letting the exact translation of the French sink in.

"You say that this...gap was filled with the form of a lion. Unfortunately, I did not see it, but the thing is, Selim Ali Pasha has a nickname, a *nom de guerre*, if you like: The Lion of Aleppo."

Andersen blinked. He noticed that Taranto's thin moustache fluttered at the edges when he reached the end of a sentence.

"Many years ago, he led a military campaign in the Arab lands, earning himself this sobriquet," Taranto continued. "Apparently, he was quite the hero."

"But not anymore?"

"No. There are many powerful factions aligned against him now. Such is the case when one minister remains in power for too long. Herr Andersen, you said that this lion might have been formed from script. Was it a reproduction of something, a lithograph perhaps?"

"Yes!" said Andersen. He had seen lithographs reproduced in France and England, and once, in Copenhagen, a newspaper editor had showed him how it was done.

"The Sufis sometimes twist prayers into animals and vases and things," Taranto continued. "Very clever, I'm sure, although I prefer to read my script straight across the page, not have it jump out of some fish's mouth."

Andersen let this go. "Could one of these Sufi prayers take the shape of a lion?" he asked.

"Yes. The Sufi community has traditionally written a lion in script. It is the Lion of Ali, compiled from the prayer, 'May God Almighty be pleased with him and honor him.' The Sufis have always referred to the *imam* as Ali, the Lion of God. If the lion you saw was meant to be Selim Ali Pasha, then the analogy would have been obvious to *Moniteur Ottoman's* readers. A man associated with such a heroic religious figure should be beyond reproach, the epitome of strength and vigor, but this does not sound like the lion you have described, Herr Andersen. No. This sounds like something else entirely."

"So the image could have been satirical?"

"It is possible, yes."

It had never occurred to Andersen that this lithographed lion could be used for political purposes; that its creator, like a Turkish version of Hogarth, might have turned his calligraphy into caricature. He pictured the lithographer employed by the *Moniteur Ottoman* pressing his grease pencil into the soft, wet limestone, forming the ear flaps of the lion, the sagging eyes and ponderous tread. Then, the treatment of the stone with acid and the cleansing with gum arabic solution. The ink rolling over the surface, seeking only the oily contours of the image, sealed by the salty residue around the lion's shape, a fossil instantaneously etched into the stone. The lithographer would dampen a sheet of paper and press it onto the stone, holding it there for a count of five before lifting the paper off like a holy shroud, and then the lion would appear in glistening lamp-black, a creature somehow greater and lesser than the sum of the words that gave it life.

$$\mathfrak{k}$$

After lunch, the men bade each other farewell, with Taranto promising to visit Copenhagen one day. Andersen walked up the hill and along the Rue de Pera to his hotel. He entered the lounge with the vague hope that the Irishman might have returned. After scanning the room to no avail, Andersen walked over to the piano and saw the music from yesterday's prelude still resting on the stand. He sat on the piano stool, humming the opening bars to himself as he read. His hands hovered over the keys, but the mood felt too unsettled for Chopin; street noise permeated the room and fingers of sunlight streaked the surface of the piano like grease from a child's hand. He decided to play a few bars, softly so that only he could hear. But his hands felt too heavy on the keys, and the notes sounded oppressive and ominous: a moment of failure he could have laughed over with the Irishman, had he ever appeared.

With the afternoon unfurling before him like a blank scroll, Andersen thought he might as well go across to the Irishman's hotel; if he wasn't there, Andersen could leave a note of apology for his behavior in the Grand Bazaar and perhaps suggest a meeting. He scribbled a few lines at the reception desk and had an idea. What if he were to express an interest in buying the man's work? This might tempt the Irishman into the open, especially if he were short of money. Besides,

Andersen was curious to know how the work of other calligraphers compared with Zeynep's script. He finished the note and told the receptionist he would be gone for fifteen minutes, should any messages arrive.

With some difficulty, he found a plaque announcing the Irishman's hotel, which, due to the erosion of the last three or four letters, said only 'Hotel O.' There was nobody in reception, a small area serviced by a narrow wooden counter displaying a bell and a dusty ledger. Andersen brought the side of his fist down hard on the top of the bell. No answer from behind the counter. He tried again, but still no response. He would have to find the man's room on his own. But it was a small establishment and, knowing the position of the Irishman's accommodation in regards to his own room, Andersen had a good idea where to look.

He climbed the stairs slowly, wary of the chipped stone. When he reached the sixth floor, the same level as his room in the Hotel de la France, he found himself on a landing with four doors, once painted blue but now chipped, the original wood showing through. How did the Irishman put up with such squalor? A single wine glass, smeared with claret-colored drops as thick as wax, had been abandoned outside one of the doors. The maid service was slack indeed. Andersen felt a wave of smugness over his well turned-out room, the bed crisply made, the soft towels draped over the rails.

He knocked, imagining the Irishman leaping in shock on the other side of the door. "Excuse me," he called, his voice lingering in the small space like a threat. No response. He picked up the glass and held it to his nose—no trace of a bouquet. He said in a softer voice, "Is anyone there?" When no one answered, Andersen replaced the glass on the floor and slid his note under the Irishman's door.

He hurried down the stairs, not wanting to stay another second in this cold, abandoned-looking establishment. The Hotel de la France greeted him with the smell of roasting coffee and pipe smoke; there had been no messages during his brief absence.

CHAPTER 13

"Who was he?" the green dervish asked the calligrapher as they made their way to the *tekke* gate.

"He looked like someone I used to know. A friend."

The green dervish rubbed his beard. "Perhaps you will see him again. Is he interested in storytelling?"

It hadn't occurred to the calligrapher that, like her, he might have been biding his time in the garden until the contest began. She remembered the days when he traveled halfway across the city, determined to track down a tale involving this or that flower. If a tulip's ancestors had traveled in the saddlebags of warriors, or bloomed in a sultan's private garden, his customers would pay more for the bulbs.

They joined the crowds pushing into the coffeehouse, which was located in a courtyard with a sunken marble fountain at its heart. The owners of the establishment had decorated a low wooden stage with thick *kilims* on which a number of distinguished figures—judges, she assumed—sat in flowing silk robes and intricately-wound turbans. Waiters hopped up and down the two steps leading to the stage, bearing coffee and plates of sweetmeats. After the judges finished their repast, a servant brought writing paper, pens, and inkwells to the stage. The judges tested these with vigor before pronouncing them satisfactory.

The calligrapher and green dervish found a secluded spot under a magnolia tree at the back of the courtyard. They sat on tiny stools with people smoking *nargiles*. Away to their left ran an arcade of striped stone, and beneath the archways, shadowy silhouettes paced back and forth, muttering and gesticulating. "Storytellers," said an old woman from a nearby stool, nodding at the arcade. "They're warming up, getting ready to holler at us like we're all deaf. Sometimes I wonder if it is only about noise nowadays. In all that commotion, who pays attention to timing or the turn of a well-crafted phrase?"

The calligrapher nodded, but the green dervish seemed not to hear. He craned his neck this way and that, peering at the other tables in search of his red friend.

The first competitor took the stage without fanfare. He was a thin, worried man in a grubby fez who launched into a story about a wolf, a maiden, and a shepherd, a familiar tale of lust and bravery on the steppe. The man employed an actual sheep as a prop, driving the creature around the stage with a branch, much to the distaste of the judges. Next was a woman with a lute and a sad tale of her fisherman lover who, due to advanced and irreversible deafness, could no longer hear her laments. The audience watched the judges, trying to discern from the furrow of a brow, the way a pen skipped across the page, or the number of times a nib was re-inked, whether the judgments were favorable. Each competitor was allowed ten minutes, with a restriction of no more than two props—everything from cudgels and swords to a cauldron of soup and a withered white rose. That afternoon, the calligrapher heard tales of love and deceit, of fortune seekers and chameleons, of caravans bringing silk and Islam to heathen lands, of dervishes and ancient saints. Tragedies and comedies and burlesques of impotent emirs and sultans with bad teeth.

After each tale, the calligrapher waited for her old friend to pull up a stool and settle his eyes upon her. What would he have to say after all these years? She thought of the stories he'd once told, stories about tulips: the sultan who named Beloved's Face for the tint and texture of his first wife's skin; the fervent Rose's Arrow, who, if forced to share the soil with its fragrant cousin, caused it to wilt and die. Or the tale of The Tulip with the Unbreakable Stem (which strain had that been?), which a grand vizier had tried unsuccessfully to destroy, enraged by the knowledge that its blooms would outlast him.

The first storyteller, the man with the sheep, was back on stage, remonstrating with the judges. "That's the trouble with these storytellers," said the old woman sitting near the calligrapher. "They can never leave well enough alone when they've finished."

The calligrapher nodded her agreement, but she was thinking of her friend and the tulips that had all but consumed him. Flowers with slim waists and narrow, finger-like petals. She hadn't thought of them in years, trapped as they were in that old notebook, that book of tulips they had once worked on together.

There, too, was the *baraka* he believed her letters contained: the spirit of those old flowers inked in singing reds and spring yellows, or where she had fused her colors in such a way that no one could tell when one began and the other ended.

Her friend believed she had captured the very essence of the flowers in this book, their spirits and souls. He used to say that only she, through her writing, could bring about the rebirth of the old strains, the incredible tulips that had once graced the gardens of the city, the ancient blooms people sewed into their clothes just to feel the petals against their skin. He believed the calligrapher's *baraka* would one day flow from the page and into the flowers themselves, imbuing them with the spirit and energy of her letters, reminding them of what they were and how they could grow again. He had promised her they would harness her power together and resurrect the old tulips. She had waited for that day, and for her friend to keep his promise, but it had never happened.

Each flower had an identity beyond the name of its species and strain, and it could be expressed in a single word that the calligrapher would delicately render with the sharpest of nibs into its inner structure. Piety, Benevolence, or Hope. Grace, Tranquility, or Reflection. Her friend described a tulip's origin and appearance, and she felt that if she knew everything about the tulip— its lineage and how it had touched people's lives through the ages—that word would come to her, the linguistic embodiment of the flower and all its ancestors. Once she sensed its epithet, transcribing the flower was easy.

The Book of Tulips. She would love to see it again. If for no other reason than to remind herself of the work she had once done.

A man, perhaps the proprietor of the coffeehouse, addressed the patrons, shaking the calligrapher from her reverie. "The honored and respected gentlemen will now retire to ponder," he said, motioning toward the judges. "And do not think they have just been doodling all this time! Did you not see the ink they expended, the concentration on their faces?" The audience murmured, nodding their heads. The old woman beside the calligrapher *tut-tutted* and sucked her pipe while the green dervish's eyes darted like fireflies around the courtyard, still hoping to catch a glimpse of a red kaftan. It was useless, the calligrapher thought, to pin one's hopes on the return of old friends.

She touched the green dervish's shoulder, but the shrewd, gray eyes of the old woman were upon them. "That writer *hanim*," she was saying. "You know, the one who could make letters change shape even as you were looking at them, right on the paper before you. You'd be reading a simple prayer, and then *whoosh*, it became the petals of a tulip, or a man's face. Funny business, that. My memory is not what it was, but you look so much like her, I would swear you were her sister."

The calligrapher smiled and shook her head.

"She's long gone," the old woman continued. "Fish food by now. Most of those Sufi calligraphers ended up on the floor of the Bosphorus. The old sultan hated that sort of thing."

CHAPTER 14

There was a chill in the air as Andersen and the boy crossed the Bosphorus on their way to Musa's house. Plump, gray clouds rested atop the cypresses as if too full to move. Andersen sat on the floor of the *caique* thinking about Zeynep's scroll. "Is there any more?" he had asked Musa. He had already seen so much of Zeynep's calligraphy: the golden paper tulip the Turk had brought to his hotel, the practice books with their compulsive letters, and the scroll with its tiny, feathered creatures—all marked by Zeynep's beneficent calligraphic face. Andersen also wanted to ask Musa about the lion in the pages of the *Moniteur Ottoman*; he longed to tell his friend how this beast had also moved him, albeit in a very different way. But he had nothing tangible to show Musa, to prove he had not imagined the creature.

Taranto had suggested the calligraphic lion was an unflattering rendering of the Grand Vizier. Andersen pictured the newspaper's calligrapher shading the lion's swollen eye, etching his drooping whiskers, creating an animal burdened by troubles of state. But Andersen had never seen Selim Ali Pasha, so could not tell whether the image of the lion bore a resemblance to the man or not.

Saturday afternoon…when the sun is full and strong. Andersen hoped this would be the time when Musa told him everything, especially about Zeynep's arrest and the nature of her alleged crimes. But he could not shake the feeling that Musa was toying with him, as if he were an audience to one of the Turk's tales. Andersen glanced at the sky. On this chilly *caique*, the sun seemed a distant friend—what if it didn't pay them a visit this afternoon?

¶

Musa's house was a simple stone cottage in Uskudar, not far from the *tekke* they had visited two days before. When Andersen arrived, the Turk was busy with a needle and a swath of cotton, attempting to fit a tiny corset over one of his tulips.

"For those with a discerning eye, the bloom is a little portly," he told Andersen. "It needs to be restrained or its petals might end up puffy." Musa rethreaded the needle and pulled the corset tighter. "If I leave it for a day or two in this fleecy jacket, *T. armena* will be ready to show to customers."

Andersen joined Musa on the floor of the salon. In front of them sat a large silver tray containing the tools of the florist's trade: bulbs in sealed packets, tweezers, nail scissors, a magnifying glass, a measuring tape, and a scorpion-shaped implement with a series of tiny mirrors. The room had striped cotton rugs and a divan pushed back against the wall, and a brazier or stove in the middle of the floor that kept both food and the room warm. A small, framed drawing of a flower hung to the right of the single window. Andersen fancied there was one more room—Musa's bedroom?—on the other side of a red and green tapestry, which hung steadfastly, blocking his view.

Musa pruned and packaged his seeds and bulbs, explaining the properties and provenances of each one to Andersen as his fingers moved. These lessons did not feel conversational, but rather forced and urgent. Andersen, as he had when Musa was translating examples of Zeynep's work, felt a tingling along the length of his spine. Was this tulip instruction part of the story Musa wanted him to tell? Was Musa trying, as he expounded on the virtues and beauty of each flower, to recreate the time he had spent with

Zeynep in the *tekke*, as if Andersen himself was the Turk's new muse?

Musa had risen and entered a small alcove at the back of the salon, which functioned as a sort of kitchenette. He retrieved a large sizzling pot and placed it on the stove. An overpowering, tangy aroma filled the room, unsettling Andersen's stomach.

"*Patlican*. I am not sure if I can translate it," Musa said, when Andersen continued to look worried. "But I am sure I can't poison you with it." He fetched a bulbous, purple vegetable from the kitchen: larger and flatter than a swan's egg and capped with a green fringe. *Aubergine*, thought Andersen as he picked up the vegetable. A bitter nightshade, which his grandfather had believed induced madness.

The meal Musa cooked, though, was delicious: a fusion of red onion and garlic, ripe tomatoes, chopped mint, and green chilies, as well as the fleshy strips of aubergine. There was fresh bread to soak up the juices and hibiscus juice to wash everything down. When they finished eating, Andersen waited for Musa to tell him why he was here, why Musa had chosen him, ahead of any other writer, to pay tribute to Zeynep's life. But the Turk just dabbed his beard with his napkin and said, "I would like to show you my garden."

He brought Andersen outside to the smallest flower garden he had ever seen. Two carpet-sized terraces behind the house led down to a pond stippled with white dots, which Andersen fancied were an exotic variety of water lilies. There were tiny beds of narcissi and carnations, thumbprints of purple and white. Musa named each flower as they passed, slowing their progress so it seemed as though they were walking through a far bigger garden. At the end of the lower terrace, a hexagonal glass house came into view. Andersen could not see inside, but around the perimeter were beds filled with hundreds of tulips, blooms shifting in the breeze like cups in an earthquake. Andersen shook his head in wonder. In reality, the L-shaped bed contained no more than a dozen tulips, but the mirrored wall of the glass house behind had reflected them into dazzling infinity.

"I call it my reflection of paradise," Musa said.

Beyond the glass house was still more land and a tantalizing glimpse of the Bosphorus in the distance, silver and smooth. Like the rest of the garden, this back space was condensed, packed with tiny pots of flowers, an overspill, perhaps, from the glass house.

At the very edge of the garden, Musa showed Andersen a small plot marked with a black stone. A grave. "This was my father's house. I arranged for his remains to return here. He died in Sinop on the Black Sea, cold and hungry, as far as I could tell." He said this with an absence of emotion, an indifference that reminded Andersen of how he'd spoken of Zeynep's death, with a peculiar lack of curiosity.

"My father wanted to recreate, in miniature, the terraces of the palace gardens," Musa continued. "He thought such pretension, such grandeur reminiscent of the past, would help his flowers to bloom. As if they could sense his great plans for them."

"Did your father know the palace gardens well?"

"Not well. But he went there on business—to trade bulbs and occasionally buy the seeds discarded by the palace gardeners, at inflated prices, of course."

Andersen bent to study the gravestone. A tall-stemmed flower had been etched into the granite above a line of calligraphy. The flower had a single, undulating leaf and six petals honed to spidery points. "We once called this tulip Mahbub, or 'Beloved,'" Musa said. "A century ago, it was the chosen bulb of Sultan Ahmed, who insisted that a single flower be cut and placed in a filigree vase and deposited in his private chamber each night. The species has all but disappeared since then, although my father once claimed he saw a bed of Mahbub still growing on the palace grounds. A case of wishful thinking on his part, I believe. It was a species my father always dreamed of raising. They say its bloom was the color of the setting sun."

As they returned to the glass house, Andersen thought again of Musa's coolness, his lack of emotion regarding anything but his precious tulips. He was holding something back, Andersen thought, and it would be difficult to write this story without Musa's full cooperation. After walking for what seemed an age, and arriving at the glass house again, Andersen had decided that if the Turk did not open up—if, by the end of the afternoon, he had not conveyed something approaching the full story—he would withdraw and never see Musa again.

"What is it about tulips, Musa?" he asked, remaining, for now, on safe ground. "Why are they so important to you?"

"Have you ever kept a garden, Herr Andersen?" Musa sat on a small bench nearby and motioned for Andersen to join him.

"No."

"In many ways, you are lucky. A garden will find a way to spurn the care one gives it, to mock a gardener's ambition. Two hundred years ago, the sultan, in his desire for the perfect bed of tulips, for the perfect tulip garden, ordered his men to gather 300,000 bulbs from the Crimean Steppe and replant them in the palace gardens. Can you imagine the trouble this caused? Hundreds of young men scrabbling at the scrub grass, uprooting the bulbs; remember, these flowers could only be collected as bulbs, never while they were blooming. These poor men could not possibly have known which ones to gather, so in their confusion, they gathered them all. But in the end, they fulfilled the order, and the *Padishah* got his treasure chest of bulbs to plant."

Musa rose from the bench and began to pace. "How is it those Crimean tulips grew in the royal gardens, thousands of kilometers away from the cool, crisp air of the steppe? Istanbul is damp and heavy, nothing like where the bulbs had come from. Still, they grew. We have evidence they grew. Stories of their beauty abound, and I can show you a hundred glorious tulip miniatures adorning manuscripts across the city. There are witnesses too, Europeans among them, who waxed lyrical on their beauty in a variety of languages.

"But today, attempts to grow the old strains beget only misshapen stems, crinkly leaves, wilting blooms. In the rare event a blossom does survive, the gardener still has the unpredictability of the tulip to deal with and its chameleon qualities, which sometimes cause it to evolve and crossbreed into an entirely different species from its parent bulb.

"Let me give you an example. There are wild tulips that grow on the side of the road between Edirne and Burgaz. They cluster together, flowers of every color you can imagine, some striped with yellow on a red background, others fringed with mauve on a canvas of cream. You can find rounded petals in the shape of half-spheres, or petals flipping over like an upturned bell. You would not even think them the same species. But if you were to visit the same road the following spring, these very same tulips would have evolved again, their new blooms sporting different colors and textures. In the same way you Europeans change your wardrobe according to the latest fashion, so do the flowers change. A gardener can never tell what a tulip will look like from one year to the next."

"Has anyone succeeded," Andersen asked, "in growing the old strains?"

"No. Even my father failed, and he tried everything: cross breeding, mixing shapes and colors, planting seeds with offsets, fertilizers. He even spent a winter nursing seedpods in the salon by the fire. He let the seeds go wild, and then he planted them in tight formation. He coaxed and bullied and prayed with his bulbs, scorched them in the sun and abandoned them to the frost. I once saw him cut two bulbs in half and tie them together with thread. But the old strains remained elusive, as they had to his father before him."

"So it can't be done?" Andersen asked.

Musa motioned with his hand. "Come," he said, and opened the door of the glass house, causing the mirrored walls outside to reflect their images in ever-diminishing pairs. The interior of the glass house, though, was like any other. There were the usual tools and accoutrements of the gardener's craft: seed trays, canvas awnings for shade, and various trowels. A large terracotta pot packed deep with earth had been placed in the middle of the floor, where it could catch the full force of the sun, now emerging from behind a bank of clouds. Musa walked directly over to the pot. Andersen caught his breath. It couldn't be, he thought.

From the dark soil grew a slender stem with two thick outer leaves, like a swan that has borrowed a stork's wings. Two inner leaves guarded the flower, whose tapering bud was the shape of a candle flame. Musa had lain two very thin strips of wood across the width of the pot, and placed a neat circle of tiny shells around the pot's edge. "This seed came from the Crimea," Musa said. "My father found a family who had been growing the old tulips for generations, without knowing what they had. He persuaded them to send a few bulbs, and when they arrived, my father planted them right here in this pot. The oyster shells collect the excess moisture. They're layered throughout the pot at various depths."

Andersen found himself confronted by an enormous brown eye. From the table beyond, Musa had picked up an oversized magnifying glass laid in a brass setting. "Take a closer look," he said, handing Andersen the glass.

Andersen pulled the inner leaves back and felt a silky, viscous quality to the light-green overlay coating the outer petals. He lifted the glass and saw the green yield to a reddish blush halfway up the bud. It was a strange and unexpected change of color. Andersen felt that he had caught the tulip in a private moment, as though it were deciding between two different dresses. He averted his eyes and passed the glass back to Musa.

The sun shone, warming the glass house. Droplets of sweat beaded along Andersen's brow. He looked back inside the pot. His spine tingled. *Saturday Afternoon. When the sun is full and strong.*

He cleared his throat and tried to concentrate. "When was it planted?" he asked.

"Seven years ago. The usual time for a tulip to flower from seed."

"But…"

"Yes, I know what you're thinking. Why should this one be any different from the others? What is so remarkable about this plant when others failed so miserably? I have a reason to be optimistic, Herr Andersen. Let's go back to the house and I'll show you."

In the cottage, Musa led Andersen into the salon and over to the drawing of the flower on the wall, which Andersen had noted on arrival. The image was mounted in a cheap-looking balsa wood frame. The flower was a tulip, drawn from calligraphic script like the one in his room, with the *alif* forming the stem and two undulating leaves. But this tulip, like its sister in the glass house, was only a bud, its head a dark green capsule yet to blossom and reveal the petals hiding within.

"What do you think?" asked Musa.

"I am curious," Andersen said, examining the image. "Why would Zeynep draw a flower that has not yet bloomed?"

"I will explain, but first let me tell you how I acquired this image. As I said before, Zeynep would have been guarded by *bostancis* or gardeners during her time in prison. Such men also acted as the palace jailers, and occasionally, as its executioners. I know some of these gentlemen. I deliver bulbs to them. I've listened to their complaints about drainage and the destructive nature of the fruit fly. But after Zeynep's arrest, I was afraid to go near them. They would have feigned ignorance about what had become of her, as was their duty. But any flicker of the eye or quiver of the voice would have told me everything I did not want to know.

"Finally, I summoned the courage to approach a palace gardener I knew well. He told me the Bostanci-Bashi, the Chief Gardener, had taken a special interest in Zeynep during her captivity, and that he had been seen bringing writing materials to her cell.

"He also told me Zeynep was curious about the palace gardens and asked a series of unexpected questions: What grows here? Is the soil crumbly or firm? How do you irrigate? Which flowers grow best together? I was intrigued because she had asked me similar questions during our work on The Book of Tulips. She needed to know *everything* about a flower before she felt ready to set it on the page.

"But I learned little more about what became of her. About a month later, I heard that the Chief Gardener had been forced to leave his post. There was all kind of speculation—an allegiance to the wrong minister, the wrong brotherhood. I don't know what happened to him, but I don't think it had anything to do with Zeynep. She was one prisoner among many, and a woman too, which would have made her doubly insignificant. Still, I had my suspicions. The same gardener told me about a drawing that had been found in Zeynep's cell, an image of a tulip. He and his friends were anxious to sell it; they knew I would pay the best price. When I saw the image, I knew immediately it was Zeynep's even before I found—"

"Her signature face!" Andersen burst in. What a marvelous time he could have with it if he wrote Zeynep's story! It would appear unexpectedly, like a tiny fairy or a wandering spirit. It would indicate the authenticity of her work like a hallmark indicates the quality of gold.

"Exactly, Herr Andersen," Musa said. "But please let me continue. The fact that Zeynep had had the time to draw this image while incarcerated puzzled me. Custom dictates that women prisoners are executed straightaway to make room in the cells. Yet, the Chief Gardener not only allowed her to remain in the cell, but granted her a privilege rare for any prisoner—the chance to write. So why did he do it?"

Why indeed, wondered Andersen. In his mind, he could clearly see the Chief Gardener leaning through the bars of Zeynep's cell to offer her a *kalem*, perhaps a single leaf of paper. Andersen had been thinking of that dungeon, the shafts of light grudgingly filtered by the bars, the smell of damp stone. Zeynep's slow and deliberate gestures as she ate or shuffled around the cramped space. The Chief Gardener would have been slightly stooped, older than Musa, but with the same softness in his cotton kaftan and wound turban. Did he and Zeynep come to some kind of agreement? Did the Chief Gardener want her to write something in particular? Andersen did not know what this writing would have entailed, or what Zeynep might have gained by displaying her skills. After all, what could a condemned prisoner hope to gain other than freedom, or at least a stay of execution?

Musa curled his lip in a thoughtful smile. "You asked why she drew the tulip as a bud. The simple answer is that she did not know what the tulip would become."

"What do you mean?"

"You will recall the petals of the tulip I gave you at your hotel are composed of the words, 'God the Generous.'"

"Yes, of course."

"Here," Musa pointed at the framed picture, "the letters of Allah form the stem and leaves in much the same way, but we do not yet know which of God's ninety-nine names the petals will bear. It reads like an incomplete sentence."

"But how did Zeynep know what letters to use for the tulip you gave me?"

"Because, Herr Andersen, as immodest as this sounds, she listened to *me*."

"To your descriptions of the old strains?"

"Exactly. And the Chief Gardener, despite his exalted rank, or perhaps because of it, did not take enough time to explain what this tulip once *was*—its provenance and place in the floral hierarchy of the palace gardens; he did not linger on its beauty, nor reflect on its power. It was only when Zeynep knew and understood everything about a tulip that she was able to sense the holy word that identified it."

"And would Zeynep have listened if the Chief Gardener had taken the time to explain?"

"Perhaps." Musa smiled. "I must ask for your patience, Herr Andersen. I'd like you to examine the tulip again." He crossed the room to where the silver tray containing his tools rested, returning with a smaller version of the magnifying glass he had offered Andersen outside.

"Try this."

Andersen held the magnifying glass close to the calligraphic tulip. There was no protective glass over the image, so he could see clearly, without a glare. Toward the top of the bud, the green ink seemed a shade lighter, and he thought he detected a hint of red, although he couldn't be certain.

"You can detect a touch of color?" Musa asked.

"I'm not sure."

Musa shook his head as if disappointed by this answer.

"Musa," Andersen said. "You told me the gardeners found this image in Zeynep's cell. Could she have been transcribing a tulip she saw in the palace gardens?"

"Let me return to your previous question, if I may, Herr Andersen. You asked if Zeynep would have listened to the Chief Gardner's description of the old tulip strains."

"Go on."

"I believe," Musa said, "that the Chief Gardener had Zeynep arrested because he needed her help. He needed her to channel her *baraka*, the spirit and energy of her letters into a tulip he was trying to grow. He might have believed he had one of the old strains, which had still yet to bloom and reveal its true identity. If so, he would have asked Zeynep to draw it, to help it on its way. Or perhaps she drew this image and only then did he believe. It is immaterial, either way, because the Chief Gardener didn't understand her power. He thought of Zeynep like a snake charmer, who could tease and tempt the ancient strains out of their bulbs with the power of her calligraphy."

The image tickled Andersen: Zeynep holding her pen like a snake charmer's flute; the flower responding to her calligraphy by rising and twisting from the earth.

"But that is not how Zeynep's *baraka* works," Musa said, interrupting his reverie. "She cannot simply will it to appear. As well as knowing everything about a tulip—its lineage, the optimum conditions for growing—she would have to trust the gardener to grow it. She could not let the flower bloom, even in ink, if she did not believe the Chief Gardener was the right man. If she didn't believe in *his* potential, as well as the tulip's, she could not set it down on the page."

"So Zeynep didn't listen to the Chief Gardener because she didn't trust him?"

"Exactly. Only in the presence of a worthy partnership would Zeynep seek the holy word, the single word that would decide the flower's fate, the letters she would use to form the tulip's petals. I believe my descriptions helped her find this word when we were at the *tekke* together, but in the end, despite the beauty of her images, we were writing a book about tulips, not growing them."

"But now," Andersen said, "you believe you can succeed where the Chief Gardener failed?"

"I have tried to make myself worthy of Zeynep's trust. I have treated my tulip well, recreating as much as possible its ideal growing conditions. But, unlike the Chief Gardener, I do not expect Zeynep will help me because of this. I must reach out to her as well. I need her to harness the *baraka* that is present in this written tulip."

Andersen felt uneasy. Musa was talking of his old friend as if she were still alive, as if she were still able to help him. "But without Zeynep here," he said, "how can she transfer her *baraka* from this image to your tulip?"

"I have done what I can to pacify her spirit," Musa said. "This past week, I have celebrated Zeynep's memory by sharing her work with you, a professional storyteller. You are here, Herr Andersen, because you have the power to immortalize her with your words."

It should have been Zeynep standing here in this small house with her *kalem* and paper, putting the finishing touches to her flower, giving it an identity, Andersen thought. Not he. But she was gone and Musa wanted him. He shivered at the thought of it, a tingling at once exhilarating and frightening. Musa wanted him to record something transformative. Something he believed would occur in this simple calligraphic image and, consequently, to the budded tulip outside in the garden.

Andersen looked at the drawing and considered its similarity to the tulip in the glass house. "I understand the power of suggestion," he said. "But you and Zeynep created images based on tulips that had already been grown. What makes you think she had any influence on something that hadn't happened yet? Like a flower yet to bloom?"

"When I used to describe the old strains to Zeynep, I was often surprised by the images she produced," Musa said. "I had studied miniatures of Diamond's Envy, for example, and Light of Joy, and I had seen one or two of the wild species on my travels, so I had a good idea of what they looked like. But Zeynep's letters, the way she developed personalities for these flowers, went far beyond my vision of them, let alone any description I had offered. I once asked her if she had ever seen a Diamond's Envy, because the image she created had such vitality, such a strong *baraka*, it was almost a living thing in its own right."

"And what did she say?"

Musa smiled. "She laughed. 'Where, my friend, would I have seen such a thing?' she said. 'I have barely left my neighborhood, let alone the city.'"

Andersen turned back to the image on the wall, the stem and the leaves, the candle-shaped capsule of the bud. It represented thousands of tulips across the city—the simple, colorful promise of spring. And maybe something more. Andersen tried to imagine the glass house tulip in full bloom: the upright posture of the stem as it thickened and grew, the stiff but smooth texture of the outer petals curled against the spring chill, the sturdiness of the leaves. If the old tulips were anything like those he had seen dancing on the tiles in the mosque, there would be six petals opening and stretching into dagger points, identical in length, leaving gaps too small for even an aphid to crawl between.

Diamond's Envy. Light of Joy. These were wonderful names. "What about your tulip," he asked, thinking of the story he was to write. "Is it one of the old strains? Does it have a name that distinguishes it from others?"

"*Nazande al*," Musa said. "Flattering Red. It is the same tulip I believe the Chief Gardener asked Zeynep to draw while she was his guest in the palace prison. Flattering Red, Herr Andersen," Musa repeated, as if Andersen hadn't paid sufficient attention. "When this tulip blooms, you will see a red so perfect it will stop your heart."

"A red as perfect as the tiles in the Sokullu Mehmet Pasha Mosque?" Andersen asked.

"The same red as those men of Iznik would have seen three hundred years ago."

Musa glanced out the window, shielding his eyes against the glare. "The time is approaching. While we wait, would you like some more tea?" Andersen agreed, and Musa busied himself in the kitchenette.

It was early afternoon, and Andersen could not get the Turk's words out of his mind. *When the sun is full and strong.* Soon. It would be soon.

Musa returned with a samovar and placed it on the stove. "Please make yourself comfortable," he said. "I will call you if there are…developments in the glass house."

"But what am I supposed to do?" Andersen asked.

Musa walked up to him and placed his hands on Andersen's shoulders, his brown eyes parallel with Andersen's own. "Ask," he said mysteriously. "Ask if Zeynep will help me."

And with that, he returned to the garden.

ʃ

Andersen poured himself a glass of tea and waited for its strength to revive him. He could still feel the imprint of Musa's hands on his shoulders. A strange and effusive confidence flowed through him, along with the black, bitter tea. His thoughts drifted out of the room, down through the tiny, terraced garden, and to the glass house. From there, he had briefly glimpsed the Bosphorus through the tall cypresses. He imagined himself standing between those trees on a spring night, looking through opera glasses across the water, to the peninsula where the sultan's palace stood. He could see two men loading a heavy, shapeless sack onto a small boat and pushing off from the royal dock. The craft drifted in ever-smaller circles, oars hanging over the sides. Andersen watched the sack writhe and thrash on the deck between the boatmen's feet. The executioners waited for the moon to break free from behind a cloud and give them a lozenge of light to work by. Then, bathed in a pale glow, they lifted the bagged prisoner, who had stopped moving. She may have fainted, or fallen into a drug-induced coma, or maybe she gave off a final, exhausted scream, begging for mercy in short, clammy breaths, only to hear the executioners laugh as they heaved her over the side.

CHAPTER 15

That night, the calligrapher wriggled inside Red's cannon, pinging her elbows against the iron. She woke once with her friend's name on her lips but silenced herself, choosing instead to write the letters of his name in her mind, to arrange the lines and loops, to place the diacritical marks with all the precision of her training. It was easier that way.

Eventually, she fell asleep and dreamed about a tulip growing on the side of a mountain pass.

On horseback and wrapped in animal skins to keep out the cold, she spotted the bright petals of a tulip bed hidden amid a patch of scrawny grass and brown rock. She dismounted and clambered up to the flowers, her breath escaping in chilly puffs. Only some had bloomed; others huddled inward against the cold. She took her time examining them until she saw the tulip she wanted—one with a deep red color, almost scarlet, standing low to the ground. Its almond-shaped petals had sharp points, and she was sure if she had applied even the slightest pressure, the tips would have drawn blood.

She awoke with a start, haunted by the red of the tulip. Sliding along the cylinder of the cannon, feet first into the light, she felt stiff and unrested. The Prophet's birthday celebrations would begin that evening at sunset, but even at this early hour, she could sense the expectation— the way people moved along the Bosphorus and smiled, the thousands of lanterns and candles that hung from the roofs, waiting to be lit.

She tried to concentrate on the tulip from her

dream, but her mind kept returning to the garden in Eyup where she had seen her friend. She had recognized the look that crossed his face, a look at once pleading and demanding. He hadn't seen her, she knew. If he had sensed her presence at all yesterday, it had been as a phantom, light on her feet, rustling the heads of flowers as she passed.

The calligrapher looked over at the cannons. She could hear the green dervish's metallic snores, while Blue had already departed for the morning, leaving his notebook and pens on her cannon. Now that she had an audience who appreciated her work, she wanted the tulip of her dream to be her parting gift to the green and blue dervishes. She could think of no better way to thank them. But could she render it without her friend's guidance, his commanding knowledge of its history and myths? She would have to find a way, because she could not return to him now. She would not be able to bear the look of fright and confusion her presence would conjure on his face. And even if he were to describe the tulip, she might not trust his description. Not after all that had happened.

Think, she ordered herself, think of the tulip in the cold, growing on the steppe of Central Asia, from where the Turks first migrated a thousand years before. What had become of the tulip's lineage? The bulb would have burrowed its roots deep into the ground to survive the frosts of winter, and at the summer's zenith, scattered its seeds. Once discovered, the bulb and its descendants would have been plucked from the soil by merchant hands, and made the long trek across the plains, nestling among the dried fruits carried by women who painted thick black lines across their eyebrows and rimmed their eyes with kohl.

In Istanbul, the species would have woven its way through the freshly planted gardens of the city, proclaiming itself from the towering domes and gutterings of mosques, and emblazoning itself onto the city's famous tiles.

With tiny strokes, she began her work, her pen scratching against the page of Blue's notebook, which she cradled in her lap. She thought of The Book of Tulips and tried to picture herself in the *tekke*, sitting in the garden or in her room. Her friend ushering her to a quiet corner, his eyes full of excitement. 'I have it,' he would say. 'I have the perfect specimen for our book,' and she would rush to fetch her writing materials, the two of them as happy as children, resurrecting the lost tulips of Istanbul.

{

Ask if Zeynep will help me. Andersen sat on Musa's divan and ordered his body and brain to relax. He would not discover anything if his heart palpitations started again. He closed his eyes and took a series of deep breaths. He tried to remember Musa's statement, something about words on the page, the images they form, how they are always changing. An interesting thought—that images could evolve, and maybe even devolve, like the lion in the newspaper, so old and careworn. Andersen opened his eyes and shook his head. Thinking this way would surely drive him mad.

A cool breeze worked its way under the partially open window, sending a shiver through him. Musa had left a clean tea glass for him next to the stove. He filled the glass from the samovar and stirred in two spoons of sugar. Sipping his tea, he cleared his mind of everything but the bitter liquid coating the back of his throat, the flow of warmth into his system.

Musa had invited him here to celebrate a horticultural feat. Another gardener or florist, just about anyone would have been better qualified, would have appreciated the sanctity of the event, more than a writer from Denmark. But Musa had asked for him. Andersen walked quickly over to the tulip hanging in its thin wooden frame. Did Musa expect him to keep watch over it, as if his proximity to Zeynep's calligraphy would enhance its power like wind filling a boat's sails?

A strong light played over the stem and leaves and the bud looked fuller than before—lighter too. Andersen smiled. This fantasy of a paper flower *becoming* something. Ink was immutable.

But as Andersen leaned closer, he couldn't deny the tip of the bud had a newfound reddish glow.

It was probably a trick of the light. Perhaps he hadn't seen the hint of red before because the sun had been at a different angle.

He took a sip of tea. Was there really something in this spiritual energy, this *baraka* that Musa saw in Zeynep's work? He thought of the small mosque near the Hippodrome where the tiled flowers had taken on the guise of silken dancers and performed for him. He remembered the glimpse of the Lion of Aleppo on the back of the city's newspaper. Did that mean that he, too, could feel this unexplained phenomena?

From out in the garden, Musa called for him. Andersen stepped outside and onto the terrace. He judged it to be mid-afternoon by the position of the sun. The mirrored wall of the glass house now reflected not only a multitude of tulips, motionless now that the breeze had disappeared, but also the bright glare of the sun. Shading his eyes, Andersen made out Musa's form through the glass. His back was turned, arched over his flower pot like a question mark.

Andersen stood in the doorway and coughed. "I was a little overzealous with the watering can," Musa said, his voice emanating from the depths of the pot. He raised his head, lips puckered as he blew a warm stream of air over the flower, encouraging the excess drops of water to fall from the joint between the bud and the stem.

"Short, sharp breaths are the best," Musa said. "That way the drops don't spread over as much of the leaves."

He began a new blowing cycle, ending it with a low incantation, a prayer of urgent, half-formed words. He lifted his head and Andersen saw that his face had undergone great strain: lines were etched under his eyes and his face gleamed with perspiration. Andersen looked quickly into the pot. It looked stronger: the bud had nuzzled its way clear of the inner leaves and the green overlay on the backs of the petals was fading fast, leaving a deep red flush.

The tulip—with its slightly elongated shape, its deepening red glow—would be special,

Andersen thought, a flower that would turn heads. But to call it a Flattering Red before it had bloomed seemed a leap of botanical faith.

Musa moved the pot outside. "Where it will have the best light," he said with a nervous smile. He sat down with the pot in front of him, legs crossed. Andersen crouched beside him, thinking how the *bostancis* in the palace gardens must have once sat and held their breath in much the same way.

‡

The calligrapher went for a walk after breakfast, and when she returned to the cannons, she found the green dervish sitting cross-legged by the Bosphorus, waiting. "My friend said I should see your work before you leave," he said.

The calligrapher nodded and, flushed from her walk, knelt by the water and dabbed her face. She went to fetch Blue's notebook and writing materials.

"Where will you go?" the green dervish asked

as the calligrapher made herself comfortable beside him. But she didn't know, so she smiled and said nothing.

"It's hard for the exile," said the green dervish. "He is a stranger in each city he visits, but if he goes back to the old places, the haunts of his youth, if he seeks the loved ones of his memory, he will be like a lost traveling trunk returned with someone else's clothes inside."

The green dervish opened the notebook and turned the pages slowly. The calligrapher had hoped that one day, all three dervishes might gaze at the book together, the sky deepening to crimson and mauve behind them, a drowsy moon seeking its reflection in the water. How would Blue and Green describe her work to Red, the dervish in whose cannon she had slept for the past three nights? Would she become, in their imaginations, a character like those created by the storytellers at the coffeehouse? She supposed it would be easy for the dervishes to call upon her memory in one of their homilies, delivered amid the detritus of human life.

The green dervish found the page she had dedicated to Blue and his lost singing voice. She had rendered the scene in a *Bismillah* of a gray nightingale with its beak open but no notes or words visible. The green dervish looked at the nightingale for a long time. "Yes, yes," he said quietly.

Next was the page she had written on their return from the puppeteers' house. While selecting her inks, she had thought of the empty cotton screen, the fading memory of the green dervish's audience. And then she had written the *sura—Everything is perishing except the Face of God*—as the mirror image of two swans, the words intricately braided into the birds' plumage. The tiny faces of the green dervish and his apprentice rested on the *alifs* of the swans' slender necks, turned away from each other and silhouetted on the page.

The green dervish chuckled at the hint of cunning the calligrapher had woven into his miniscule eyes and said of the *sura* that this was what they were put on this earth to learn.

When he turned to the page with the calligrapher's drawing of Red, the green dervish fell silent. She had divided the page into quarters and drawn the wooden toy, the *haciyatmaz*, once in each section, every version dipping and spinning on its axis in a different direction. The figure seemed in perpetual motion, a restlessly wandering spirit.

"It is my dream that one day we will find him happy enough to be still again," the green dervish said, but with only the faintest flicker of hope.

They looked at the book together. On one side of the pages was Blue's impenetrable script, and on the other, the calligrapher's faces and animals, her lanterns and boats and mosques. When he'd turned the final page, the green dervish congratulated the calligrapher on her holy gift.

"There's only one thing I don't understand," he said, opening the notebook to the first page and pointing to the top right-hand corner where the calligrapher had drawn the green shoots of a tiny tulip. At the top of the next twenty pages, too, in exactly the same position, the calligrapher had drawn a miniature tulip from script, slowly maturing, so that as the green dervish flicked the pages forward with his thumb, the stem grew stronger and straighter, sprouting leaves, and gradually formed the curve of a bud until an almond-shaped capsule of dark green lay half-hidden among the leaves. "The flower. It's a marvelous trick, but it disappears halfway through the book."

The calligrapher nodded. Toward the middle of the notebook the green faded, and for three pages, a pinkish-red tinge started to play around the tip of the bud. But then she had stopped.

The flower consisted of four letters: *alif*, for the stem, the first letter; a pair of *lam-alifs* for the leaves, the second and third letters, one on each side like the wings of an ungainly bird. As the tulip grew stronger, she had thickened and tapered the top of the *alif* into a smooth oval. The shading had been hard. The outer petals of a tulip-bud only imply the color green, a hue closer to gray, like the color of a man's cheeks when he has eaten too many mussels. Finally, she had threaded a needle-thin *ha* through the pale midrib on the backs of the petals, running from the base and disappearing into the top of the bud. *Ha*: the fourth and last letter of God's name.

"It's been a while since I watched a tulip grow," said the calligrapher. "It's very hard to capture that moment, when the green flush washes away and the color breaks through. I don't know if one can see it with the human eye, but sometimes, if I concentrate hard enough, I sense that first hint of bloom."

"But you stopped before the bud had a chance to open. And now you are leaving us."

"If God blesses my pen, the tulip will reveal itself before I leave."

The green dervish looked into the calligrapher's eyes and placed his hand on her shoulder. "Thank you," he said. The weight and warmth of another's touch felt strange, at once judgmental and empowering, like her father's hand. Throughout her youth, he had observed her work silently, never interfering, but his touch had expressed first judgment, then pride. She closed her eyes and tried to picture her parents' smiling faces, but they had gone. All that remained was the memory of her father's presence behind her, the slight pressure of his hand. She must have had a thousand chances to look up at him as she wrote, but her concentration was unwavering and she never did.

$$\int$$

Andersen and Musa watched the tulip grow. It was tranquil, staring at a living entity, filling one's eyes with it to the exclusion of all else. The stem with its slippery finish, the sinuous leaves, the faint glow of the bud.

After an hour, when Andersen thought he could hear the faint call of a nightingale drifting in on the breeze, Musa spoke. "You asked me earlier, Herr Andersen, if anyone had ever grown the old strains. I wasn't entirely frank with you when I answered—there *was* one person who almost managed it."

"Who?" Andersen asked. "Your father?"

"It was I, Herr Andersen," he said flatly. "Yes, my father's obsession infected me like a damp chill infects the lungs. Once, I had been happy enough simply describing the old tulips, telling their stories and witnessing their form and color in Zeynep's calligraphy. But my father had failed so often and become so disheartened, I wanted to help."

Without shifting his gaze from the tulip, Musa told the story of a warm autumn day when he had gone on a breeding frenzy, transferring the pollen from the stamens of various tulips to the stigma of others. There had been little rhyme or reason behind the cross-fertilization, he said, other than attempting something his father had not tried. He paired vermillion reds with buttery yellows, merged feathered tulips with flamed, coupled unblemished whites with tulips that had blotches on their bases, like the onset of a man's beard. "I suppose I was trying to recreate the indiscriminate environment of the steppe," he said, "where so many different species and strains grow together. In truth, it was the act of a desperate man."

He sowed the seeds without a thought for the position of the bed in relation to the sun, or the quality of the soil. Squirreled away in the corner of his garden, away from his other flowers, he left the seeds to their own devices as one season followed another.

"Despite my neglect," Musa said, "a solitary stem emerged after seven years, and I watched it, every day, as we are doing now. In bud, the tulip was dark green. The backs of the petals had the texture of satin. After a week the flower opened, a brilliant white veined with crimson through the midrib and along the borders. It was thinner than the other tulips in my garden, pinched at the waist, with six spidery fingers for petals. But its classification, its identity, was a mystery to me, Herr Andersen: Remember, I had paid no attention to parentage when I carelessly scattered those seeds.

"I reached for The Book of Tulips to see if, by some chance, I had raised one of the old strains, if the flower matched one of Zeynep's illustrations. She had done a few depictions of blooms in this earliest phase, but nothing resembled the finely feathered markings of the flower before me. Why had I planted it so far from the warming sun? Such careless and impetuous gardening would have infuriated my father. Distraught, I sat down and waited for its fate to become apparent."

Musa wiped his brow with the back of his hand.

"At sunset, there was a knock on the garden gate," he continued, "but I was in no mood for company, so I ignored it and stayed watching my tulip. Hours later, I made my way back to the salon. The house was completely dark, but through the window I saw a figure standing in front of the house—Zeynep, a splash of moonlight on her face. She couldn't see me, so I remained still, curious to know what she would do next. I did not know why she had chosen this moment to appear; it is not the custom for a woman to arrive unannounced on a man's doorstep, and moreover, Zeynep rarely left the *tekke*. She held something against her leg, which in the twilight appeared like a shadowy extension of her hand. But even in the dark I recognized that cylindrical case, the varnished pine container that held her pens, an inkpot, and the plate she used to sharpen her nib. I'd told no one about the tulip, not even my father. How had she known? I was irritated. I knew that if she saw this new tulip, it would be so easy for her to transcribe that she wouldn't need my words to shape her letters into the angle of the stem, my imagination to fashion the lean curve of the petals. It would all be there for her, whereas my father had spent a lifetime working toward this single moment. I returned to my vigil in the garden and quite forgot about her."

"Musa," Andersen said, pointing at the Turk's brow.

He had rubbed a streak of dirt into the lines of his forehead. Musa spat on his hand and tried to wipe the dirt away with an abrasive swipe that left a reddish-brown smear in its wake. Andersen felt for his handkerchief, but left it in his pocket.

Musa's disdain for Zeynep had shocked him, the hardness in his tone.

"That first night, the tulip began to weaken," Musa continued, ignoring the stain on his forehead. "The leaves showed signs of mottling; the stem stooped and the petals withered. I did not sleep, praying the dawn sun would save the plant. In the morning, something extraordinary happened. The tulip was still dying, but its crimson borders and veins had leached through the edges and midribs of the petals in perfect symmetry. As I looked on, the tulip flushed purple, its white surface like a strip of cotton bloodied by a slow wound.

"Zeynep should have been there. I needed her to write the flower onto the page before it disappeared. I tore out of the house, wildly searching up and down in the hope that she might still be on my street. I ran to the *tekke*, each step taking me further from the tulip, which I knew was in the throes of its final act.

"I opened the door to Zeynep's room and found her sitting in the dark, the writing case unopened in front of her. I begged her to return to the house with me. I thought if she saw the flower, even in its distressed state, she could transcribe its image with her holy letters. Something inside me believed that this act of tribute, this rendering onto the page, would comfort the tulip as the words of a loved one can sometimes bring clarity to a man consumed by fever. But she just looked at me pityingly, as one might a madman—as if I understood nothing at all.

"I walked out of her room, out of the *tekke* and back to my house, heavier with sorrow than I have ever been.

"No doubt you will say I deserved nothing less. After all, it was I who refused to let Zeynep inside. You will castigate me for ignoring her offer of help, for that's what it was, Herr Andersen. She came to help me." Musa stared at the terracotta pot, his mind replaying that evening he'd left Zeynep standing in the moonlight; or perhaps, Andersen thought unkindly, still thinking of his precious flower.

"Why, Musa?" Andersen said, adding Musa's rejection to the tragedy and cruelty Zeynep had endured in her life. "Why did you turn her away?"

"I don't know, Herr Andersen," he said quietly. "Pride, I suppose. The belief that I could do for my father what no one else could, and that I could do it alone, without the help of another."

"What happened when you got back?"

"By the time I returned to the house, the tulip had wilted and shriveled—dead before I could identify it," Musa said in a low voice. "In a fury, I tore up the flower bed. I could not have endured another loss of that magnitude. After my father died, I gardened only for myself, on a very small scale, and continued my trade as a florist."

Andersen felt Musa was expecting a consoling phrase, but he could not shake the image of Zeynep waiting outside that window. To be turned away by an old friend, a collaborator, and the only other person who understood those old tulips—what must it have done to her?

And besides, Andersen didn't like the

coldness that Musa had attributed to Zeynep when he arrived at the *tekke*. As if she had deliberately punished her old friend for his vanity, withheld her compassion as well as her skills. It was not how Andersen wanted the episode of the failed tulip to end.

"Did you see her again?" he asked. "After that night?"

"No," Musa said, and treated Andersen to his half-smile.

There were albatross on the Bosphorus. Wandering, the green dervish said, between hemispheres as he and his friends strolled from one sea village to the next. In early summer, the birds would continue northward, but the green dervish hoped a few would remain until autumn, when the winds blew down from the Black Sea and chilled the air. "After all," he said to the calligrapher, gesturing at the blue water, "they have everything they need right here."

They were splendid birds, powerful in the air and resplendent in the water with their pristine white feathers. Closer inspection, however, during their curious waddles along the sea front, revealed almost as much black as white, delicate shading under their necks and wings, a dark tinge to the tail.

A pair skipped and splashed near the shore, dipping their bills into the water, riding the swell of passing boats. The calligrapher and the green dervish sat by the water's edge and watched. The latter had produced an ancient water pipe and puffed on it contentedly while the calligrapher stared at Blue's notebook. The green dervish had asked if he could sit with her while she worked on the tulip, with the strict understanding that he wouldn't disturb her. But the calligrapher struggled to concentrate. The tiny tulips she had drawn seemed vulnerable, as though Blue's closely-knit script could, at any moment, spill across the page and bury her work. She had tried unsuccessfully to read Blue's musings. Occasionally, she made out the odd word:

'jasmine,' 'driftwood,' and four or five repetitions of a word that might have been 'hyacinth.' But mostly the markings were undecipherable, an ancient coded system that only Blue could understand.

The albatross swam closer to the bank and caught her eye. One lifted its large wings out of the water, as if debating whether or not to soar into the air. The other bird opened its bill to squawk, two refined notes, lower in register than a seagull's. The calligrapher stretched the letter *sin* across a blank page of Blue's notebook, forming the outline of a bird bobbing on the water, elongating its beak. A couple, she decided, the female drying her wings in the sun, the male hurrying her along with an anxious squawk. The birds splashed out of the water and landed on the paved bank, wobbling on sea legs. They regarded the green dervish with yellow eyes. Their orange webbed feet were translucent enough for the calligrapher to see a thousand letters veined under the skin.

The calligrapher drew the second bird, its

eyes tiny *ayns*, the feet *dahls*. The birds hopped a little closer, barely more than an arm's length away now. She lifted the notebook and turned it round so they could get a good look at themselves. The calligrapher felt their gaze, strong and severe as the *usta* from the *tekke* who had first granted her the permission to write. He had ruined one eye through years of scrutinizing his letters and concentrating on the page, but his good eye, like that of the albatross, never moved as it evaluated her work. The calligrapher imagined many a poor student succumbing to the power of that black pupil.

The birds hopped to the left and the male let out a low hum, almost a growl, the bottom of its bill vibrating slightly. Then they were airborne, the thick flap of wings, the effortless glide.

The calligrapher turned back to the last tulip she had transcribed in the corner of Blue's notebook, but her mind kept wandering. On the Bosphorus, a sailboat with billowing masts passed by.

"Perhaps if you tell me about the tulip, it

might help," the green dervish said, his eyes still on the diminishing albatross.

The calligrapher told him something of her dream, of her imagined history of the red tulip. "There was…is a man who wants to grow it," she said.

"The man we saw in the flower garden at Eyup?"

"Yes."

"And does this man have the skill, the knowledge to achieve this?"

"That is a question I have asked myself," the calligrapher said. "There was a time, before my exile, when he almost succeeded. He was working in his father's garden and grew a white tulip with six slender petals, each one marked with crimson around the edges and through the midribs, like the veins of a leaf."

The green dervish smiled at the description. "Not a flower one could find easily nowadays."

"No. And I can't explain it, but I *sensed* he had grown this remarkable tulip. He didn't tell me about the flower himself."

"Why not?"

"I don't know. This man and I had created tulips before, calligraphic tulips, when we were hardly more than children. I transcribed them in a book. He knew all the old species that had grown in the city. He told me their stories, described their forms and natures, and as I listened, I pictured them and tried to recreate them in ink.

"Time passed and I suppose we had become strangers, with nothing but memories between us. But I had a strong feeling about this tulip, and I wanted to see it. So I went to his father's house, taking my inks and paper with me. You see, I hadn't given up hope that he would grow one of the old strains. I thought that one day, I would take up The Book of Tulips again and transcribe a living specimen, one we could touch and smell."

"What happened?"

"I knocked on his door and he refused to let me in."

The green dervish shook his head but said nothing.

"I went home," the calligrapher continued. "I felt the loss of my friend's faith twisting inside me and I sat in my room, unable to move. But then, a few hours later, he came to the *tekke*. It seemed he wanted to see me after all."

"Because the tulip was in trouble?" the green dervish said.

"Yes. And he begged me to go with him to record its presence, to find the letters, the holy word, that would capture its essence and help the flower to recover. He told me that the tulip's life was in my hands, that if I didn't act quickly, he would not be able to protect his father's reputation as a gardener."

"So what did you do?"

"I went to his father's house. I stood in front of that crimson and white tulip the same way I had once stood in front of him, waiting for his voice to tell me the story of its species, its heritage, and the journey it had made to arrive in the shadiest corner of his garden. I asked him to talk about the tulip as he had in the old days, as if he had planted and nurtured it in his imagination.

But he said nothing."

The calligrapher tugged at the sleeve of her *ferace*. "He had turned cold. He said we had no time for paper dreams; this was a real species, one that could make his father's name and put his legion of doubters to shame. And it was dying in front of our eyes. 'Write it!' he demanded of me. 'Write it before it slips from our consciousness; write it so it can grow strong again!'"

"He became greedy, your friend," the green dervish said. "Greedy and impatient."

The calligrapher nodded. "I couldn't transcribe the tulip," she said sadly. "Without a trustworthy gardener to tell me its story, what could I write? Rendering that flower's likeness would have been like weaving cotton without a loom. It could not be done."

"So what did you do?" asked the green dervish.

"I turned to leave and he accused me of withholding the tulip's *baraka*, as if it were mine to give. Then something happened I will never forget. We stood arguing in front of the tulip, and as our words grew harsher, the bloom turned purple, a deeply wounded blush. I suppose its pigments had started to run together, but I had the strongest sense the flower was ashamed of us, that we had disappointed it beyond measure."

The green dervish shook his head and tutted. "One must always respect the mystery of God's creations," he said. "Or they will forever remain a mystery." He gestured toward the notebook. "And now you are trying to help this man again?"

The calligrapher looked away. "Yes," she said.

"But to grow a different tulip this time," said the green dervish, recalling the flush of pink on the flower in Blue's notebook.

"Yes. Flattering Red.

"What did you say?"

"Flattering Red."

"I know it!" the green dervish said and rocked up onto his heels. "Those tiles, the Iznik tiles! They say each tiler was given a single bloom of Flattering Red to work with, one per man, and they were instructed to match the color exactly, before the flower faded. Where are those tiles again? What was the name of that mosque? I'm useless with places and names."

"Sokullu Mehmet Pasha."

He was animated, a surge of energy rippling through his green kaftan. "That's it! Those tiles above the *minbar*. A peerless red!"

‡

Musa was silent. Andersen wondered how much time had elapsed between Zeynep coming to his father's house and her arrest. And how long between her arrest and the journey in the boat with her two executioners? Musa must have speculated on how she'd upset the authorities beyond the general impurity of her writing. Andersen recalled the image of the lion on the back of the city's newspaper, how the artist, perhaps a calligrapher himself, had rendered the lion as exhausted and on the verge of collapse. Taranto had speculated the image might represent the unpopular Selim Ali Pasha, the 'Lion of Aleppo,' who had overstayed his welcome as Grand Vizier. Could Zeynep's calligraphy have been interpreted similarly? It was difficult, though, to imagine how her joyous riverbank animals could cause offence to anyone.

As they sat by the flower pot, waiting for the tulip to bloom, Andersen started to speak. "I saw this image in the *Moniteur Ottoman*, Musa," he said. "Initially, I could only make out a series of unrelated lines and markings, but when I looked again, I recognized the form of a cat, a large cat like a lion, composed of these markings."

Musa looked at Andersen and turned back to his flower.

"The thing is," Andersen continued, "there was something about this creature that didn't look right. It wasn't hunting or sleeping in the sun, as you might expect; no, it appeared weary and resigned as if it expected its next step to be its last."

Andersen paused, waiting for Musa to react, but the Turk did not lift his gaze from the flower pot.

"And the lion's face. It was... This might

seem odd, because I now know it was composed of Arabic letters like Zeynep's riverbank creatures on her scroll. But I didn't know that at the time. I didn't know how a skilled calligrapher could animate her images, make them look fresh and alive. But this lion was not full of life—anything but."

When Musa still didn't respond, Andersen spoke of the caption he had seen under the image of the lion and Taranto's theory about Selim Ali Pasha being depicted as tired and unfit to govern. He spoke until his words ran out, and when he had finished, he felt like a child who has spun a tall tale to deflect the disapproval of an elder.

Musa worked an errant shell, which had appeared at the surface of the flower pot, slowly back into the soil with his thumb. "Herr Andersen," he said. "These calligraphic images, as you describe them, are not unknown to me. I cannot tell you the identity of every perpetrator, but I could identify a hundred places in the city where one might obtain such work. Some consist of script that has been arranged, sometimes ingeniously, into the form of a human face; they bear no resemblance to living figures. A minority, as with the example you have mentioned, may have been produced for baser motives: to discredit someone, for example, or simply to cause embarrassment. At this very moment, you are trying to decide in which category Zeynep's work belongs, despite my detailed accounts of her skills and intentions, and the work that I have not only shown you, but presented to you as a gift."

"Musa, I didn't mean…"

"Herr Andersen, you need not explain. You are a professional writer and you must consider your story. I'm sure you have already formed assessments of all of us involved. You are considering our motivations, whether we are capable of unscrupulous acts. I will relate as much as I know about Zeynep's alleged crime, and if it causes you to think less of my friend, and of me, then please do not allow what I am about to say to spoil your story. It *is* your story, yes, but let me also tell you what I know, that you may be better informed as you condemn or redeem us."

Andersen reddened. It unnerved him that Musa seemed to know each step he was taking in the writing of this story. He thought of Zeynep in her prison cell and the Chief Gardner offering her writing materials. Was she resigned to her fate because she knew what she had done, or because others, like Andersen himself, had assumed she must have done something?

Condemn or redeem. It was up to Andersen now. He was the storyteller.

"Herr Andersen," Musa said, "I have already shared my theory with you. The Chief Gardener was an opportunist who knew Zeynep was special. He attempted to exploit her, to glorify his name by growing a tulip everyone believed was extinct, the very same species you see in this pot. I also believe Zeynep shunned him, barring him access to her *baraka*. Of course, the Chief Gardener realized this when the tulip died.

"The Chief Gardener, powerful though he is, could not have arranged for Zeynep's arrest. Charges must have been filed against her. The New Guard could not have come to our *tekke* and arrested her otherwise. And when they arrived at her cell, they would have needed evidence. Something tangible, incriminating. The question is what? By that time, I was no longer close to Zeynep. The night she came to my house was the first time I had seen her for many months. I knew nothing of her recent activities."

"Wait." Andersen, whose foot had already gone to sleep, now had cramp in his calf. He struggled to his feet like a newborn lamb, trying to shake some feeling into his leg and foot. Musa stood too, in one fluid movement, a look of concern on his face. Andersen waved him away. "I'll be alright," he said. "Please go on."

Musa stretched, a languid motion, as if he had just woken after a good sleep. "Days after her death," he continued, "another *bostanci* from the palace gardens showed me a series of images he had smuggled out of the palace in the confusion that followed the Chief Gardener's dismissal. Each of the images contained her signature face, sometimes so tiny it was barely visible to the naked eye. But I knew to look for them and I did;

she had signed every one."

"Images of what?" Andersen asked, his voice rising. He knew there had to be something else, something Musa had not told him.

"Faces, Herr Andersen. Renderings of public faces belonging to prominent men in the city and the empire beyond. The *bostanci* gave them to me in a pile. At first, I did not understand. But when I studied the images closely, truly took time to see them, every page struck an uncanny resemblance. It was like waking up from a dream with a familiar face on my mind and finally recalling exactly who I'd been thinking of.

"The first face I recognized was the Chief Admiral's. This gentleman has pockmarks—he contracted smallpox as a child, I believe—and always wears an expression of immense discomfort. Next came the interior minister with his look of smugness, suggesting he could solve the problem of ethnic discord in the east while smoking a cigar. I recognized a colonel, a senior officer in the New Guard, because of his glass eye rolling about in its socket, and the Chief Eunuch because of his threatening jowls. And many, many more.

"I was given only one opportunity to study these faces. My contact at the palace insisted we destroy them because of their inflammatory nature. It happened so quickly, Herr Andersen. Would I have inferred the same likenesses if I had looked again? Perhaps. Or had my imagination placed a universal sneer onto the face of someone on whom it seemed to fit? That, Herr Andersen, is for you to decide."

Andersen swallowed, his mouth suddenly dry. "Was Selim Ali Pasha among the faces you saw?" he asked. "A tired face, one that had seen better days?"

"Yes," said Musa. "Although it wasn't the face of a man, but of a lion."

$\mathfrak{f}$

The green dervish lit his pipe, sending loops of smoke into the air. "But this tulip," he said, gesturing again toward Blue's notebook, "this

Flattering Red. Without your friend, how will you transcribe it?"

"Because I have seen it before," the calligrapher said. "There was someone else, a man who once described this tulip to me, who told me of its slow and difficult journey to the city, the kind of soil it preferred, and how it coped with the warm, wet climate of Istanbul."

"A man you knew in prison?"

"Yes." A memory of crouching on swollen heels in a stone cell came to her: cheap, unburnished paper on her knees and a scratchy, arthritic pen trudging through ligatures and lines. She remembered waiting for the streak of light that filtered into her cell only once a day, an emissary of the spring sun. In that light she had written the petition that led to her outdoor privileges, and later, that strange, slow tour of the outer gardens given by an old man in a drooping maroon hat who had held her life in his hands.

She told the green dervish of the morning she stood at the door of her cell, the moment after the guards had opened it to reveal a vast, terraced garden plunging down to the sea. Everywhere she looked, there were flowers on the verge of blooming—tulips, narcissi and jasmine, hyacinths and roses—flowers about to reveal their personalities to the world.

"These are the Padishah's gardens," her guards told her as she shielded her eyes from the sun, "and you are blessed to see them before you die." Women were never executed in the prison itself. They would go directly to the gallows, or straight into the sea. But the calligrapher—gazing from her cell into this paradise of marble fountains and pavilions glazed with tiles, each tier of the gardens a self-contained world with kiosks, vineyards, and orchards of apricot, cherry, and date—believed she had died already.

She had known the old man who came to read her petition. He called himself the Bostanci-Bashi and was held in reverence by the other gardeners, who scuttled to his commands and would not meet his eye. He looked at the writing materials he had sent earlier to her cell, daring her to challenge the paucity of the ink, the bluntness of the nib. He must have recognized her but gave no sign, just examined her petition and told her to step outside her cell.

A guard pushed at her shoulder. She followed the Bostanci-Bashi until she was forced to kneel on a patch of spring-green grass. To her surprise, the Bostanci-Bashi lowered himself too, his knee joints cracking like pistol shots. He sat cross-legged and invited her to do the same.

She had only a short time to plead her case. She met his eyes, full-on, allowing her gaze to rove over his tight mouth and well-trimmed beard; she did her best to ignore his comical hat. Her look unnerved him, she could tell, because when he mentioned her petition, his own gaze turned away, landing anywhere but on her.

The Bostanci-Bashi signaled to one of the guards, who trotted forward carrying a stack of papers, each one bearing a face. Rows and rows of faces, which he spread out on the grass between jailer and prisoner like a set of giant playing cards. There were faces with *nuns* for eyebrows, thick and thin, raised at one corner in surprise or furrowed in concentration. There were *ayns* for eyes, arched in doubt or narrowed in accusation; eyes of youth and vigor, and those of unfathomable disappointment. Noses grew from *alifs*, fluted like despots or smudged across the page like a man worse off for drink. *Mims* formed mealy mouths or relaxed into smiles so wide they could have seduced an empire. Other letters and diacritical marks worked their way into a jawline or a raffish fringe, or marked the skin like the onset of a disease.

"Tell me whom they belong to," the Bostanci-Bashi said, "and it will be easier for you in the end. This one, for example," and he lifted a face at random: "Whom were you thinking of? Why did you write him in this way? What do you know of his life?"

The calligrapher smiled. "Do you remember the faces of the people you have executed?" she said. "Could you distinguish between one's look of fear, and another's of hate? Would you recognize them if they were here, on the ground in front of you?"

The Bostanci-Bashi met the calligrapher's gaze and looked away. He clicked his fingers and the guard bent to collect the faces.

She was told to stand. The Bostanci-Bashi was ready to show her the tiers of the sultan's gardens.

They walked slowly, the Bostanci-Bashi stopping to preen and sniff, pinch buds, and blow moisture off petals. He pointed to the great beds of tulips: Those that Burn the Heart, Pomegranate Lance, and Increaser of Joy. He explained to the calligrapher which of these species could be sold off to the public at the Imperial Gate, and which were picked for the sultan's quarters. They moved from one terrace to another. Fresh running water trickled from the fountains and streams, threading the gardens like lace.

The Bostanci-Bashi talked of the animals that still roamed the thickets and woods of the sultan's lands: the deer, foxes, and hares; the bears and wild boar brought in for the royal hunts. They passed a gold kiosk where Sultan Beyazit once watched a lion, sent by the king of Tunisia, fight and kill a buffalo. In the aviary, a walled enclosure by the Rose Garden, a black bird with a red eye landed on the Bostanci-Bashi's shoulder and proceeded, not unlike the old man himself, to examine the calligrapher. They did not know if she could be useful, but they had to make sure.

Gradually and with many detours, the salty tang of the sea filled the calligrapher's nostrils. A wooden fishing station came into view on the shoreline just below the palace grounds. They paused beside an isolated flower bed shaded by the wall of a stone cottage. Behind the cottage stood an open-topped tower with a series of heavy chains, looming like henchman. "That is where our prisoners wait," the Bostanci-Bashi said, pointing to the tower.

"For what?" the calligrapher asked.

The Bostanci-Bashi gave her a black look. The calligrapher had forgotten herself walking through the garden. It was time to make her peace with God. This man, she told herself, this flower-loving man, will place the garrote around my neck and tighten it until I choke. But not yet, it seemed. The tour had not finished. Her host invited her to kneel beside him and look at the bud of yet another tulip.

{

The only sound was of Musa's murmured prayers. The Turk rocked back and forth, gripping his knees, committing the tulip to God's hands. Andersen envied the man's faith. He wanted to believe, but something in him always cowed. He peered at Musa's reflection in the outer wall of the glass house, a multitude of turbaned heads bent in reverence over infinite pots.

The sun was beginning its descent to the west. Both men had resumed their sitting positions, but Andersen, feeling his foot fall asleep again, got to his feet. He wanted to ask more questions, but Musa seemed content to leave the image of the lion's face, the satirical visage of Selim Ali Pasha dangling in front of him. Was Musa telling the truth? Could Zeynep have drawn that face, and all the others? *Condemn or redeem*?

While the Turk prayed, Andersen went back inside to pour himself more tea. He had an uncomfortable feeling. He could not imagine Zeynep creating those faces unless she had been compelled to do so. What did she have to gain otherwise?

And if she had drawn the faces Musa described, he thought, then she could not have done it alone. She'd spent her life at the *tekke*, in that small room with her pens and paper. She must have had help. How else could she have captured the Grand Admiral or the Chief Eunuch so accurately? Surely they'd never come to the *tekke*.

Andersen examined Zeynep's tulip, standing close, his nose almost touching the image. The flower seemed sunken, turned in on itself now. The letters, lines, and loops had taken on an ethereal quality, as if someone had untied their moorings. Andersen checked the doorway to the garden, and finding himself still alone, lifted the image from its hook. He wanted to examine the drawing in direct light, to check for evidence of tinkering, of lines altered, colored, or erased. He ran his fingertip along the surface of the paper. Zeynep would not have been happy with the quality: the paper was quite thin and had a scratchy texture to the finish. He pressed his thumb to the tip of the tulip. The ink was dry, the pigments almost fused together so that the dark green, almost black blotch at the base of the flower merged into a lighter green, which in turn faded to whiteness near the tip.

If Zeynep had drawn this in the palace gardens, then the image was now seven years old. Yet the inks had not faded and the paper wasn't jaundiced the way one would expect, especially being exposed, the way it was, without a protective sheen of glass.

If Zeynep hadn't drawn the image, then Musa must know another remarkably skilled calligrapher. He turned the frame over and found a brown protective card tacked to the frame and covering the back of the paper. According to

Musa, Zeynep often signed her work on the reverse side. Andersen loosened the tacks with a fingernail and in his haste, ripped the top of the card. More carefully, he threaded the paper with the image on it, bit by bit, through the gap he had made at the top of the frame. The paper was much whiter on the back side; smoother, too.

Andersen was ready for the signature face—the slightly mocking brows, the curious eyes—but instead found a face with its lips firmly set. There was a hardness about it: the eyes shrunken and wary, the cheekbones less pronounced. As if the face had aged. Andersen ran his finger over its tiny constituent features. Its ink had begun to fade and flake around the edges.

He glanced out the window again, nervous Musa would catch him with the picture out of its frame. Musa had moved forward onto his heels, his head almost inside the pot. Andersen fitted the paper back into the frame, reflecting on how a signature could change, take on a different character over time. The paper hadn't gone in straight, but Andersen hung the frame anyway.

He needed something more of Zeynep, and thought immediately of The Book of Tulips. Where could Musa have hidden it? Somewhere here, in this small house. Andersen couldn't imagine Musa entrusting the cherished object to anyone else's care.

Over in the corner of the salon was that curtain, leading, Andersen had assumed, to where the Turk slept. It would be a violation of privacy, but now the curtain taunted him; it was slightly parted as if daring him to enter. *Ask if Zeynep will help me.* Andersen put his hands on the fabric and went inside.

$$\mathbf{\imath}$$

As swiftly as it appeared, the calligrapher's memory of that day in the palace gardens faded. She told the green dervish she wanted to be alone, that she would be able to reveal more about Flattering Red once she had finished transcribing it.

The green dervish nodded and got to his feet.

"The afternoon before the Prophet's illuminations are always a good time for a walk," he said. "People like to get things off their chests, clear their minds before they feel ready to celebrate."

She studied the last tulip she had transcribed, the backs of the petals huddled and taut in a protective green flush. The tulip had grown from a nail-sized slip to almost the length of her finger. She pushed up from her seat on the ground into a squatting position, swaying on the balls of her feet, her calves pressed against her skin the way her *usta* had taught her. It wasn't good to be too comfortable, he used to say. You need to feel the earth tugging at your vanity. You are not ready to pick up your pen until your blood has proclaimed its mortality by jabbing its pins and needles into your every extremity.

The notebook wobbled across her thighs. The writing case lay open beside her, the inkwell dappled with tiny pools of color: gold and silver, red and blue, yellow and green, various hues in between. Blue must have spent an age preparing the inks, and yet, the whole time she'd been with the dervishes, if she used even the smallest amount, she found the pigment replenished by morning. Beside the inkwell, Blue's six pens were laid out in order of size: the largest measured twice the length of her hand, and the smallest— the one she had used to draw the earliest versions of her tulip—she could fit within the lines of her palm. They were made of finely-shaved reed, polished to a dark brown, and rounded at the edges of the shaft so as not to hurt or rub the fingers. The calligrapher held the smallest pen to the light: a slight groove was carved in the center of the nib, with an opening on the left and another on the right. The groove was meant to hold a bubble of ink, and she could vary the width of each stroke by pressing either to the left or right, or sometimes both together, as when forming the thick curve of the tulip's leaves. There was also a penknife with three separate blades and a small cutting plate made of ivory, but she'd had no call to use these items, not once; Blue always cleaned and sharpened the nibs before she opened the case.

The calligrapher turned the pages of the notebook very slowly. She did not flick them with her thumb, as the green dervish had done, to create the illusion of rapid growth. She wanted to examine each iteration of the tulip, study the changes in form and tone from one image to the next, just as an anxious gardener might scrutinize a prize specimen. On the eighteenth and nineteenth pages, a pink hue appeared at the tip of the bud, although she had to tilt the image toward the sun in order to see the pigment. She'd added the tincture with a tiny dab of Blue's remarkable pink ink, the color of grapefruit flesh. And then she had overlaid one of the lighter greens. She was pleased with the result: a pinprick of color like the promise of warmth and light.

She concentrated fiercely, her mind searching for the proper phrase, the word that would best describe the waiting tulip. She skimmed Blue's notebook, looked over the unintelligible script, hoping something would lift off the page. But this would not do. The word would have to originate with the tulip itself—and if she had coaxed this secret from the flower seven years ago, she couldn't remember it now.

Her thoughts kept returning to The Book of Tulips. Would one of her old creations trigger a memory or provide the inspiration she needed? In her mind, she went back to her friend's room and to the place where he kept the book. She imagined the soft texture of the cover and felt the creamy surface of its pages on her fingertips. She tried to picture the creations as she had once rendered them, page by page. She did this because despite everything that had happened, the tulips still haunted her.

$$\mathfrak{t}$$

Andersen found a small room with rugs laid out as a bed, a pitcher of water, and a bowl. He closed his eyes and imagined Musa reclining on the stack of rugs, a bare forearm stretching to pour water into the bowl.

He waited for his heartbeat to settle. In the

corner opposite the bed was a chest made from finely lacquered wood, emboldened on the front by three multi-colored, prancing lions. Andersen lifted the lid. Inside, he found the mundane possessions of a bachelor: a lemon-colored mouthpiece for a pipe, a length of worn silk, some coins, and a battered Koran, the pages barely clinging to the spine. He rummaged around blindly, touching something metal with sharp edges. Andersen lifted an antique tool from the chest, shaped like a trowel. It was made of burnished copper, gilded with arabesque around the scoop and along the handle. Musa, or perhaps his father before him, had polished it well—a ceremonial piece rather than a practical implement.

At the bottom of the chest was a bundle of papers. Rough-looking Arabic script plodded across the pages, weighed down by fat strokes and ink blotches. Letters, Andersen thought, from the format and the appearance of numbers that he recognized from the grandfather clock in his hotel, written where one normally put the date.

Were they from Musa's father to his son?

Andersen picked up one of the letters. In contrast to the heavy calligraphy of the other sheets, he found a curvaceous and fluid script, borne along by swooping curls and the constant switchback of thick and thin lines, as if a racing snake were sloughing its skins. Even Andersen could recognize the work of a skilled calligrapher.

He explored the chest more earnestly, digging beneath sheaves of paper and fabric scraps, all the way to the bottom, where his fingers brushed against a soft leather cover and the curve of a book spine. Andersen removed the volume and balanced it on his knees. His hands were damp and he had to wipe them on his trousers. "The Book of Tulips," he said softly.

He felt a tingling along his spine and looked up. He sensed the particles in the room had changed their alignment, as if someone had moved behind him, displacing the air. Instinctively, Andersen turned toward the curtain, expecting to find Musa, but he was alone. The curtain hung heavy and still. He shivered, thinking of the strange draft that had brushed the back of his neck at the mosque with the dancing tiles.

Andersen held the book to his nose. The fragrance was at once familiar and elusive, as if it had been part of a dream or memory. A smoky, resinous smell; a spiciness that lingered unobtrusively. And he realized the fragrance had been with him since he first arrived here, a constant and comforting partner. He pictured the trees that plunged to the Bosphorus shore at Uskudar. Straight and solemn, he thought of them as guardsmen on parade, eschewing any needless movement, resistant to the stiffest breeze. He remembered the aroma of the arrow-straight evergreens that lined the walkways of the cemetery at Zeynep's *tekke*, and of the intricate bird cage Taranto had presented him as a gift.

The fragrance of the cypress tree.

He closed his eyes and inhaled, picturing Zeynep with the book on her lap, the nib of her pen lightly caressing the page, Musa recalling the tulip's adventures, summoning the powerful breeders who fought to possess it. Could Andersen imagine writing this scene? Perhaps— if the story turned out as Musa hoped; if Zeynep made her presence felt and guided him toward the bloom he so craved. Then she would have forgiven him, Andersen supposed.

He opened the book. Each page was just as Musa described. Flowers bobbed on delicate stems, one or more on every page: apricot, orange, vermillion. Almond-shaped petals tapered into six points. He ran his fingers over the tulips' curves and ligatures, thinking of their cousins planted in the garden outside. Each specimen was carefully labeled. Andersen had no need to check the script against the letter he had found to know they'd been written by the same hand.

Halfway through, the tulips came to an end. Confronted with blank sheets of paper, Andersen was bereft. Staring at the white pages, his own imagination ran dry. For a moment, he was back at his desk in Copenhagen, in those weeks and months when he'd tried desperately to finish *The Moorish Maid*, snowflakes melting on his window pane, his mind blank as a sheet of ice.

He flipped back to the final tulip, and there, in the top right-hand corner, he noticed two miniature figures: one male, one female. How had he missed them? Outside, the dusk had thickened. He needed more light to make sense of the images. He lit a nearby lantern. Its glow skittered across the room, forming shadows that dared each other to get closer, like children around a bonfire. He lifted The Book of Tulips closer to the flame.

As with the lion in the newspaper, the ink looked fresh, the figures newly drawn; there was a glistening quality to the firm lines of their bodies and the brightly colored fabrics of their clothes. Both were as tall as his hand, the man dressed in a maroon hat with an extended pouch that drooped over his shoulder and a kaftan of the same color, the woman in a simple green headscarf and robe. He recognized the woman immediately, instinctually. Zeynep.

The calligrapher had finally settled in her favorite spot under the Judas tree, the trunk molded into her back. She was glad to be alone. No fishermen rode the sea, no couples gnawed on corn cobs or pointed at boats. All were home with their families, resting and preparing for the festivities. Now she was alone and undisturbed. The shaft of the pen felt as natural as a finger. Blue's inkwell had the colors she needed. She leaned into her work and heard only the sounds of her labors— pen to ink, pen to paper—the tulip growing in imperceptible stages, page after page. Repetition, extension, color.

It was rhythmic, the way her hand moved through the stem to the leaves to the cup: the *alif* to the *lam-alifs* and back to the *alif*, woven through with the *ha*. On each new page, the flower stood a little straighter, the leaves gained another curl, the tips of the petals grew more pointed.

Seven years ago, she'd been ordered to draw this very same tulip. The Bostanci-Bashi told her everything he knew about the strain, and then set himself to watch her work, leaning against the ramshackle stone wall of his cottage. "What is it?" he asked when she had finished drawing and held it up to him. "What will it become?"

The calligrapher pressed the sheet of paper into his hands. The eyes of a greedy, frustrated child peered through the cracks and grooves of the Bostanci-Bashi's face. He had not expected this. She had given him a work in progress, a budded tulip with its bloom still unknown. She was giving herself precious time, waiting to see what the Bostanci-Bashi would do next.

"What will it become?" The Bostanci-Bashi's repeated question hung in the air, faint and plaintive, like the song of a departing bird.

She would not tell him. The holy word that would form this flower could not be squeezed and forced like juice from a lemon. She could not be compelled to use her gift. And even if the flower were to bloom, a tulip grown under duress would not survive.

The calligrapher knew the shape of the tulip the Bostanci-Bashi wanted her to draw, because she had lettered many similar tulips before as a free woman, formed their six dagger petals from the loving description of a friend, a man who knew so much about the old tulips of Istanbul. She knew the color too, the peerless red the craftsmen of Iznik once used to paint their tulip tiles. She knew it, but the Bostanci-Bashi did not. And if her petition worked, she would be a half-day's walk away before he realized his prized specimen had flattered to deceive.

"Go," the Bostanci-Bashi had said, his spirit ebbing and flowing in front of her eyes. "Go back to your cell and wait for me. I grant your request."

The calligrapher wrote in Blue's notebook for most of the afternoon, the scene with the Bostanci-Bashi replaying in her mind, when all of a sudden, she came to the end, the last page of Blue's notebook. She lay down her pen. Releasing the instrument was like waking from a troubled sleep: her neck ached and a dull pulse throbbed at her temples.

One thought filled her head: She could write it as a single word, if she wanted, one of the ninety-nine names of her creator. She could thread its letters into the anatomy of the tulip in Blue's notebook, merge its spirals and ligatures with the flower's reproductive heart.

Now that she knew it, she could take a finely bristled camel-hair brush and transfer the word onto this tulip and a thousand more. She imagined sending this army of paper tulips back to the *tekke* where she had first studied their stories and discovered her gift. Perhaps her friend would return and find a dazzling paper garden. She lifted her head, smiling at the thought of her friend, how he always had the story of an ancient tulip on his lips.

The word was *ulfet*. Intimacy. When the calligrapher tried to write it, tried to sense its warmth and softness, the ink on the nib dried and hardened, and her heart hardened with it. She and her friend, they had embarked on a journey together. But he had deserted her when their intimacy was at its height. She could not allow this tulip to fall under the care of such a man.

The calligrapher closed Blue's notebook. Let

the green and blue dervishes skim through the pages and follow the tulip's progress as far as they could. She did not care to know the flower's fate. God would decide its destiny.

{

Andersen turned the page. The two figures appeared again, but this time, the man was bent over with knees flexed, while Zeynep, now slightly behind him, had arched her back and pushed her shoulders forward. Both looked downward, as if focusing on something beneath their feet. Under the image of these crouching bodies were two lines of text written in Zeynep's unmistakable script. The third, fourth, and fifth pages also contained two lines of text. Were they telling a story? Meanwhile, as Andersen turned the pages, the man in the maroon hat and Zeynep grew further apart, their images moving spasmodically, as if a puppeteer controlled their limbs.

On the eleventh page, a tiny tear appeared

through the sleeve of Zeynep's robe. Andersen held the book close to his face. Had the figures become disheveled, grubbier in the last few pages?

He turned back to look at the previous images. No doubt the man had begun to wear the pinched look of someone in great pain, while Zeynep remained fresh-faced despite her exertions. What were they doing? Were they executing steps in an enervating dance like the worshippers in Musa's *tekke*?

Andersen felt he knew the man, or had seen him in a dream. As the pair continued to move throughout the book, it became evident the man was too old for such strenuous effort: he looked on the verge of collapse. His hat, which at the outset had looked as cheerful as an English nightcap, now hung limply over his ear.

Worried that Musa would return to the house, Andersen turned the next pages more quickly, watching the subtle shifts in movement and gesture. The man and Zeynep drew closer, until by the final few images, their bodies merged, entwining in a dramatic collusion of limbs and fabric. Immediately, Andersen returned to the first page. He used his thumb to flick the story forward, animating the characters so that he saw in an instant the sum of their parts, the whole scene. At this rapid pace, the script also took on a life of its own, the loops and sloping edges of the words undulating like a flock of gulls. If the accompanying text provided details that he could not translate, it didn't matter. Andersen's story, the story of these miniature figures *in extremis*, was already taking shape in his mind.

Zeynep sitting in the palace dungeon. Clammy walls and moonlight slipping between the bars. At dawn, the door of her cell opens and the Bostanci-Bashi stands before her in a droopy maroon hat. She notices his hands, lumpy silhouettes in the murk. Execution in such hands, Zeynep thinks, will be as quick as the deadheading of a flower. But the Chief Gardener speaks to her in a low, soothing tone. They leave the cell together and follow a pathway lined with plane trees and geranium bushes, which look to

Zeynep like a thousand red eyes. They are walking uphill, the air noticeably chillier, the soil scrubby beneath their feet.

Then someone cried out—a primal, distraught sound—tearing Andersen from his vision of the two characters on their walk through the darkness. The cry had come from the garden. Musa.

Andersen reached the salon in two steps, still holding The Book of Tulips. Through the window, he saw Musa on his knees, arms draped around the pot. Andersen returned to the bedroom, intending to replace the book and close the chest, but first he had to know the outcome of Zeynep's dawn walk with the Chief Gardener through the sleepy tiers of the palace's outer gardens. He had to know what the executioner had planned for his prisoner.

He thumbed through the pages again, making the figures move with indecent haste. This time, he understood their movements more clearly. They were running down through the gardens, stumbling and scrabbling at thorny bushes and darting between trees. The letters in the accompanying texts arched their backs and flattened their heads, lacerating Zeynep's green robe, snatching at her headscarf like the bristly arms of a fir tree. He had thought Zeynep was escaping with the Chief Gardener in pursuit. But a few pages later, the Chief Gardener overtook Zeynep, running ahead of her, only for Zeynep to catch up and take the lead again a few pages later.

Of course. They were *racing*. Just like Atalanta's foot race against her potential suitors, where victory granted her freedom from marriage. And Zeynep's prize, Andersen decided, if she won this race against her executioner, would be her life.

Andersen prepared to flick the pages forward again, and then gasped.

Musa stood in the doorway, the heavy pot cradled in his arms, gazing at Andersen. A moment passed in which Andersen might have said something in mitigation, or condemned Musa for not sharing what he had known. Why hadn't he told Andersen about these finely painted figures racing through the palace gardens toward the shoreline? But before he could speak, Andersen's eyes were drawn to the pot in Musa's arms. He saw a pearl of red, a pinprick, at the very tip of the bud, as if the flower had cut itself and bled. The tulip was in trouble, the roots visible, the stem bent like the back of the porter who had hauled Andersen's baggage up the hill to Pera. Musa must have broken the tulip, snapped its spine when he realized it wasn't the Flattering Red he so craved.

Musa stood there with his face resting on the pot, and it was as if he had suddenly aged. Lines marred his brow and a yellow tinge was evident on his skin. Gray hairs spiraled free from the turban, which had come loose for the first time since Andersen had met him. Exhausted from his vigil, grimy and distraught, Musa reminded Andersen of the miniature Bostanci-Bashi running down the hill.

Musa's arms turned to string. He could no longer bear the pot, heavy with its baked clay and its earth and its exhausted hope. Andersen, who would find terracotta shards and crumbs of soil in his hair and clothes for weeks, could only watch as the vessel crashed to the floor.

CHAPTER 16

Andersen guided Musa into the salon and sat him on the divan, the Turk as limp and lifeless as a puppet in its box. He did what he could to sweep up the fragments of pot and clods of soil. In the kitchenette, he made fresh tea, fumbling with coals and the lid of the samovar, trying to recall how Musa had manipulated it so expertly, releasing the steam at exactly the right moments.

He filled the glasses, arranged the sugar, and found a tray. Musa slumped on the divan, his head tilted back. If he was asleep, then Andersen would have to wake him, if only to fetch the boy to lead him back to the dock. But Musa straightened as Andersen entered the room, a look of panic passing across his face as the events of the past few hours returned.

"Drink this," Andersen said, and passed him the glass. He went to the lantern and lit the wick. "Musa," Andersen began, "I should not have gone into your room. It was a terrible abuse of your hospitality."

Musa dropped cubes of sugar into his tea and stirred mechanically.

"If you can't accept my apology, then so be it. I may be wrong, but I think you *wanted* me to find The Book of Tulips." Andersen waited. "Do you understand me?" he said.

Musa stirred his tea again. "Herr Andersen," he said, his voice grave. "I have lost my ability to grow tulips, not to converse in the German language."

Taken aback, Andersen busied himself with his tea, dropping sugar cube after sugar cube into the steeped liquid. When he glanced up again, Musa was smiling, his green eyes suddenly bright and alert. For a moment, Andersen thought he was going to laugh as he had in Zeynep's room after translating the *usta*'s caveat in her practice book.

"When you invited me to your room, Herr Andersen," Musa said, "I remarked that you had a sorcerer's look. No doubt you recall why I said this."

"Yes," Andersen said, sliding into the familiar pattern of confirming Musa's flat assertions.

"I noticed on the steamship you sat apart from the other Franks. You did not conform to their way of dress: the fez and the cheap kaftan worn over their Western suits, as if they could shed the skin of each country they visited."

Andersen had felt ignored on the ship because he had not been wearing such garb, both by the other European passengers and by Musa himself, at first.

"After you made that paper cut for the child," Musa continued, "the boat with funnels like minarets and the holy man with a bird perched on his head, I'm sure you cannot guess what I did."

"I cannot."

"I bribed the child to let me borrow it. For an hour or more I studied it, trying to understand how such intricate shapes could have been made without measurements or plan. And then in your room, when I asked you to make the same paper cut, I watched your hands, marveling at the dexterity of your fingers. But, Herr Andersen, I couldn't resist peeking at your face. And when I did, I saw that look again."

"The sorcerer's look."

"Exactly."

Musa sipped his tea. "I was envious of your creations, Herr Andersen," he said. "And I came to your hotel thinking I, too, could acquire this paper-cutting skill."

"I could have taught you," Andersen said sadly.

Musa shook his head. "But I can tell you, it was at that moment, when I looked at your face in your hotel room, that I knew you could help me."

Musa leaned back on the divan. As quickly as his old self had bubbled to the surface, it sunk and dissolved, like the many sugars Andersen had put into his tea.

"Musa," Andersen said quietly. "You said the way I cut paper reminded you of the way Zeynep worked."

"Yes," Musa confirmed.

"So because of my paper cuts, did you think I possessed some kind of magic, an energy perhaps, which could bring your flower to life?"

Musa sighed. "Not exactly," he said. "But I thought your presence here tonight might pacify Zeynep's spirit. I harmed her greatly. With you here, the way you were curious to know her, your keenness to convey her virtues through your story, I thought she, she might—"

"She might forgive you."

Musa hung his head.

Andersen rose and brought The Book of Tulips into the salon, placing it beside Musa on the divan. He solemnly turned the pages, hoping

Zeynep's exotic flowers would encourage the Turk to talk, but although Musa turned his head to look, he remained silent.

When they reached the middle of the book, Andersen searched for the racing figures. But three more tulips appeared: each with the same tall stem, the pointed petals. "I thought…" Andersen began, and turned another page.

There, in the top right-hand corner, he found the man and the woman standing finger-tall: the man, dressed in a pristine burgundy kaftan and floppy hat; the young woman in her green robe. Relieved, Andersen continued to turn the pages, marveling again at the intricacy of these painted miniatures, the wealth of detail in their every gesture, the progress of the race, the gradual dishevelment of their hair and clothes. At this slow speed though, the scene was less like a race than a pair of mechanical toys winding down.

Still Musa said nothing.

Andersen returned to the first images, gripping the pages in a clump between his thumb and forefinger, bending them back. Then he released them with a sound like the panicked fluttering of birds' wings.

Musa let out a small, carefully wrapped cry. Andersen flipped the pages forward again and then again. He wanted Musa to see this race a hundred times, a thousand, until the Turk had it imprinted on his mind as a testament to his desertion of a friend.

"Stop," Musa said.

Andersen flattened The Book of Tulips on his lap, open to the last page. On his first viewing in Musa's bedroom, he'd thought the race too close to call, but now he could see Zeynep standing serenely on her own, in her green robe, looking out at a series of wavy blue lines. The sea! She stood by the shoreline. The man in the burgundy robe, a hand's length to her right, was still running, moving between two trees, a spiky branch clawing at his face.

"It was a race, wasn't it, Musa?" Andersen said. "And if Zeynep had won, she would have been allowed to go free?"

"Yes," Musa said. "She would have been

promised her life. As long as she left the city."

Andersen tried to collect his thoughts. How long did her exile last? Where did she go? Did she ever return? He would ask Musa all these things; his readers would want to know.

"He was too old," Musa said, jabbing a finger at the tiny figure of the Chief Gardener. "Too old to be racing through the palace gardens, and too stubborn to understand the old tulips."

Andersen looked at the Chief Gardener, his minute face etched with lines, pinpricks of red on his cheeks. Musa was shaking his head, his finger still pressed over the man's figure. As if he wished to obliterate him.

"Did you know him, Musa?" Andersen asked quietly.

Musa lifted his finger off the page, gently. "I knew him," he said. "But we lost contact. He was exiled to Sinop."

"Sinop? But when we were standing by that gravestone in your garden, you told me someone else used to live in Sinop."

"Herr Andersen, please." He moved to stand,

but he had no power left in his legs.

"Who was he?" Andersen pressed. "Who was the Chief Gardener?"

"He was my father."

Musa fell back in the divan. But Andersen had a story to write and, like a bloodhound, he would pursue his prey to the end.

"If the Chief Gardener was too old," he said as gently as he could, "why did he run the race himself? Why did he not order a younger man, one of the *bostancis*, to race Zeynep?"

Musa placed his palms on either side of his turban, massaging his head in slow, rough circles.

"Musa."

"Because he needed to lose and no *bostanci* would have agreed to lose the Executioner's Race. Their code would not allow it. This was not a common race. It was a privilege allowed only of high-ranking notables, and even then, only if they knew to ask for the honor. To allow a woman to compete was unheard-of. I doubt if any of the *bostancis* were aware the race had even taken place."

"Why did the Chief Gardener lose?" Andersen asked.

"For the sake of *that*." Musa pointed to the picture of the budded tulip on the wall, now slightly askew. "He was a gardener," Musa said ruefully. "And gardeners never think how foolish a flower can make them if it refuses to bloom. That's why he let Zeynep race, because she represented his last hope, like a stick to a drowning man."

"But the Chief Gardener didn't succeed?" Andersen said, looking at the budded tulip on the wall.

"Oh, he didn't grow Flattering Red. He failed as I have failed. Repeatedly. From the time he first worked in the palace gardens as a young man, to this, his ultimate failure."

Andersen picked up The Book of Tulips and looked at the final image of Zeynep by the shoreline. He forced himself to take a deep breath, gave himself the time to find the right words.

"Couldn't you have done something, Musa?

Couldn't you have interceded on her behalf?"

Musa was silent for a long time.

"I did not help her because I assumed she would share her *baraka* with my father. That's why I told him. I assumed she would do as he asked, and win her freedom."

"Told him what? What did you tell your father?"

"I…reminded him that we had a skilled calligrapher in our *tekke*. I showed him The Book of Tulips, and I let him believe Zeynep would help him."

Andersen shook his head. Musa had known all along why the New Guard soldiers arrested Zeynep. And he had said nothing while she sat in that prison cell. He had discarded her then, at the moment of her death, as he had discarded her in life.

And what about those faces, Andersen wanted to ask, the ones Musa's *bostanci* friend had smuggled from Zeynep's cell? Did they exist? But he remembered the last time they had talked about those who corrupted the calligrapher's art.

In his mind's eye, he could still see the hint of cunning in Musa's eyes, the flicker of amusement around the lips. *At this very moment you are trying to decide in which category Zeynep's work belongs.* Andersen knew the answer and he would write a story that showed the calligrapher at her best.

But Andersen needed Musa to tell him one more thing.

"If Zeynep won the race against her executioner," he said, "why wasn't she set free?"

"Herr Andersen…"

"Why go to the trouble of staging the Executioner's Race at all?"

Musa took the book from Andersen's hands and closed it.

"Herr Andersen, how is this for an ending to your story? Zeynep was taken back to her cell after the race. Oh, she wouldn't have been locked up again, of course. A nice chair would have been found for her and placed outside where she could gaze at the gardens. A *bostanci* would have brought her a glass of tea. 'It won't be long now, Zeynep *hanim*,' he would have said. No doubt they told her a boat needed to be found, that a *bostanci* could not be released from his other duties to escort her to the jetty.

"And my father would have gone to his tulip and studied it. He would have waited for a few hours, just in case the waning afternoon sun brought it to bloom. As the sun set, he would have searched again, hoping to find a flush of red, the stem standing a little straighter. When he realized there was no hope, he would have been furious."

"So he killed her. He killed Zeynep because of his own failure as a gardener?"

Musa said nothing.

"How do you know this? You weren't there. You didn't see what happened."

"Herr Andersen, I…"

"Your father could have released her. He could have sent her away from the city."

Musa raised his head and clicked his tongue. "No. It couldn't be."

"Tell me *why*."

"My father's reputation as the Chief

Gardener was predicated on his ability to revive the old strains. The sultan would have expected it. Flattering Red was the flower of our empire, Herr Andersen, a symbol of a time when we had wealth and power. Growing it again would have returned our pride. My father's failure, the scale of it, left no room for mercy."

Andersen grew angry. Zeynep could not be dead. She had won the Executioner's Race! He snatched the book, found the first page of the race, and, bending the corners back much further than he had before, replayed it again. Four glorious seconds of hope played out between his hands.

"Look Musa! Look what happened!

Musa put his hands to his head and rubbed those slow circles again. In the thin, spectral light of the lantern, he looked as pale and broken as the budded tulip Andersen had picked off the floor.

"Herr Andersen, it is your story now. To do with as you wish. All I ask is one thing. Allow my father a little dignity. When you write the tale of the calligrapher, let one of the *bostancis* run the race. To be defeated by a woman would be regarded as the ultimate stain."

CHAPTER 17

*D*usk fell and people left their houses to walk by the Bosphorus, gazing expectantly toward the city. After the call to prayer, an army of men would emerge from the mosques, and, torches in hand, slowly illuminate the great chains that hung between the minarets. Across the Bosphorus a thousand lights would burn. She remembered watching, as a child, the silvery shadows of fish, sliding and skimming through the surface of the water as if they knew, for this night only, the fishermen would not touch them.

The calligrapher dreaded these illuminations. Something about the smell, the heat prickling her skin. In strangers' eyes she saw the reflection of the flames that had burned her parents' house. When the rest of the *tekke* was out celebrating, she had always stayed home.

Blue returned and went immediately to the top of his cannon, where she had left the notebook for him to find. From her spot under the Judas tree, the calligrapher watched as the two men, Blue and Green, settled themselves to examine her work, just as she and the green dervish had done earlier. They lit two lanterns, one green and one blue, and placed them on the plinths of their respective cannons. And even though she could not hear their conversation, the great shadows the lanterns cast behind them made her feel she was watching another of Green's puppet shows and receiving a gentle, silhouetted lesson in life.

The dervishes must have first studied the drawing of Red; they became still as they gazed at the page, heads bowed. The calligrapher realized Blue's extended absences had been spent in search of Red, and that his cannon, the smallest and sleekest of the three, would remain empty until another traveler asked for shelter.

She watched them turn the pages together. The green dervish pointed out one or two things of interest, and then leapt to his feet to re-enact the ungainly waddle of the albatross after they had emerged from the water. Blue laughed in his soundless way.

Next, she sensed they were examining the *Bismillah* of the nightingale, and at one point, Green turned to Blue with a look of tenderness in his eyes.

For a few minutes Blue retreated, his body slumped and shrunken, and then, in a burst of strength, gripped the notebook, his eyes fixed on the nightingale.

He took the deepest breath the calligrapher had ever seen anyone take.

He rolled his shoulders and stretched his neck.

He looked at the notebook and danced his finger through the air.

At first, the sound that emerged from his throat was low and guttural, as if he were channeling energy from the earth with his body. The growls became words, murmured and unintelligible. His hum sharpened and migrated a few intervals up the scale. Then his voice focused, like the lens of a telescope, and his words became familiar words, holy and reassuring. The first phrase she understood was *Al-Jabbar*, The Compeller. Then came more monikers: The Judge, The Just, The Subtle One. He recited the ninety-nine names of God with such a light inflection the calligrapher could not discern where one name ended and another began.

The blue dervish kept his eyes on the notebook as his voice dipped and soared, tracing the lines and markings with his fingers, occasionally turning the page. With a start, the calligrapher realized he was looking, not at her work, but at his own script. Her nightingale had helped him to remember how to read it—musical notes that he now sang in joyous memory of his past life.

When Blue stopped singing, all of Istanbul went quiet.

The calligrapher stood and smoothed the wrinkles from her *ferace*. The two dervishes, Green and Blue, sat by the cannons with the notebook between them. She knew they had seen her rise, but they would not turn to watch her go.

For the last time, she looked over the Bosphorus, at the outline of the city where her life had been. But there was nothing left to see. Her parents were gone, her home. Only the *tekke* remained. She regretted the shame she had brought her old friends and teachers, but she didn't regret anything else. She had taken pleasure in every image she had fashioned with her *kalem*, every flower and bird, every lantern and mosque. And if others had chosen to read into her faces their own fears and prejudices, the calligrapher hoped that one day they might look again and realize their stupidity. For, as with everything she transcribed, those faces had formed in her heart. And no one could condemn her for that.

Cannon shots blared from the top of Istanbul's seven hills, commemorating the hour of the Prophet's birth. Children cheered, their cries echoing across the Bosphorus as the calligrapher walked toward the wooded hills above the fortress, beginning her long journey out of the city.

CHAPTER 18

Andersen laid his cream suit on the bed and stood in his underclothes in front of the mirror. He promised himself, as he always did in a state of undress, that he would add meat to his collection of loosely entwined bones, include more starch in his diet. He selected a fresh lemon-colored shirt and knotted his tie. The jaunty attire seemed appropriate for the eve of the Prophet's birthday, the festival of light. After all that had happened at Musa's house the previous evening, Andersen wanted his final night in Constantinople to be a happy occasion.

The suit could do with a press, but Andersen, still without his boots, distrusted the hotel. He did the best he could by smoothing the imperfections with his hands. His missing boots would have completed the outfit nicely, but now they were nothing more than a sweet memory. Andersen had written a letter of complaint, detailing the hotel's failed attempts to locate the boots, which he intended to present to the manager before he left.

He picked up the burgundy leather folio he'd purchased that morning and opened its soft flap. Inside, on hotel notepaper, he'd written Zeynep's story. After leaving Musa's house and returning to the hotel, he'd scratched away with the nib of his pen for most of last night and today while everything was still vivid in his mind. He thumbed through the pages, so official-seeming in the folio, wondering what Zeynep would make of his curly, slightly sloping handwriting. It had none of the disciplined uniformity of her trained hand, but Andersen had tried to make his letters a little more assertive than usual, bolder in their execution. Without an editor, he'd done the best he could.

He returned to the mirror with the folio tucked under his arm. 'Dear Musa,' he would write in the letter he hoped would one day accompany the published story, 'I enclose a small gift for you. I hope it will help you remember the woman you once called your friend.'

And how would Musa remember *him*? As the man he had caught ransacking his possessions for the heart of the story? Or as the writer who had not only provided that story with its ending but given Zeynep the send-off she deserved?

Andersen picked up Zeynep's paper flower, which Musa had presented to him in this very room. What a charming front cover it would make for the book of Zeynep's story! At least this tulip would remain as she had intended—in its prime, yellow petals infused with the glow of the spring sun.

A loud rap on his door brought Andersen out

of this reverie. Had the hotel finally found his boots? He quickly put on his trousers and reached the door in three strides. He found himself face-to-face with a hotel employee. But instead of a pair of boots, the man gave him a battered-looking manila envelope. "From the gentleman downstairs," he said cryptically, and before Andersen could enquire further, the man clicked his heels and walked briskly away.

Andersen looked at the envelope. Had Musa decided to apologize formally for his behavior the previous evening? It was all Andersen could do to resist running downstairs to check if the Turk were still in the hotel. But he considered the envelope more carefully. It was old and possibly reused, and his own name was scrawled across the front in a barely legible hand. That didn't seem like Musa at all; he was so meticulous.

Andersen sat on his bed and opened the envelope. He pulled out seven sheets of paper, all of which seemed to contain childish scrawls fashioned into shapes and images he could not discern. He laid the sheets of paper in a straight line on the bed and took a step back to gain a better perspective, an uneasy feeling creeping over him.

The images took shape before his eyes. He saw a rogue's gallery of disfigured faces: squinty eyes and onion noses, mouths fashioned into sneers and snarls. Like the newspaper lion and the animals on Zeynep's riverbank scroll, Andersen guessed they were compiled from Arabic script. Yet their features were stiff and awkward—drawn, it seemed, with a heavy hand, to say nothing of a poor-quality nib. Two were not even complete; they were abandoned as if the author could not bear to go on. One contained a pair of eyes and the beginnings of a nose; the other depicted a man missing a mouth. Even the completed ones had a shifty, unfocused look, and none of them would meet his eye.

Andersen picked up one of the images and saw that a number had been scrawled into the corner, alongside a denomination. The others, too, bore the same or similar numbers— ridiculous amounts that only a greatly disturbed man would charge with any expectation of payment.

From the gentleman downstairs. Was the Irishman sitting in the lounge at this moment expecting Andersen to pay for his work? There was nothing he could do. He would have no dealings with a man who had debased the art form Zeynep had pursued with such courage.

What had Musa said about those people who tried to make a living selling their calligraphy? *I cannot tell you the identity of every perpetrator, but I could identify a hundred places in the city where one might obtain such work.* Was there a network of black-market calligraphers producing faces such as these, each with a market value according to its embarrassment factor? But the only person who should feel embarrassed about work like this, Andersen thought, was the man who had produced it.

He recalled the Irishman's sketchbook at the Grand Bazaar; had he been trying to sell these images to the scribes? In any case, the men of letters had refused. They must have known that such work was not calligraphy and could serve no noble purpose.

Andersen would have torn up the images and burned them right away if he hadn't heard the piano notes coming from the reception room. He opened the door to check he wasn't imagining it. A Chopin Nocturne played so slowly that the listener would surely grow old and gray by the end of the piece. The Irishman was taunting him with this leaden music. Andersen could imagine the gaunt figure leaning on the keys, bushy eyebrow undulating in time to the ponderous notes. He gathered up the images and stuffed them back into the envelope. Within a minute he had reached the lounge and was walking through a forest of Franks bustling to and fro in their ill-fitting kaftans, their ridiculous fezzes. He hadn't even put on his jacket.

When he saw the figure sitting at the piano, Andersen described an arc around the room so that he was positioned behind the Irishman. He took a deep breath and walked up to the stool, leaned over the Irishman, and slammed the envelope down on the piano's music stand. As he turned away for his room, Andersen was aware of only one thing: the edge of the Irishman's enormous eyebrow ascending to the top of his forehead as he turned in surprise.

Andersen rested for an hour before he went downstairs again. During this time, he heard not a single note from the piano. Dressed in his cream suit and carrying the folio, Andersen went first to the desk to check for messages. Nothing from Musa, but Jensen had invited him to join his party for the celebrations tomorrow. There was to be a procession through the streets of guilds and dignitaries, with the sultan himself bringing up the rear. Andersen declined by writing a note at the desk. With his steamer, *The Fernando*, due to depart from the Galata dock that same evening, he wanted to stay close to the hotel, where he could easily receive word of unexpected developments or delays.

He remembered his letter of complaint and gave it to the desk clerk, insisting it be placed in the manager's hand at the first opportunity. Then he strode off to the lounge.

He found a seat where he could see the main entrance to the hotel, as well as the reception desk. The hotel had made an erratic effort to recognize the impending holiday. Lanterns appeared throughout the lounge: some behind armchairs, imbuing the occupants with a halo-like quality, others on window ledges next to the bird cages, casting a tawdry glow.

Andersen opened the leather folio containing Zeynep's story. What would they think in Denmark if he told them this tale in front of the fire, as they sipped their brandy and toasted their feet? How would he convey the calligrapher to them, her animal-shaped prayers and her long search for home? Perhaps he could draw a tulip while they watched. He took a piece of paper from his jacket pocket and tried to render a tulip with the Danish letters for the word. But the letters were stiff and unyielding, like children yanked from their beds on a cold winter's day. The 't' toppled into the 'u' and the 'p' clung for dear life to the side of what he had managed to form of the stem.

As he crumpled the piece of paper, the grandfather clock in the lounge chimed seven times. Men removed their fezzes and called for waiters. Andersen ordered hibiscus juice and sipped it slowly. The call to prayer came and went.

It was too late for a stroll before dinner. But a walk would not have been the same without Musa anyway. He pictured the Turk standing tall in his burgundy gown, the carefully etched lines of his face and beard, the soft certainty of his turban. They would have made a good pair this evening, strolling together arm in arm as the city illuminated around them. He didn't want to think of the man who had stood holding that accursed flowerpot. He would remember Musa as he was at the *tekke*, the way he stood behind Andersen and turned the pages of Zeynep's practice book, the brush of his breathing, slow and calm, against Andersen's ear.

It was Andersen's last evening in Constantinople. Taranto had promised the city would light up more than heaven itself on this night, the eve of the Prophet's birthday. Perhaps he would take that walk after all.

He got to his feet. At the reception desk, two of the clerks were laughing at something. Andersen was convinced they were looking his way. They were probably having a joke at his expense, the fool who could not find his boots. Andersen was angry, and not just because he had loved those boots. The clerk who had been looking at him opened an envelope and read its contents. His eyes slid from the letter to Andersen's face and back, his mouth still grinning broadly. No doubt about it, the fellow was reading Andersen's sealed complaint!

Andersen walked toward the desk. Brazen to the last, the fellow kept reading. Andersen opened his mouth to speak but was suddenly distracted by the gray curl of hair on the man's head, a curl which, in the three days since he had last seen it, had grown considerably. It was the impudent clerk who had suggested he write about his own boots.

"Good Evening, Monsieur!" the man said. "And what a fine evening on which to celebrate the birth of our great Prophet!"

"Good Evening," Andersen said, and pointed at the letter. "Look, is that the letter I entrusted to the manager? About my missing boots?"

"Indeed it is, Monsieur!"

"Well, are you the manager?"

"No, I have not attained such an exalted position. But the manager is not the gentleman who can help you now, Monsieur."

Andersen was nonplussed. "I'm afraid I don't understand."

"Indeed you don't, Monsieur!"

The man's smile vanished. He said in a low voice: "You're a storyteller, Herr Andersen, not a functionary writing a report." He pointed to the letter. "This isn't storytelling. This is a litany of moans, a saga of a man unshod and uninspired."

"What does this have to do with my boots?"

The receptionist narrowed his eyes and the curl fell over his forehead, forming the question mark Andersen remembered from before. "Go outside, Herr Andersen," he said. "It is the eve of the Prophet's birthday, a time for illuminating the soul. Why waste such an evening talking to me?"

"But I...I don't know where to go."

"There is a cemetery on the side of a hill. Near the Galata Tower. I'm told it is the most peaceful place in the world to experience the Prophet's illuminations. But take a lantern to guide you, so you don't lose your way. The lanterns for our guests are just by the main entrance."

Andersen spun round to look.

When he turned back, the man with the gray curl was gone. On the counter stood a pair of calf-length riding boots of deep, luxuriant cherry-brown, so pliant his fingers sank into the leather. A darker fur trim around the rim of the boots, and brown tassels down the front. They were the most beautiful boots he had ever seen, even though they were not his own. He put them on anyway, and they cushioned and caressed his bony feet. They even matched his cream suit.

{

On Hans Christian Andersen's last night in Constantinople, he walked in his new boots through the illuminated city. He carried the leather folio in one hand and a paper lantern in the other. Turks, Greeks, Jews, and Franks cast eerie shadows with their lanterns and candles. The palaces of the foreign embassies burned with pyramids of light.

On the bay of the Golden Horn, the masts of ships glowed from the lights on their decks and in the mouths of their cannons. Sailors clambered over rigging and masts, mounting yet more flames. Across the water, the mosques of the old city smoldered, minarets stretching upward, "like colossal flowers of fire on white stems," as Andersen would later write. Only the gardens of the seraglio remained dark and aloof. Sultan Ahmed's great mosque had rows of lights suspended between its six minarets like a holy chain. Andersen, fascinated throughout his life by flight, imagined God uprooting the mosque and floating it over the city, a vast balloon powered by prayer, the minarets spread like the wings of a bird.

Below the Galata Tower, a cemetery set amid coal-black cypresses stretched to the shoreline. He looked at his pocket watch. In only a few minutes, cannon shots marking the hour of the Prophet's birth would boom out over the city. Andersen followed a path through the trees, breathing the familiar fragrance, marveling at his lack of fear. Here he was in a foreign city making his way in a dark cemetery, quite alone! His new boots and Zeynep's story had given him courage. Candlelight sparkled like fireflies among the graves as Turks knelt by their loved ones. He recalled something Musa said about Turks and their graveyards: that one day the city would become a vast cemetery, with the living pushed further and further away from the metropolis, until the moment they, too, could return and claim their spaces underground.

Wandering among the cypresses, he passed gravestones shaped into turbans and fezzes. The mourners were peaceful, the lanterns at their feet casting flickering patterns on their faces. He nodded as he passed them. The clerk was right: it was the best place to mark the Prophet's birth. A cool, fragrant Garden of the Dead surrounded by those celebrating the memory of their loved ones: a hand laid tenderly on an arm, a line of poetry whispered into an ear.

Andersen moved deeper into the cemetery and turned to the right. The foliage was denser now, branches reaching down to brush against his neck. The trees felt older here; gravestones were scattered all around their trunks.

He approached one of the graves and set down his lantern. The slab was thin, bent with age. He ran his fingers along the surface—a rough surface that was blank apart from the lotus blossom carved delicately into the corner. A woman's grave. Only her loved ones would know her name. Even in death, anonymity veiled her.

It had grown very dark. No other lanterns or colored candles bobbed close by. No one, it seemed, wanted to share this night with the women in the graveyard. Only the cypress trees watched over their forgotten souls.

An idea struck him, as perfect as the beat of a swallow's wings. Zeynep's body might have been tipped into the Bosphorus, but her spirit was surely here among her sisters in this quiet part of the cemetery. He wanted to do something, to honor her in some way, but he would need the right words, the right gesture. He needed to find the right place.

He walked for a while, searching for a stone that felt right, though they all looked the same. He had to hold the lantern in front of his face to stave off the growing darkness.

Soon, he would have to turn back, before his lantern burned out and he was lost for good amongst the thickening trees and crumbling stones. A branch raked itself across his hand and he cursed.

As he examined the wound, the moon

appeared from behind a bank of clouds, a dramatic vista of light, as if it, too, were waiting to pay homage to the Prophet. Andersen emptied his mind, tried to be still like the men and women he had seen at the cemetery in the *tekke*.

Calmer now, he continued deeper into the graveyard, coming ever closer to the sea, the soft leather of the folio still snug in his hand. In this new light, he could see the silvery tips of his boots leading him forward. He could dedicate any one of these silent, unacknowledged stones to Zeynep, he thought, but he would choose carefully, perhaps one with a view of the Bosphorus glinting through the trees.

He found a stone that stood a little straighter than its neighbors and knelt to put his hand flat against it. It felt cool against his fingertips, the lotus blossom raised a little on the surface as if it had been freshly carved.

Andersen sniffed. The woody, spicy fragrance was stronger here and he was suddenly back in Musa's room, laying his hands on the Book of Tulips for the first time. He took a deep breath. This was the place, he told himself: secluded but close to the sea; a spot to observe and contemplate life.

Placing his lantern and the leather folio on the ground, he took out his scissors and paper and sat cross-legged. He wanted to create a paper tableau for Zeynep, something to make her smile. He worked steadily, mesmerized by the serpentine motion of the blades until the profile of two figures, a man and a woman, took shape. They sat at a table on which a single tulip grew from a filigree vase. The man was Musa, wearing his usual turban and kaftan, and the woman Zeynep, lightly veiled with pen in hand, poised and waiting to transcribe. As an afterthought, Andersen made a few more snips and added himself to the tableau, complete with domed forehead and beaked nose. After all, he had written the story.

As he finished, cannon shots rang out in violent unison: from the seven hills of the city, from the Hippodrome where the young sultan waited in his carriage, and from the European warships at anchor in the bay. Andersen closed his eyes, feeling the earth shift under him with the impact of each shot.

He placed the paper cut in front of the stone and weighed it down with some loose soil. As he rose, his feet felt numb. Pins and needles surged through his toes. And then a tingling, the sense of a presence again, the sense that someone was brushing their fingertips up and down the length of his spine. Lightheaded, he gripped the sides of the stone, flakes of masonry crumbling beneath his palm.

The presence wanted something from him, something more weighty and substantial than a paper cut. Andersen opened the leather folio.

He would bury the story of the calligrapher here, two thousand kilometers away from those who would damage it with their ignorance and prejudice. But first, he would read the tale out loud, into the bright night of the Prophet's birthday, for Zeynep, wherever she might be. He cleared his throat and delivered the first line.

THE EXECUTIONER'S RACE

Women in the sultan's capital, no matter their rank, tended to die uneventfully: strangled in the dead of night, sewed neatly into weighted flour sacks, tipped into the Bosphorus along with the rest of the week's refuse.

A calligrapher, imprisoned for reassembling the word of God, might have expected the same treatment. She had drawn human and animal forms from holy words and invocations, compact chronograms with diacritical marks for eyes and letters for limbs, but the holy men didn't care to see the *Bismillah* reflected in their own faces. Their God belonged on the page, as immobile and resolute as a citadel. They sentenced the calligrapher to death.

Her jailers talked of the Executioner's Race. She begged them to pass a message to the Bostanci-Bashi, the Chief Gardener, who doubled as the sultan's executioner.

"Let me race," she said. "Let me die an honorable death. After all, as a woman I have no chance of winning, and think of the spectacle you would have on your hands as I flounder through the bushes, thorns, and weeds."

Her jailers shook their heads and said the race was the privilege of condemned notables—a deposed vizier, perhaps, or a chief eunuch—not for someone as ordinary as her.

The calligrapher scratched a petition on the walls of her cell with the husk of her reed pen. She called in the jailers and they, unlettered and afraid, ran to the Bostanci-Bashi. The Chief Gardener examined her markings by candlelight and clucked his tongue.

"Is this the way you honor your master's profession?" he asked. "By daubing God's script on prison walls?"

"I'm sure you are right, sir," the calligrapher said. "Women are always impatient. I simply couldn't wait for the right conditions."

"The right conditions?"

"As a gardener, you wouldn't plant and sow unless the soil was favorable?

"Of course not."

"And you wouldn't use an inferior spade and hoe?"

"No."

"And as an executioner, you wouldn't slice off my head with anything but the sharpest blade."

"Woman, what are you saying?"

"That you, sir, possess infinite patience and expertise. A lesson I would do well to learn."

An hour later, a sheet of paper and a tortoise shell full of ink arrived at her cell.

The calligrapher licked and spat on her right hand until her mouth drained dry. She removed the grime and dead skin of the dungeon the best she could with the hem of her *ferace*. She looked down at the materials sent by the Bostanci-Bashi and sighed. The ink was thinly mixed and flakes of soot floated to the surface like crumbs of bread in a bowl of soup. The paper was coarse and unburnished, lacking the shiny finish of the quince kernels and egg white she was accustomed to working with. The pen was unkempt; she longed for a penknife to trim its rough edges, to hone it in preparation for the words forming in her head. She sat cross-legged and balanced the paper on thigh and knee. She felt it tremble a little and waited for it to settle. She began to write.

When the Bostanci-Bashi looked at the bold strokes and curving letters climbing the page, he had to blink twice before he saw that the calligrapher had woven her petition into the shape of a flower, of a type that his predecessors had once grown in the palace gardens. In his dreams he had felt the texture of this flower on his fingers, breathed its slight scent. He arranged for the petition to be framed. Eventually he sent word that the calligrapher would race against a *bostanci*, a junior gardener. They would begin on the top terrace of the palace's outer garden and run down to the fish-house gate in the sea wall. If the calligrapher reached the gate first, her life would be spared.

{

The calligrapher stood at the apex of the palace gardens and looked down at the sea. Half-starved, eyes burning in the sun's glare, she could barely stand. Her green *ferace* was torn, her shoes and veil had long since disappeared, and her hair, hacked off by the jailers, grew like black gorse across her skull. Only her hands remained defiant. Her fingernails were dark, henna-stained tips. On her left palm she had painted the letters of her name; on the right, the words *Insha'Allah*— God willing. The junior gardener stood at her side, broad-shouldered, his bare arms a document of cuts and scratches from the flora in his care.

At midday, a cannon boomed and the two figures began their descent to the shoreline. The young gardener was racing for pride; it had been many years since his brethren had lost the race against a condemned man, let alone a woman. The runners passed through and around thorny rose bushes, woods of guarded cypress, and, massed like vast armies reposed after battle, beds of hyacinths, narcissi, and tulips. *Bostancis* stood guard at each tier. Men dressed in similar sleeveless tunics and blue breeches were differentiated by the color of their belts: red for the Corps of Vine Grafters, yellow for the Corps of the Haystore, and blue and green for the rival Corps of Okra and Cabbage.

If the calligrapher veered from the path onto the sultan's flower beds, she would be struck down by the axe of the nearest *bostanci* before the race had run its course. She weaved around the aprons of attentive tulips, moving sideways and sometimes backwards to find a path, constantly thwarted as she tried to break into a steady run.

The junior gardener had already passed between the ranks of the Grand Turk's tulips— the Delicate Coquettes and Pomegranate Lances with their taut stems and silken petals. He knew the narrow paths well; he had worked this soil since he was a boy. His mind began to wander. Tomorrow he would be permitted to collect, cut, and place five of the finest specimens in filigree glasses in the sultan's private kiosk on the top tier of the gardens overlooking the Golden Horn. The sultan himself would choose one of these flowers to be placed in his private chamber. It would be a great honor for the young *bostanci*, a mark of the respect he could then expect from his colleagues.

But something was happening behind him. The calligrapher had arrived at a bed of the sultan's most prized tulips: the reddish/orange *Mahbub*, or Beloved, a single bulb of which a collector once offered one thousand gold coins to possess. The sultan himself had named this particular cultivar; its petals reminded him of the curve of the new moon that crested his beloved city on spring evenings. The calligrapher stopped dead in her tracks and stared. To the observing *bostancis*, it seemed she had given up on the race and decided to spend the remaining moments of her life enjoying the tulips' beauty. The calligrapher took a few steps back as if to gain a better perspective. The young gardeners nodded to each other. The woman was misguided and perhaps crazy, but she could appreciate beauty and was courageous; she would die a noble death. Then, without warning, she dashed toward the tulip bed, *ferace* billowing around her, hennaed fingers glinting in the sun.

The *bostancis* drew their axes; it seemed, after all, that the woman was a reprobate and would care no more about crushing the sacred flowers than stepping on a beetle. As they advanced toward her, the calligrapher began to dance, spin, and skip between each row of tulips. There was certainly no path cut through the meticulous flower bed—even a rabbit could not have forged its way between the tight ranks—but she pointed her bony toes downward and landed on the tiny strips of earth that separated each line of flowers. The *bostancis* raised their axes and waited for the calligrapher to crush even a single petal. The Mahbub swayed and dipped their heads as if caught by a sudden breeze. In a few seconds, the calligrapher had traversed the flower bed without damaging a single bloom.

When the calligrapher passed in a flurry of silk and skin, the *bostanci* felt the earth exhale. Standing in her wake, he understood, for the first time, the true nature of the soil.

The *bostanci*'s colleagues, not believing the evidence of their own eyes, surrounded the calligrapher. They prodded her with their rakes and hoes as if she were a snap-jawed plant. They might have returned her to the earth had not the Bostanci-Bashi arrived on the scene. He hadn't seen the calligrapher dance over his precious tulip beds; he had been waiting for her at the fish-house gate, garrote in hand, a woven sack crumpled at his feet like an exhausted dog. The reaction of his men told him that he would not have the pleasure of tightening the knot around the woman's neck and consigning her memory to the Golden Horn. But he restrained his young charges in case the calligrapher had some strange, magical attribute to use against him.

A week later, after the calligrapher's sentence was commuted to a seven-year exile, an envelope arrived at the Bostanci-Bashi's quarters. It contained one sheet of thick, creamy paper, emitting the faintest aroma of quince. He recognized the loops and curls of the script immediately, the elasticity of letters that could not be contained. Above a short note that read simply, 'from the beneficiary of your expertise,' the Bostanci-Bashi beheld a stork in full flight, its plumage a network of loops, lines, and dots, its fragile, fluted neck curving into a tipped beak.

ARABIC ALPHABET

ا   ب   ت   ث   ج

ʾalif   bāʾ   tāʾ   t̲hāʾ   ǧīm
                                  (θ)

ح   خ   د   ذ   ر

ḥāʾ   h̲āʾ   dāl   d̲āl   rāʾ

ز   س   ش   ص   ض

zāy   sīn   šīn   ṣād   ḍād

416

ṭā’   ẓā’   ʿayn   ġayn   fā’

qāf   kāf   lām   Mīm   nūn

hā’   wāw   yā’

hamzah

GLOSSARY OF TURKISH & ARABIC WORDS & PHRASES

Alif: The first Arabic letter.

Ayn, Dahl, Ha, Lam-Alif, Mim, Nun, Wah: Arabic letters.

Baraka: A spiritual energy.

Bismillah: 'In the name of God.'

Borek: Flaky pastry with spinach or cheese.

Bostanci: Palace gardener.

Bostanci-Bashi: Chief Gardener who also acted as the Chief Executioner in the Sultan's palace.

Caique: Small boat used to transfer passengers across the Bosphorus; similar to a gondola.

Effendim / (Bey) Effendi: Honorific titles for males, corresponding to 'Sir' or 'Mr.'

Ezan: The call to prayer.

Ferace: Female shift or cloak.

Grand Vizier: Head of Ottoman government.

Hanim: Honorific female title, used after first name, corresponding to 'Miss' or 'Mrs.'

Hocam: Honorific title meaning 'my teacher.'

Imam: Prayer leader in mosque.

Inshallah: 'God willing.'

Iznik Fayans: Tiles from Iznik.

Kaba: Holiest site of Islam and focal point of Muslim pilgrimage in Mecca.

Kalem: A reed pen.

Katabahu: 'She wrote it.' The master's seal of approval for his apprentice calligrapher.

Kilim: A handwoven rug.

La illah illallah: 'There is no God but Allah.'

Mihrab: Prayer niche in mosque.

Minbar: Pulpit in mosque.

Muezzin: The man who calls the faithful to prayer.

Namaz: The holy prayers required by Muslims five times a day.

Nargile: Water pipe.

Nastaliq: A style of Ottoman calligraphy.

Ney: Reed flute.

Padishah: Sultan.

Sen: Informal use of 'you' in Turkish.

Siz: Formal use of 'you' in Turkish.

Sunnet: Circumcision ceremony.

Sura: A chapter of the Koran.

Tabouret: A small table or stool.

Tekke: Religious brotherhood or lodge.

Tughra: Sultan's signature or seal.

Ulema: Islamic scholars.

Ulfet: 'Intimacy.'

Usta: A master craftsman and teacher of apprentices.

Yali: Wooden summer house.

Yashmak: Woman's two piece head and face covering.

Zikr: The Sufi recital of the ninety nine names of God.

THE NINETY-NINE MOST
BEAUTIFUL NAMES OF
ALLAH

Allah: The Greatest Name

1. Ar-Rahman: The All-Compassionate
2. Ar-Rahim: The All-Merciful
3. Al-Malik: The Absolute Ruler
4. Al-Quddus: The Pure One
5. As-Salam: The Source of Peace
6. Al-Mu'min: The Inspirer of Faith
7. Al-Muhaymin: The Guardian
8. Al-'Aziz: The Victorious
9. Al-Jabbar: The Compeller
10. Al-Mutakabbir: The Greatest
11. Al-Khaliq: The Creator
12. Al-Bari': The Maker of Order
13. Al-Musawwir: The Shaper of Beauty

14. Al-Ghaffar: The Forgiving

15. Al-Qahhar: The Subduer

16. Al-Wahhab: The Giver of All

17. Ar-Razzaq: The Sustainer

18. Al-Fattah: The Opener

19. Al-'Alim: The Knower of All

20. Al-Qabid: The Constrictor

21. Al-Basit: The Reliever

22. Al-Khafid: The Abaser

23. Ar-Rafi': The Exalter

24. Al-Mu'izz: The Bestower of Honors

25. Al-Mudhill: The Humiliator

26. As-Sami: The Hearer of All

27. Al-Basir: The Seer of All

28. Al-Hakam: The Judge

29. Al-'Adl: The Just

30. Al-Latif: The Subtle One

31. Al-Khabir: The All-Aware

32. Al-Halim: The Forebearing

33. Al-'Azim: The Magnificent

34. Al-Ghafur: The Forgiver and Hider of Faults

35. Ash-Shakur: The Rewarder of Thankfulness

36. Al-'Ali: The Highest

37. Al-Kabir: The Greatest

38. Al-Hafiz: The Preserver

39. Al-Muqit: The Nourisher

40. Al-Hasib: The Accounter

41. Al-Jalil: The Mighty

42. Al-Karim: The Generous

43. Ar-Raqib: The Watchful One

44. Al-Mujib: The Responder to Prayer

45. Al-Wasi': The All-Comprehending

46. Al-Hakim: The Perfectly Wise

47. Al-Wadud: The Loving One

48. Al-Majíd: The Majestic One

49. Al-Ba'ith: The Resurrector

50. Ash-Shahid: The Witness

51. Al-h Haqq: The Truth

52. Al-Wakil: The Trustee

53. Al-Qawi: The Possessor of All Strength

54. Al-Matin: The Forceful One

55. Al-Wáli: The Governor

56. Al-Hamid: The Praised One

57. Al-Muhsi: The Appraiser

58. Al-Mubdi: The Originator

59. Al-Mu'id: The Restorer

60. Al-Muhyi: The Giver of Life

61. Al-Mumit: The Taker of Life

62. Al-Hayy: The Ever Living One

63. Al-Qayyum: The Self-Existing One

64. Al-Wajid: The Finder

65. Al-Májid: The Glorious

66. Al-Wahid: The Only One

67. Al-Ahad: The One

68. As-Samad: The Satisfier of All Needs

69. Al-Qadir: The All Powerful

70. Al-Muqtadir: The Creator of All Power

71. Al-Muqaddim: The Expediter

72. Al-Mu'akhkhir: The Delayer

73. Al-Awwal: The First

74. Al-Akhir: The Last

75. Az-Zahir: The Manifest One

76. Al-Batin: The Hidden One

77. Al-Walí: The Protecting Friend

78. Al-Muta'ali: The Supreme One

79. Al-Barr: The Doer of Good

80. At-Tawwib: The Guide to Repentance

81. Al-Muntaqim: The Avenger

82. Al-Afu: The Forgiver

83. Ar-Ra'uf: The Clement
84. Malik al-Mulk: The Owner of All
85. Dhul-Jalali Wal-Ikram: The Lord of Majesty and Bounty
86. Al-Muqsit: The Equitable One
87. Al-Jami: The Gatherer
88. Al-Ghani: The Rich One
89. Al-Mughni: The Enricher
90. Al-Mani': The Preventer of Harm
91. Ad-Darr: The Creator of the Harmful
92. An-Nafi: The Creator of Good
93. An-Nur: The Light
94. Al-Hadi: The Guide
95. Al-Badi: The Originator
96. Al-Baqi: The Everlasting One
97. Al-Warith: The Inheritor of All
98. Ar-Rashid: The Righteous Teacher
99. As-Sabur: The Patient One

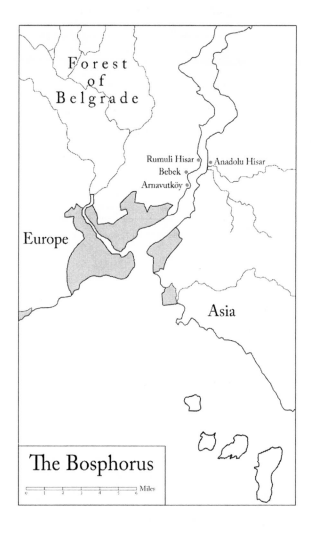

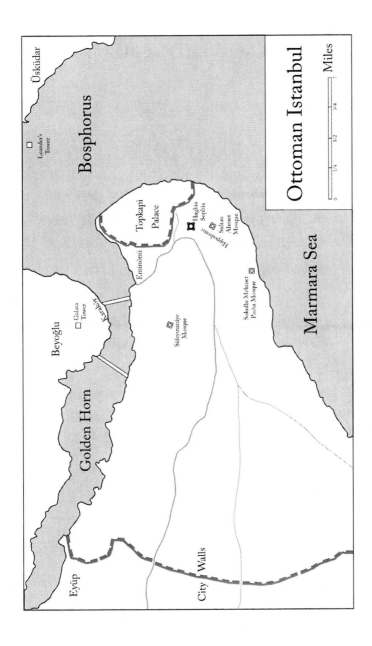

Ottoman Istanbul

Miles

0   1:4   1/2   3:4   1

Üsküdar

Bosphorus

Leander's Tower

Topkapi Palace

Hagia Sophia

Sultan Ahmet Mosque

Hippodrome

Eminönü

Marmara Sea

Galata Tower

Karaköy

Beyoğlu

Süleymaniye Mosque

Sokullu Mehmet Pasha Mosque

Golden Horn

Eyüp

City Walls

ACKNOWLEDGEMENTS

Hans Christian Andersen's *A Poet's Bazaar* was the starting point for this novel, particularly his remarkable chapters on the Istanbul of 1841. For background on Andersen's work and life, I am indebted to Jackie Wullschlager's expertise, especially her masterful editing of *Hans Christian Andersen: Fairy Tales*. For the architecture and geography of Istanbul, Michael Pereira's 1968 travelogue *Istanbul: Aspects of a City* was poignant in that much of his description would be unrecognizable today. Orhan Pamuk's *Istanbul: Memories of the City* helped me peer into this lost urban soul.

Cynthia Reeser, the publisher of Aqueous Books, was the first to give this novel a chance; she is also a fine editor. Cynthia's press and others like it not only allow writers to compete on a level playing field but enrich the lives of so many readers.

I am grateful to Ali Abdulaziz Aljubailan and Mohammed Alobaida for their help in lettering the tulip image on the cover, and to Paul Sloboda for his skill in drawing the cover image. Hale Yilmaz and Roger Deal provided much invaluable insight into Ottoman Istanbul and were a great help with translating some Ottoman Turkish words. Kay Carr painstakingly created the maps to reflect Andersen's progress around Istanbul.

Marshall Klimasewiski, Kellie Wells, and Katherine Davis were skilled guides in this novel's early incarnations. Betsy Dougherty, Stacey Sloboda, Carol Hurlburt, and Saundra Weddle provided many helpful suggestions during the various drafts of the book. And I owe much to my friend Alena Wilson (1967-2007), whose memory has stayed with me throughout the book's creation.

Nurhan Ozer continues to be my dear friend and go-to person in Istanbul. Jennifer Fandel helped me understand the world of publishing from much closer to home.

My parents, Anthony Bynom and Irene Nash, have always inspired as well as recommended great books to read.

Finally, my wife and partner, Holly Hurlburt, who, after reading the first paragraph of this book, urged me to write the second. You are brilliant as always.

ABOUT THE AUTHOR

Andrew Bynom graduated from the MFA Fiction Writing Program at Washington University in St. Louis in 2006. His work has been published in *The Tusculum Review* and in *Phoebe*, which awarded his story, "The Burial Party," first prize in its 2010 Winter Fiction contest.

CPSIA information can be obtained at www.ICGtesting.com
Printed in the USA
LVOW06s1806200915

454947LV00003B/52/P